NOISE

A Novel

Jane Everist

Logtown Press

ISBN-13: 978-1-7349103-1-5

Printed in the United States of America

NOISE

A NOVEL

JANE EVERIST

I can't see because there is too much light.
I can't hear because there is too much noise.
Zack Ewing

PART I

CHAPTER 1

13 June 2017

I have appointed myself to write my sister's story; she could not write it if she tried. And I believe in my heart I can do it justice because Sheila shared everything with me. Crushed between her son and her husband was hard enough, but the noise was deafening.

What I did not observe myself, I learned from interviewing reliable sources—a simple thing to do in Gower, Louisiana. For what is assumed, I rely upon an educated guess and the doctor who guided our family through a shattering experience.

Carl Ewing, my sister's husband, could not tolerate criticism or teasing of any sort, and he never forgot a grudge. But his flaws were overshadowed by his charm. He could charm the whiskers off a cat or the pants off his neighbor's wife, but his goal, laser-sharp, was to become wealthy and powerful. This afternoon he was expecting a welcome, not a lawyer's trap.

The sidewalk, in front of the law office belonging to Wilson and Tucker, baked in direct sunlight. It was 108 degrees. Trent Wilson, looking out of his window, nodded "yes" to himself before reaching for his sunglasses.

Across the street, Carl parked his truck on the curb. So far, their partnership was friendly and courteous.

Carl was the sole contractor, and Trent supplied money and legal expertise for a residential development. When Trent scheduled a meeting on Tuesday, Carl agreed without hesitation.

Seeing Trent on the front steps waiting for him, Carl waved before looking both ways to weave between the slow-moving cars.

Wilson, waved back, then checked the time on his watch, and straightened his tie.

Minutes later, Carl stood bolted to the sidewalk, refusing to retreat, while his partner barred the door.

"MY LORD, CARL, INSURANCE FRAUD—WHAT WERE YOU THINKING." People passing by turned their heads. "I'M MORTIFIED THAT YOU WOULD COMMIT SUCH A CRIME." Trent, standing on the steps, looked down at Carl.

Carl fumed in the sun, while Trent, perched under an awning, enjoyed the shade. On days like this, kids try to incinerate ants with a magnifying glass. Carl, if given a chance, would have incinerated Trent, but curious onlookers surrounded them.

"YOU ARE AN IDIOT; I DIDN'T DO ANYTHING WRONG."

Trent's office was a block from the courthouse and next door to a bail bondsman. At four in the afternoon, the foot traffic was at its peak, which finally explained why he met Carl outside. Tomorrow, half the town would talk about it.

"YOUR WIFE COMES FROM GOOD PEOPLE, BUT YOU ARE CON MAN."

Carl's white hair stuck to his head with perspiration. The sweat stung his eyes and blurred his vision. A small crowd formed to gawk at the two men, one calm, the other red hot.

"YOU KEEP MY WIFE OUTTA THIS." Carl tried to turn Trent's words inside out, but he seemed to have an unintended effect. Trent's demeanor changed, his eyes shifted, and a bemused expression took over his face. Carl felt a tap on his shoulder and heard a man's voice behind him.

"What's going on?" said a policeman. "Trent, is everything all right?"

"We are okay," Trent said. Carl took off his glasses and wiped his eyes with a white cotton handkerchief. The lawyer continued to provoke him.

"I'll see you in court."

The officer stood close while Carl put his glasses back on, carefully folded his handkerchief, and slid it into his back pocket. His hand stroked his mustache.To anyone looking at him now, Carl appeared to be a harmless grandfather staring at the ground until Trent opened the office door. Carl looked up just in time to see it shut.

"What was that all about?" The policeman asked.

"Nothing. Us two are like oil and water. We can't do business together." Carl attempted a smile. "Thanks for cutting him off. How's your family doin'?"

"We're fine. My wife's wishing for school to start already, but other than that..." Fred said, laughing.

"Can you believe it? My boy is headed for college in two months."

"Zack? That's impossible; just yesterday, he was pitching balls in middle school."

"Yep, he sure was."

They both ogled a pretty girl in a short skirt, wearing stilettos.

Carl whispered in Fred's ear. "The shorter the skirt, the lower the heel should be on the shoe."

Fred giggled.

"You are the worst." The policeman's eyes brightened with appreciation, informing Carl that Fred was on his side now.

"Are you getting off soon? I'd like to take you out for a beer." Carl put his hands together and swung like he was hitting a golf ball.

"Sorry, I got a few more hours of policing. Speaking of which, your truck is parked too close to a fire hydrant."

"Oops—I'll move it right now." He saluted Fred and crossed the street. When he drove away, he grabbed his phone and left a message for his wife.

"Sheila," he said in a voice he used for funerals, "my friend Bob's real messed up. Some of us guys are going to take him out so he can share with us what's going on with him and Anita. Don't expect me until eight."

Sheila's phone rang while she and her sister, Jean, sorted laundry. It was a scene from the 1950s, washing, ironing, and mending Zack's old clothes. She was wearing a full apron with a bib and two front pockets. The self-belt crossed in the back and tied in a front, a signature style for her and others who are thin enough to do it. Sheila Ewing, nee Hayward, got along well with her large family, but Jean was her best friend and confidante.

"That's Carl," Sheila said when her phone rattled a version of "Second Line." Jean picked it up and handed it to her.

"Let it go to voicemail. I'll call him back later." Sheila swept her fingers through her curly brown hair. It was a habit she had since childhood, an effort to relieve tension. Her siblings used to tease her, claiming the hand was checking to see if the hair was still there.

"What's the matter? Why wouldn't you take your husband's call?"

"I'm sick of his theatrics." Sheila put the stacked tee shirts into a cardboard box.

"Try living with Bill, he has to have the last word on everything. Throw me the tape and a marker."

"I'm serious," Sheila pursed her lips in determination, "No one knows Carl the way I do."

"Are you and Carl having trouble?"

"No, no trouble, just a gnawing feeling of regret on my part." Sheila sank into a chair opposite Jean. "Carl is not the man I thought he was."

"I think it is normal for people to change when they get older; it's a form of adaptation." Jean was a high school guidance counselor—and back then, she thought she knew everything.

"My question is: what will the next thirty years be like?" She looked around the elegant dining room with twelve place settings, a chandelier, and a handsome portrait of her family. It was hard for Jean to feel sorry for Sheila.

"Is it because Zack is leaving for college soon?"

"Partly, no more children at home means I am freer to choose how I spend my time."

"What is the other part?"

Sheila shrugged. "The lies alone are enough to drive me insane."

"What lies?"

"Senseless, juvenile distortion of fact; I feel like I'm sharing my life with a four-year-old."

"Do you mean tall tales?" Jean liked to guess the diagnosis. "Maybe he is getting dementia or having micro-strokes."

"No, nothing that grand. White lies that have no purpose."

"Let's listen to his message." Jean shoved the phone closer to Sheila, and their heads hovered over it.

"Sheila, my friend Bob's real messed up—some of us guys are going to take him out so he can share with us what's going on with him and Anita. Don't expect me until eight."

"I see nothing melodramatic about this message." Jean said, enamored by the husky voice of a whiskey drinking country music singer. "He is telling you what he is doing and who he is doing it with. Bill's message would be shorter," Jean imitated the tenor voice of her husband. "I'll be late."

"No, I'm sure you hear nothing out of the ordinary, but what I hear is a lie."

Carl's magnetism was so powerful even Jean wanted to trust him.

"What is the lie here?"

"I know for a fact that Bob and his wife don't have any problems. Carl is making an excuse to go out drinking with his friends on a weeknight. And the word 'share'—men like Carl don't share their feelings with each other. Who does he think he's killing?" She hastened to correct herself, "I mean to say, kidding." Sheila shook her head at her mistake.

"I believe you. I do. But from the outside looking in, people think you and Carl have the perfect family."

Sheila changed the subject by scooping up the folded jeans, and putting them into a plastic bag, "I hope this helps you make your quota for the Junior League."

"If it is a lie; it is a white lie. And the purpose of a white lie is to be kind, even if it misses the mark."

The sisters, arms full, walked to Jean's car.

"I know in my heart that Carl loves you; He has never been unfaithful; that is saying a lot."

"I suppose, but adultery is hard for men to pull off in a small town, and if caught, they are in hot water."

"Have you prayed about this?"

"I pray about it, but I don't get any answers."

"Maybe it is not the answer you want to hear."

"Maybe," Sheila wrung her hands. "But we are not talking about Santa Claus or the Tooth Fairy. Carl's lies are disrespectful and stupid because it is so easy for me to check. All I have to do is call up Anita, right?" Sheila waited for Jean to unlock her car. "One other thing, I can guarantee; he will not be home at eight."

After Jean left, Sheila selected a package of monogrammed note cards off the sideboard.

"Dear Mrs. Nash," she wrote. "Thank you for the Old Spice After Shave (and for teaching me in fifth grade). You were one of my favorite teachers. Love, Zack." She placed the note in an envelope and addressed it. Taking another blank note from the pile, she wrote: "Dear Dr. and Mrs. Batson, Thank you for the wonderful Cross pen. I am looking forward to using it at Hillcrest College. My Best, Zack." She had four more to write when footsteps came near, and Zack appeared, peeking in from the living room.

"Mom, what are you doing?" He hesitated at the door. Zack was the spitting image of his father at the same age, sandy hair, blue eyes, and thin lips. He was taller, though—about two inches taller. Today, he seemed to be in a rush.

"Would you turn on the light, Zack?"

The warm chandelier light enhanced the sheen on the cherry veneer of the table.

"Come sit down with me." Sheila felt as though she hadn't talked to him all week. Zack came in the room, but did not sit down; he remained standing between the family portrait on one side of him and the sheer draperies on the other.

He's in a hurry to be independent, she thought. It's true, all teenagers manifest worrisome phases. Her daughters were no exception. There was a time when Aimee would wash her hair once a month. And Renee left one morning in her car, picked up her boyfriend, and drove three hundred miles to the French Quarter for lunch. If it hadn't been for the souvenir napkin, Sheila would never have known about it. Zack's phase was to become more distant.

"I can't, Mom, I'm already late for Jennifer's party." It seemed awkward to Sheila that he spoke from such a distance, as if he were avoiding a physical closeness to her.

"Is the family having something fancy?" Zack needed a haircut and shave.

"No, they are cooking outside—hamburgers, I think." He turned and looked at the family portrait. "Ralph was the best dog a family could have. Look how happy he was when we won Family of the Year."

"If you are going to the party, you had better get ready. Didn't it start at five? It's six-fifteen now."

Zack still lingered by the portrait. He's scruffy, he's distant, and he is forgetful, she thought.

"It's okay, Zack," she said, reading his mind. "I have a few more to write, and then we won't have to worry about them."

CHAPTER 2

25 August 2017

Gower, Louisiana sits on the east bank of the Ouachita River. To the west of town, hills and pine trees, the "piney woods," stretch to Texas. To the east, an alluvial plain extends seventy miles to the great Mississippi River. The junction of forest and fertile land creates a marvelous diversity of wildlife and plants—*a sportsman's paradise.* But Gower is insular, separated from Baton Rouge and New Orleans by outdated meandering highways.

Zack who lived in Gower all of his life, was eager to leave. One more day, a nod to his parents, and then free to go to college.

"Mom," he touched her shoulder. His mother opened her eyes. "Dad, good morning, I made you coffee."

His mother rolled over and propped up her pillow. His Dad put on his glasses and looked at the alarm clock. It was 5:30.

"You're up early, Son."

"I'm going to work with you this morning. Thanks for letting me have the summer off."

"That's great," his mother said, "but this afternoon, we pack."

"Yes, ma'am."

Zack slept through breakfast senior summer, avoiding his parents because he did his best writing at night. Mr. Abernathy, his English teacher, called him a prodigy and begged his parents to give Zack time to polish his work before college life took its toll.

While his mother poached eggs and his Dad read the newspaper, Zack sat at the kitchen table, attempting to make a list. He found it harder than he expected. It seemed impossible to think of everything he took for granted at home.

"Mom, where are my swimming trunks? I can't find them anywhere."

He was holding his cell phone in one hand and a fork in the other.

"Did you try the bottom drawer in your bureau?"

"No, I'll look." Zack stirred four teaspoons of sugar in his coffee. "I'm looking at the college website now. We should be there at nine." He used his finger to scroll down the page.

His mother stood up and grabbed two envelopes from the kitchen island. "Here's a check so you can open up a bank account in Troy."

Zack was still staring at his phone, but he reached out his hand.

"And here is a credit card for emergencies and books."

Zack took the card from her and stared at it.

"Visa should put your picture on the card."

"It would make sense, but they don't. Your roommate's Mom said they have a refrigerator and want you to bring your television." His mother joined them at the table.

"What does he need a television for?" asked his father, who had a knack of entering a conversation and leaving it without warning.

"Well, he has a television in his room, so he might as well bring it." His mother stood up to get the orange juice, and as she passed Zack, she bent over and hugged him. He shuddered.

"Dad, I'm ready to go when you are...," Zack rearranged the food on his plate with the fork. When his father slapped the newspaper down on the table, Zack jumped.

"Let's go make some noise," his father said.

"Yes, sir!" While his father gave his mother a perfunctory kiss goodbye, Zack picked up his plate and shoved the uneaten breakfast down the sink disposal.

The morning's weather, for August, was perfect, clear skies and not too hot—yet.

"Thank goodness for the weather; I always worry it will rain when I schedule a foundation." His Dad offered him a breath mint and produced a set of house plans from the back seat.

The plans, consisting of ten sheets of paper, twenty-four by thirty-six inches, rolled up like wrapping paper, required a suitable table, so Zack held them unfurled in his lap. They drove without speaking until the truck turned left onto a narrow road that Zack knew well. He and his friends fished from the bridge he and his Dad crossed.

Zack tried to sound enthusiastic. "This is a really nice location for a house, Dad."

"You bet. This house has only one neighbor, so the spillover of birds and animals from the refuge is significant, deer prints everywhere, and wait til you see the view of the bayou."

The road passed a public boat dock before coming to a fork. Going left would take them to the Department of Wildlife and Fisheries Office, but they veered right to a new residential development.

When they arrived at the job site, the owners, John and Bess, were serving mimosas to their friends, and Steve, his father's foreman, waited on the street. Carl stuck his arm out of the cab to hail Steve but did not stop. Instead, he drove to an empty lot, parking twenty feet away. Steve, waiting at the opposite end of the groundwork, smiled as if they were celebrating his birthday, but he said nothing. He knew his place. Zack knew his place, too. As the heir apparent, he had to greet the homeowners.

The white party-tent stood out in stark contrast to the myriad shades of green, gray, and brown on the bayou bank. Zack thought the spot was breathtaking in the natural state where cypress trees and knees commanded the view vertically, while the Bermuda grass carpeted the ground. The early morning sun sprinkled patches of light through the tree branches, but its reflection off the water was spectacular. The full sun and steady breeze made the bayou glitter like a lake. He and his Dad stood side by side taking in the view, and Zack smelled Carl's peppermint breath when he leaned in close to whisper.

"Never build a white house on the bayou, because white will overpower everything. Come on, I'll introduce you."

Zack could sense the excitement by the pitch of the conversation and laughter flowing over him with the wind.

Carl shook the husband's hand and nodded to the wife.

"Good Mornin'," he said.

Zack saw his Aunt Jean and Aunt Martha with their husbands and waved to them.

"The cement truck will be here in about ten minutes. The foundation always looks smaller than you'd expect, but it is an optical illusion. Don't worry, the measurements are correct."

"Carl, would you like a drink?" the husband asked.

"No thanks, I keep my eyes on the work." Carl chuckled. "But, please, you might as well drink one for me."

The homeowner grinned at this remark, and his eyes met Carl's eyes to signify respect.

"You can relax and enjoy the day. I know how hard you worked for this house." Carl turned to Zack. "This here is my son, Zack."

Zack smiled while he shook hands with the husband and the wife.

"I saw the plans," he said. "Your home is going to be beautiful." Zack was quoting a standard phrase from the residential contractor handbook. If there is such a thing, his father wrote it, he thought.

"I love an Acadian house." This much was true.

"Zack's here to help me put them anchor bolts in." His Dad pointed to four boxes of giant screws lying on the ground. "Tomorrow he's leaving for college."

"That's great," said the husband. "Good luck with your studies."

Zack followed his father to a picnic table where they unrolled the plans. A set of builder's plans should remain at the job site at all times, but in the early stages, a job site lacks a place to put them.

"Don't forget. Nothing makes a greater impression on a homeowner than the huge concrete trucks and the man who controls them." Zack had heard this before.

"They are a fleet of dinosaurs," Zack said as the first truck came into view.

Before Zack hated the construction business, he loved it. By the age of five, he memorized names of heavy equipment: backhoe, excavator, front-end loader, and so on. But he agreed with his father. Nothing was more amazing, or louder, than the cement mixer truck with a boom that could rise as high as 124 feet, pumping cement at a rate of 30 cubic meters per hour.

The first truck arrived within minutes, followed by another, and another, until the entire area of red clay, steel rods, and pipes drowned in a gray soup. The floor was a moonscape perforated by vertical white plastic water pipes, and smaller gray metal conduit tubes to convey electrical wires. A wooden mold would be removed later.

Zack followed his Dad around the perimeter, watching him drop the anchor bolts into the wet cement, not more than twelve inches from the corners and no more than four feet from the center. The concrete cures for at least thirty days before the framing crew can secure the wooden exterior walls to the foundation by threading a horizontal board onto anchor bolts and topping each with a hexagonal nut.

"Nothing is more satisfying than pouring a foundation," his Dad said. "Oh, and if you see any of those garter snakes with the yellow stripe, try to catch one of them—your Mom wants one for her garden."

"Mom's scared to death of snakes." Zack never understood why his father enjoyed aggravating his mother.

"No, she is afraid of poisonous snakes; garter snakes —they are good for the garden."

Zack distinctly remembered his Mom telling him she did not want any kind of snake in her yard. "Even though a snake may not be poisonous, they can still bite you," she cautioned.

"Your mother's smart, Zack, but what I love about her is the lack of common sense. I got a bag in the truck if you find one." Carl plopped another anchor bolt in.

When the parade was over, there was nothing left to do. Steve took over now, allowing Carl to stand near the homeowners to claim success.

"Hey, Baby. Everything went great, no glitches whatsoever; I wish my Daddy had been here to see it." he held the phone to his ear, nodding his head, and walking in place. "I'll have Zack home in a few minutes."

On the drive home, Zack had one burning question.

"Why are they pouring the foundation in August? It's going to be too hot."

"Rich people are always in a hurry. They can't wait. If I told him I wanted to pour it in February, he'd hire another builder."

"Okay, but doesn't he mind taking a chance?"

"By the time he notices a crack in the foundation, he'll be ready to upgrade. Makes you wonder how they got their money in the first place," his father laughed. "Come on, Son, I've got to take you home."

When Zack entered the house, the odor from the kitchen was sickening. The smell of chicken frying in a pan conjured a panoply of disgusting images. *Why would the Motherboard sacrifice a chicken, and the Nazi pour a fragile foundation on his last day at home?* He told his mother a lie: the homeowners served brunch, and he wasn't hungry. While she ate alone, he rested in his room, glad to get away from his parents—nothing was more annoying to the muse than living in their house. When his mother knocked on his door, he willed himself to allow her to help him pack, and when they finished, he excused himself to spend time on his laptop.

Flushed from the exertion, his mother managed to create one more task.

"I'll get my car," Zack said, "and wait for you out front."

Soon his mother appeared at the front door, still wearing old blue jeans and a long-sleeve shirt, but now carrying her purse and a legal-sized envelope boldly labeled HAYWARD FARMS, INC.

"Uncle Martin wants to see you before you leave." Sheila settled herself in the car. "I think you are his favorite nephew."

The thirty-minute drive to uncle Martin's house was a familiar one for both of them. Six generations of the Hayward family had farmed the homeplace. They quickly reached the city limits of Gower, and once in the countryside, Zack focused on the scenery. He wasn't planning on coming back.

Sheila opened the envelope and reviewed the invoices she had scanned into her computer. The corn, cotton, and soybean fields reminded Zack of his grandfather. Both of his grandfathers were dead now, but Zack had a relationship with Granddad Hayward. He was too young to remember Mr. Ewing.

"I'm wondering how things will be for you when I'm gone," Zack said while he drove.

"That's sweet, Zack, but I will be fine. We always knew you would grow up, didn't we?"

"Don't let Dad put snakes in your garden."

Sheila ran her fingers through her hair and rubbed her neck. "Where did you get that idea?" She drew her chin in and cocked her head forward while she stared at the road ahead of them.

"Your God can't protect you from him."

"Honestly, I don't know what you are talking about. Concentrate on your studies. I will be fine." Sheila put the paperwork back in the envelope. "Be sure you don't miss the turnoff for Martin's house."

"No way would I miss it."

Before Zack could pick up a hammer, he and his cousins spent hours at the farm, jumping in a truck filled with raw cotton, riding in the voluminous cab of the cotton picker, or playing hide-and-seek in the cornfield. Granddad could pack four small children in his picker. Those childhood memories of the farm, his cousins, and his grandfather were unblemished. No matter where he went, he vowed never to forget any of the details.

They turned left into Martin's driveway, a primitive gravel road leading to a grove of trees and three houses. From a distance, they appeared to be moving toward an island in a sea of cropland. Beyond the grove, a shop the size of a warehouse blended in with the cornstalks. There were no windows or distinguishing features of any kind creating a monolith, but its color erased it from the sweeping view. The eye is drawn to row upon row of verdant green cornstalks which slam into the edge of dense woods.

Martin's house, a red brick California bungalow, was the original Hayward home. Sheila, her two sisters, and her brother grew up in that house. Two modest wood-frame cottages, one on either side, were empty, but well maintained. Mr. Hayward built them for his farmhands in 1977, before mechanization took over those jobs.

Martin sat on the porch, his feet propped up on a chair, drinking iced tea. He did not wait for them to stop; instead, he ran down the steps to meet them. Zack thought his uncle looked as though he couldn't be happier.

"I am so glad you could stop by," he said as he hugged his sister and shook Zack's hand. "Come on inside. Don't mind me. I was washing the car and didn't have time to shower." Martin was rail thin and dressed in tattered jeans, a yellowed dress shirt, and well-worn cowboy boots. Sweat and dust covered his clothes, and his face reminded Zack of the black and white pictures of men living during the depression.

They followed Martin to the front door which he held wide open as they walked from the porch into the house.

"It's a lot cooler inside," he said.

When Martin divorced, he let his wife take most of the furniture. The living room looked empty except for a sofa and a massive bookcase stuffed with books. There were no lamps, no coffee table, no nick-knacks, and no pictures.

"Can I get you a coke or water? I've learned to make tea." Martin, frugal in most of his affairs, was the consummate host.

"Nothing for me," said Sheila.

"How about you, Zack?" Martin's face softened when he looked at his nephew.

"Huh," Zack's mind was miles away. He imagined a story set in an empty house like this one, except the fictional house was in Vermont. In Martin's house, he could hear the muse, but there was something in the Ewing house that ravaged her.

"Do you want a coke?" Martin broke his concentration.

"No, thanks." Zack took a seat on the sofa. "I like the changes you made."

"It's called bachelor roulette." Martin laughed, still standing. Sheila sat next to Zack, and he inched his way to the opposite side.

"I bought you a graduation gift," his uncle said. "It's in the bedroom—wait here, and I'll get it." Martin returned with a package the size of a hardback book, wrapped in the cartoon section of the newspaper.

Zack opened the gift, keeping the wrapping paper as intact as he could, and held the book up for them to see.

"It's an old copy of the Odyssey," Martin showed him the title page. "See, it is one hundred years old."

"Thank you so much." Elated, Zack flipped through the pages. "They don't read classics in high school anymore, uncle Martin." The book was leather bound and perfectly preserved.

"Martin," Sheila passed the HAYWARD FARMS, INC envelope to him, "here are the invoices, all stored in the cloud."

"Thanks for keeping me modern. When we finish up with the corn, I'll distribute the checks."

By the time Martin took it over, the Hayward farm was a substantial source of ongoing income for the Hayward children: Sheila, Jean, Martha, and Martin.

"Zack, you sure you don't want a coke or something?" Zack's knee was jumping up and down, and he tried to make it stop.

"No, I'm fine," Zack felt the need to move his legs; his good mood was dissipating. Embarrassed, he stood up to shift his weight from one foot to the other while holding the book in both hands. It was a relief to walk in place.

When Sheila suggested that they should go, Zack walked out the door to the car where he waited for Sheila to say goodbye.

His mother did not take long, and soon he was enjoying the drive, but wishing they were driving to college instead of home. After about five miles, something dark crossed the road, grabbing Zack's attention. He couldn't make it out, but it wasn't a deer, maybe it was a small bear.

"Did you see that, Mom?"

"What? I was checking the time just now."

"I think I might need glasses," Zack brushed his hair away from his eyes.

"Do you want me to drive?"

"No, it's not that bad—kind of comes and goes." Zack shrugged it off.

"We should have your eyes checked."

"Everything looks fine now."

"Good."

CHAPTER 3

26 August 2017

Sheila awoke to the smell of burnt toast.

"Zack, honey, what are you doing?"

"What does it look like I'm doing?"

"Well, to me, it looks like a disaster."

An open box of pancake mix was on the floor and six slices of bread burned to charcoal lay on the kitchen counter.

"The toaster's not working."

"It's the setting on the toaster; you've turned it up too high." Sheila opened the broom closet to clean up the flour. "I'll take care of breakfast. Start putting your stuff in the car so we can leave on time." Sheila shook her head; teenagers, she thought. "And please wake up your Dad."

The family drove two cars to Hillcrest College, took stock of the dorm room, and made a cozy space out of Zack's half; his roommate would be a day late. Hillcrest accommodated 12,000 undergraduates, granting them a four-year degree. When Sheila attended, so many years ago, Hillcrest was a junior college. Soon after she finished her education, the administration built one building after another and thrived beyond everyone's expectations. All the buildings were colonial red brick now, with white trim.

"I'm so proud of you, Zack," Sheila said to him while they walked down the stairs of the dormitory and out onto the veranda to say goodbye. "Let's get someone to take a picture of us!" and then to someone passing by, she said, "Do you mind taking a picture of us—with the sign?"

"No problem," said a student wearing a bright "Can I Help You" tee-shirt. He took Sheila's cell phone and snapped a photo which included the Nicholson Honors Dorm sign. Sheila was holding back tears when she hugged him, and his Dad shook his hand.

"I think you are making a big mistake," he whispered to him. "You have a job waiting for you at home."

"Bye, Mom, take care." He turned to face his father, "Bye, Dad."

Zack spun around to return his room while Sheila watched him get swallowed up by freshman students streaming into the building.

"Well," Carl shrugged, "I guess that's it for us."

In the parking lot, Carl opened the passenger door for his wife. Sheila slid into place and checked her face in the mirror. Her mascara was intact. She had just enough time to apply a fresh coat of lipstick before Carl put the key in the motor, and soon, they were leaving the campus on a winding road encased by live oaks. Sheila kicked off her high heels and wiggled her toes. Hillcrest College was three hours east of Gower. As she settled in for the ride, she took off her gold watch, a gift from her mother, and her wedding band, dropping them in the well between the seats for safekeeping. She dug into her purse to find a small bottle of hand lotion and rubbed her hands together, allowing the cream to sink in.

When Carl eased onto the entrance to the interstate highway, he said, "Things sure have changed since I was a kid. I learned everything on the job with my Daddy, but kids these days go to college, and then they leave you."

"Are you afraid of being left?"

"No, that is just how it is these days. Kids don't want to take over the family business anymore."

"I guess we will just have to see." Sheila stretched her arms; she had suffered from a frozen shoulder in the past, and the stretches became a habit. "I'm tired, aren't you?"

"Is my blue suit clean?" Carl ignored her question. Or maybe he didn't hear it. "I want to wear it Monday while I meet with a lawyer." Carl spoke without emotion.

"Yes, it is, but why? Why are you having a meeting?"

"Somebody is always complaining in the construction business, Sheila. We ain't sure yet if we are going to court, but we might." Carl kept his eyes on the road. "You want to go out and eat tonight?"

"I have something at home if you would rather eat there. Aren't you tired?"

"Naw, I'm ain't tired. Going out is good advertising for me. Folks run into me, and they think about remodeling the kitchen."

"I didn't know that."

"Well, now you do. Baby, if people don't see me out and about, they think about remodeling the kitchen and hire somebody else."

Carl lowered the visor to block the sunlight.

"Just so you know, my lawyer and me are going to try to settle the dispute—amicably." He said "amicably," as if he had just learned a brand-new word.

"Amicably," he said again to feel it roll off his tongue, "but he don't think the guy will settle up with us."

By now, they were driving into a setting sun, which was blinding. Sheila extracted her sunglasses from her purse and put them on. Carl turned on the radio. After a while, she interrupted a staticky version of the weather.

"Are you worried about a lawsuit? You seem so quiet."

"I got a little headache, nothing serious." Carl rolled his head around, stretching the muscles in his neck.

"Sorry. I didn't know."

After a few minutes of silence, there was venom in his voice as he said, "It just pisses me off that you can't understand Zack belongs in the business with me."

Sheila did not reply.

"Do you know what my Mama used to say?" Carl raised his voice even louder.

"No, what?"

"She said, me and my Daddy was like two peas in a pod. My Daddy built the business for me, and I took it over."

"Carl, the restaurant you like, will be on the left."

"I'm looking for it," Carl gripped the steering wheel. "This log truck in front of me is throwing pieces of pine tree at us. That pinging sound—and the dancing red flags—is making me crazy." He tugged at his seat belt. "We got to get around this redneck." He jerked into the other lane and sped up to pass the truck, nearly missing the turn.

After dinner, Carl drove Sheila to the front of their house. He rubbed his eyes hard and massaged his temples.

"Baby, my migraine is coming back. While I park your car, would you run upstairs and get me some Advil? I'll be in the office crunching numbers for the meeting tomorrow."

Sheila grabbed her purse and literature the school provided to the parents. "Sure, it's been a long emotional day." Consumed by her errand, Sheila let herself in the front door.

Carl parked the car in the garage and sat frozen in the driver's seat for a few seconds, then lowered his hand into the well between the seats. He picked up Sheila's watch and cupped it in his hand.

"*Son,*" his father advised him, "*Every transgression has to be addressed. Take something sentimental.*"

***

Gower, though isolated, was a town well suited for raising families—safe, no long commutes, lots of outdoor activities, and a flourishing 4-H club. As the seat of Arcadia Parish, it is the center of parish government which provides jobs for its people and a thriving, if small, newspaper and lifestyle magazine. The courthouse, surrounded by a tree-shaded park, marks the center of town. There is just enough freedom to be content in our small town. But the residents of Gower do not condone divorce, and at this point in her life my sister was considering a divorce.

Sheila knew of only one person in the extended Hayward family, living or dead, who divorced, and he was our brother, Martin. Our mother would not even say the word divorce; she would spell it when the subject came up. In her view, D-I-V-O-R-C-E was never an option. Daddy advised: "Choose wisely and stick to your promise—till death do us part." Our parents formed these beliefs when they were poor—land poor, as Daddy would say.

Our father referred to himself as a dirt farmer. Still, by the time Sheila was ready for marriage, the family was prominent and considered by the townspeople to be wealthy. Mr. Hayward built a minor fortune, by working hard, saving, and borrowing no money. But he failed to appreciate the unintended consequences for his children.

Sheila, who was average in appearance, brown hair, brown eyes, forgettable face, and figure, became an item when the boys began looking for wives instead of girlfriends. Carl, who joined his father's business the day after he graduated from high school, became interested in Sheila a few days before she ordered her cap and gown. He had competition, but his courtship was intense. When Sheila's father announced that she could not marry Carl or anyone else until she attended college, the other boys lost interest. Carl happily agreed with him.

"One of the things I love most about your daughter," he said when he asked for her hand in marriage, "is that she is smart. I think she should go to college." Sheila accepted his proposal on her nineteenth birthday when he gifted her a set of plans—plans for the house he would build for her while he waited. Carl exceeded everyone's expectations.

CHAPTER 4

27 August 2017

Sheila loved her house. Carl designed it based upon a plantation home in Natchez, one that Mr. Hayward admired. It was not a mansion, but it was large, with four spacious bedrooms upstairs, a grand staircase, and a gorgeous wraparound porch. After a honeymoon in Hot Springs, he carried Sheila over the threshold. His muscular arms conveyed her up the stairs, placing her on the bed. Their neighbors questioned how a young couple could afford such a big house. Some suspected Sheila's father gave them a loan, and he had. Her friends wondered how Sheila Hayward snagged someone as popular as Carl Ewing.

As the children left, her decorating challenge was to make the house cozy for two people, and she thought she had succeeded until she awoke the day after Zack left home. It was five AM; Carl was sleeping, and the room was cold, sixty-five degrees exactly. He set the air conditioning at night to compensate for his daytime hours in the sun. An unexpected weariness enveloped her as she lay uncomfortable, lonely, and cold.

Too early to get up for church, her stiff shoulder prevented her from falling asleep again; she had to stretch. Trying not to disturb Carl, she reached for her robe, did a few arm exercises, and moved to sit by the window. It was a familiar pose for her, sitting sideways on the love-seat, wrapped in an afghan, waiting for daylight. She tugged at her blanket to wrap it tighter.

A friend in high school crocheted the throw for her sixteenth birthday. The girls, back then, learned to sew or knit a variety of items, but her friend was talented. Sandra created a design with different shades of blue yarn, and the color was soothing then and now. Letting these friends drift away was Sheila's biggest regret now that the house seemed empty.

Eighty students graduated in Sheila's high school class, and she knew them well as the student council secretary all four years, a record in the school's history. Lowell Graham served as president for four years, also a record. Together, they settled disputes, planned the proms, and conducted fundraisers. Everyone said they made a great team. The student government appointments kept them out of cliques and bound them together until graduation. At the end of senior summer, Lowell left Gower to attend Tulane, promising to invite her to New Orleans during the Mardi Gras holiday. They planned to see each other in Gower over the Thanksgiving and Christmas holidays, too. Lowell never called, but by the Thanksgiving recess, Carl had his hooks in her.

This morning, on a whim, she leaned forward to open her laptop and searched for Lowell on Facebook. She wondered whether he would use the name, Lowell, or his middle name, Abel. She tried Abel Graham first.

It seemed odd that Mr. and Mrs. Graham would choose that name. Everyone knew what happened to Cain's brother. At first, Sheila thought calling him Abel was bad luck. But Lowell explained her doubts away when he told her Abel was the first human born naturally.

"My parents had me first," Lowell said when Sheila met him on the first day of high school. "Adam and Eve had Abel first. Then they conceived Cain."

He spoke like a teacher.

"Abel was the first farmer, too. Did you know that?" He smiled, making his eyes squint. "We have something in common already." Sheila warmed to his easygoing confidence.

"Are you interested in politics?" he asked her when she was his date for Senior prom.

"I don't know. Are you?"

"I don't know either," he laughed, and the gym filled with the sound of him. She pictured what he would look like as an older man.

What if Abel slept where Carl sleeps now?

Sunlight filled the room, and Carl rolled over. Closing her laptop, Sheila vowed to search for Abel later.

"Baby, I've been thinking about what you said last night." Carl surprised her while they sat at the kitchen table. "I am proud Zack is going to college, and if you want me to, I can remodel your kitchen."

He looked around the room as if he were taking stock of the updates he would recommend.
"We could do it this winter," he added.

"Let me think about it; I don't remember saying anything about the kitchen yesterday." Sheila put the dirty dishes in the sink to wash them later. "Coming to church? We're planning to go out for lunch after." Sheila picked up her coffee to carry it to the bedroom.

"No, you go ahead. I'm spending the morning researching a bid."

She did not remember her ring and watch until shifting her car into drive. Surprised that she forgot them, but knowing they were inches away in the car, she blindly slipped her hand into the well. There was never a day when she dressed without those two accessories. Her fingers probed every inch of the tiny space. The watch was "something borrowed" for the wedding, which became a gift after the ceremony. She retrieved the wedding ring, but not the watch. Puzzled, she walked back into the house for a flashlight and asked Carl about it.

"Did you see my watch last night?"

"No, Baby. Are you missing it?" He had the newspaper lying flat on the table, appearing to study an article. He shot a quick sideways glance at her.

"Yes, I'm sure I left it in the car." Sheila pulled open a drawer in the kitchen.

"I bet you dropped it on the floor. Did you look under the floor mats?"

"I'm going to look now." Sheila took the flashlight and got down on her knees to shine it under the passenger and driver's seats. It was not under the floor mats either. As a last resort, she looked in the glove compartment, knowing the watch would not be there. She studied the concrete floor of the garage, the steps leading up to the kitchen door, and the floor of the kitchen. She scoured the bedroom, looking at surfaces where she might have placed it.

The missing watch caused her to arrive late to church. The congregation was already singing: "When We All Get to Heaven." Easing herself into the pew, already filled with her sisters and their husbands. she slipped past them to stand by Martin and share his hymnal.

"Where's Mama?" she whispered.

"She's got a cold."

Sheila's family filled the fifth row on the right. When the singing stopped, and they sat down, Martin pointed to dirt on Sheila's knee. She tried to scrub it off with her hand.

"Today," the preacher began, "I have prepared a sermon on Love: what is it?"

No one could have stolen my watch.

"But not to chase a rabbit: Does anyone in the congregation follow the NASCAR races?" The church members were quiet. The preacher stood up on his toes and back down, held his sermon in front of him, and never looked at it once.

It has to be in the car.

"I love to watch those guys (and gals) speed around the track. My wife tells me I should love to rake the leaves, and if I LOVED her, I would." The congregation laughed softly.

"Sometimes we use the word love carelessly. Today I want to dig down to the essence of the word. The apostle Paul's definition of Love in the Love Chapter tells us there are three things that endure—faith, hope, and Love—the greatest of these is Love. Paul is telling us that Love is constant. It's not here one day and gone the next. He tells us how to recognize Love, too. Love is patient, and Love is kind."

Did I bring it inside?

"I believe it would be correct to say that Love is never suffocating."

"Who has a child attending kindergarten this year? Raise your hand." The preacher raised his hand to show how to do it.

Was the car door locked?

"When you drop your child off at kindergarten or college, it's a poignant moment, right?" He paused long enough to survey his audience. "And who had a child leave home to get married?" Other hands went up, including Sheila's. "And finally, who has experienced the death of a loved one?" Everyone raised their hands. "I think we all know that just because we love someone, it does not mean we can keep them by our side."

Maybe Carl left it unlocked.

"Christians KNOW that learning to let go of someone you love is a fact of life. You don't stop loving them, but you let them go because it is the right thing to do.

"There is another kind of Love, but it is the Love that deceives us. This kind of Love feels wonderful because the good times are so great. Every twist and turn that causes despair is followed by a thrilling rebirth of devotion. This kind of Love is addicting, corrosive, and dangerous because your Love is pure, and the object of your Love is malicious.

"Turn away from the promise of Love when it is unkind, ephemeral, or deceitful. Turn away when obedience becomes servitude. You can still love and turn away, just as you would avoid a rattlesnake."

Sheila and the entire congregation now knew the sermon referred to the tragic death of one of their members. Everyone in the sanctuary, including her, was attentive now.

"For decades, a member of this church battled a monster with the patience of a Saint. Today we mourn her passing, but tomorrow we will go forward with Love.

"To be Christian is to love and forgive, but not to be deceived by the devil. Love is patient and kind. Use Paul's words as a litmus test and turn away from Love that is impatient and destructive. Teach this message to your children. I pledge today that you can count on this church to help you if you are in danger." He reached for his Bible to read, First Corinthians Chapter 13, verse 1-3.

> If I could speak in any language in heaven or on earth but didn't love others, I would make a meaningless noise like a loud gong or a clanging cymbal. If I had the gift of prophecy, and if I knew all the mysteries of the future... if I didn't love others, I would be of no value whatsoever. (New Living Translation)

"Wow," Sheila's sister Jean said when the family gathered on the lawn in front of the church. "I did not see that one coming."

"Me neither," said Sheila. "No telling what her life was like. I never dreamed he would kill her."

"Obviously, she never dreamed of it either."

"He is claiming it was suicide," said Bill. "It will be in the newspaper tomorrow."

"One way or another, he killed her," Martin added.

"Sis, are you going to lunch with us? You can be my date."

"Sure, Carl is working in the office all day." Sheila felt her phone vibrate a text message.

"It's Zack," she said. "He says he needs glasses."

After lunch, Sheila and Martin walked to her car. She was more relaxed now, having enjoyed the company of her family.

"With Zack gone, I can help you more, not only with the books but with other jobs as well." Sheila glanced at her bare wrist to check the time.

"I can't think of anyone better qualified." Martin opened her car door. "In that case," he said, "would you like to go to the Farm Bureau Meeting this year? It's not too late to register."

"I can't think of anything I would enjoy more."

Mr. Hayward took the entire family to New Orleans every summer to attend the Louisiana State Farm Bureau meeting. Sheila and her siblings, especially as they got older, loved the freedom only a Farm Bureau meeting could offer four preteen children. Armed with a room key, they spent hours in the hotel pool and cruising the hospitality rooms for free food and promotional giveaways. Everything was free if your Daddy was a farmer.

Sheila welcomed Martin's invitation; it kept her looking forward even though tangles formed in her brain already, and Zack had only been gone one day. She vowed to stop overthinking everything. Life was too short to spend hours in remorse or accusations. That afternoon, she turned again to Facebook. Nine or ten of her classmates left Gower, and she vowed to find them all before the thirty-fifth reunion. The good news was her generation was now free to travel, to meet up, and to remember their youth.

Lowell Abel Graham was easy to find.

CHAPTER 5

9 October 2017

Zack overslept on the morning of his first exam. When he opened his eyes, his roommate's bed was empty, and his cell phone read eight-thirty. The exam started at nine. Quickly, he dressed in the clothes he shed on the floor the night before and ran out of the dorm, hesitating on the veranda referred to by students as Nicholson Beach. Looking left and right, he surveyed the campus before loping over the steps to the sidewalk that led to the fine arts building.

Zack reached the downstairs classroom at one minute to nine, out of breath and sweating through his shirt. A cowlick caused his hair to stick up in back, and he needed a shave. Appearing at the door, he hesitated.

"You just made it." A tall withered man, with a skeletal face, waved him in and noticed the boy misaligned the buttons on his shirt, and wasn't wearing shoes.

Zack studied the room's occupants, as if he were looking for someone, before taking the nearest empty seat. A multiple-choice exam rested on the desk.

Slam! The door closed, sealing the classroom. It felt stuffy, hot, and crowded.

"Good people, you may begin."

The room, a vacuum now, sounded of rustling paper and pencils clinking together, while Zack sat transfixed, looking at a blank page. The proctor who stood nearby watching him, approached his desk and turned the test over so he could read it.

As Zack stared at the questions, the letters elevated slightly off the page, suspended in air. He detected an infinitesimal degree of motion in the words, like a trembling of the typed image no longer anchored to the paper. In an instant, the page appeared to be its photographic negative; the areas of white space were now dark spaces that coalesced into the shape of an ink stain, and all the white words blew away. Zack raised his hand, and the proctor returned to help.

"May I go to the bathroom?" he said, trembling.

Carl, after eating breakfast at the airport café, drove to his first appointment. Miss Sarah, a loyal customer for years, expected him to arrive on time and often within minutes of her call. He parked in her driveway, slipped on a Breast Cancer bracelet, put a peppermint in his mouth, and stuffed dog treats in his pocket. A benevolent smile softened his features before he lowered himself from the truck to walk down an uneven sidewalk to her front gate. Sarah's husband died, leaving her a mansion, but it was on the wrong side of town. Drug deals took place in her backyard after dark.

Six feet away, a miniature poodle, penned in the front yard by a fence that Carl built, noticed him. She whipped herself into a frenzy, barking and jumping. Sasha drew back to allow him to enter. He latched the gate behind him. Reaching deep into his pocket, he recovered a treat and held it close to her nose. Her eyes watched him as she ate it out of his hand.

The path to the porch was worse than the sidewalk

along the street. Long-standing tree roots cracked the concrete and elevated parts of it. Carl almost fell when the dog began dancing between his feet, expecting more handouts.

"That's a good way to get stepped on, Sasha." Carl bent over to hand her another treat, feeling a dull ache in his back. "Here you go, sweetheart." He heard Miss Sarah step just outside the front door.

"Good mornin'," he said, while he slowly stood up.

"Good morning, Carl."

Carl met his client at his own wedding reception. Sheila's mother and Miss Sarah shared an interest in genealogical research before computers and gene testing made it easy. Together they qualified for membership in the Daughters of the American Revolution and the Daughters of the War of 1812.

"Come on into the kitchen. Coffee?" Today Miss Sarah wore a shirtwaist dress with pumps. In her youth, she was the belle of the ball, but she was in her eighties now, and most of her contemporaries had gone home, as she phrased it.

When Carl walked in, he detected a faint musty smell. Could be a small leak in the roof, he thought, and the house appeared cluttered. Sarah was too old to do housekeeping, but she was still trying. Her maid died years ago and was "irreplaceable."

"You know, Bob could fix anything."

"He was a good man," Carl bowed his head.

"Yes, he was. He always made sure I had a proper house. How's your family? I saw in the paper that your son graduated high school."

"Yeah, we're sure proud of him."

"What are his plans now?"

"He's going to college." Carl sat down at her kitchen table. "To tell you the truth, I wish he'd join me in the business."

"It's such a change when the last child leaves." Miss Sarah filled his cup with coffee.

Carl smiled, "Honestly, I think my wife likes it, but I miss 'em."

"I wish your son the best."

"I'll tell him." Carl tried to sip his coffee, but it was too hot.

"While this coffee cools, I'll take a look at the hot water heater." He stood up, stretched his back, and walked to the hallway closet while Miss Sarah put her breakfast dishes in the sink.

"It's the pilot light, Miss Sarah."

"Can you fix it, Carl?"

"A new one is what you need. This one's about thirty years old."

"Well, I would hate to give up hot water," she laughed.

"Yes, ma'am." He took a large swallow of his coffee. "I'll get started now and install it before lunch."

He hugged her goodbye. The dog, resting at Miss Sarah's feet, tried to follow him out the door, but he gently kicked her back into the house.

"You can't go to the hardware store, Sasha."

After replacing the pilot light, he met with two prospective clients after lunch, and by three in the afternoon, he went home to put on his suit and tie. The meeting with lawyers was contentious. Nothing short of a lawsuit would satisfy Wilson.

As he drove home, a thought took form—something to take his mind off a bad day. He slowed down and circled the block, looking for a parking place. For small jobs like a pilot light, Miss Sarah paid cash. With the extra spending money in his pocket, why not buy flowers for Sheila.

In the Flower Shoppe, he asked the clerk, "What is your most romantic flower?" The young woman in her twenties was wearing a light brown sundress that flowed over her curves. Her hair was a loose tumble of curls, and her eyes were dipped in mascara. Carl noted the wedding ring on her left hand.

"I'd say red roses, but if a fella was buying me flowers, I would want white ones."

"Why?"

"They remind me of weddings." He bought a dozen white roses.

She turned to open the cooler and selected the stems while Carl counted out forty dollars, leaving him three hundred dollars left.

"This'ill do the trick." He winked at her before he left.

Skipping in anticipation, Carl entered his house through his office where he left his shoes. He could smell she started dinner, but Sheila was not in the kitchen. Armed with champagne, Carl found her in the bedroom.

"Sheila, we have the house to ourselves." He presented her the flowers, opened the champagne, and produced two glasses.

Sheila melted at the sight of flowers. He reminded her of the man she married.

"I'm glad to celebrate with you," she smiled, cradling the roses like a baby. He poured her a glass of champagne and gently took the flowers from her bosom to place them in the box.

"Come over here," she said, sitting on the bed.

If she had to pinpoint when her trouble with Carl started, she would have chosen the year her father died. Sheila attributed Carl's transformation to her failure as a wife when she withdrew overcome by grief. As she recovered, Carl got worse. The lies, the moods, the time he spent away from home peaked.

"Yes, ma'am," Carl said, and he strutted over to stand directly in front of her. She unzipped his trousers, and they fell at his feet. Slipping her hand inside his briefs, she massaged him until he couldn't stand it anymore.

"I'm dying here, Sheila."

The good times could be so great.

"I want you, too." She slipped off her panties and lay on the bed.

When he took her, she imagined they were still happy together.

After the lovemaking, Sheila opted to wait and see. She circled a random date, February 2, 2018, on her calendar. But she did follow through with the decision to contact Abel. He was living in Texas. Reuniting with him to plan their class reunion gave her a sense of purpose, a distraction. But there was another change in the family she could not have expected.

Sheila's phone rang at 2 AM.

"Mom?" Sheila sat up with a start.

"Zack! What's wrong?"

"Mom, someone is following me," his voice wavered.

"Where are you?"

"I'm in my room, but someone has followed me here."

"Who?"

"A boy in my history class."

"You mean he is inside the dorm?"

"No, I see him from my window."

"Tell the dorm parent in the morning, okay? And lock your door."

"Okay." He sounded more confident now.

CHAPTER 6

10 October 2017

Sheila did not sleep well after speaking with Zack. So many worries flooded her mind that by eight, she had to call him.

"I'm meeting someone this morning," Zack assured her.

"Good, let me know what happens."

"I will, but I have to go now."

The next day she called him again.

"Don't worry, Mom. It's a misunderstanding." Zack sounded carefree. "We've figured it out."

The last time she called, he reprimanded her.

"MOM, I'm fine, but I won't be if you keep calling."

"I'm sorry, Zack. I'm concerned."

"Don't be," his voice was terse. "It singles me out."

Sheila stopped calling. But a few days later, he sent her a series of text messages: *"They are investigating it." "Don't worry, I'm safe." "Meeting with Miss Evans." "I'm a high priority." "They are so thankful." "Don't call, just text." "Don't call, just text."*

She felt that he was sending the messages to reassure her, but they had the opposite effect. Two weeks after the middle of the night phone call from Zack, she received another text from him: *"The Dean is getting ready to call you."*

On the same day a secretary from the Dean of Students Office called to request a meeting *before* they took Zack home.

She begged Zack for an explanation. *"Did you fail your courses?"* *"Did you do something wrong?"* *"Can I call you?"*

"NO!!!! Some students don't like me; and I have to leave."

"But why don't they like you?" He rang her phone.

"For God's sake, can't you trust me?" Zack called her. "The Dean is trying to keep me safe. I don't leave the dorm anymore." Zack sounded as if he was about to break down when he asked, "Are you and Dad coming tomorrow?"

"Should we come today?"

"No, I'm safe in my room, and I've got some work to do. Please don't come today."

"Zack, did you make someone mad?"

"No, Mom, I swear I didn't do anything. But I may have to do something if they don't stop."

"Stop what?"

"FOLLOWING ME."

Carl, shrugged it off when she called him.

"A bully only picks on a weak person; I'll straighten him out." He hung up as soon as he said, "We'll talk about it tonight."

But they didn't talk about it. Carl came in late and went to bed early.

"We'll find out when we pick him up," was all he said.

The next morning Carl backed Sheila's car out of the garage in the dark. He parked in the circular drive and watched her lock the front door. Humiliated at the thought of picking up an eighteen-year-old boy because he was homesick, Carl started the day in a foul mood. His wife, carrying her coat, a large handbag, and snacks, settled into the passenger seat.

"I hope I have everything," she said as she tossed her coat behind her into the backseat.

"Zack's always been nervous, Sheila," Carl hugged the steering wheel. "Sensitive, that's what I would call him: sensitive and weak."

"I don't see him that way at all."

"He's not cut out for college," he said as he turned onto the interstate highway.

"How can you say that? He's smart and likes to study."

"Yeah, and his friends are a bunch of oddballs, too." He could hardly bear to listen to her.

"He played basketball; He had lots of good friends."

"I knew all along he was different, but it was you who made him this way."

When people feel bad, Son, it's a good time to make them feel worse.

"How is he different, Carl?" Sheila's face was so constricted she looked like a prune.

"I told you. Zack's too sensitive."

They started the trip in the dark, but now there was a beautiful sunrise behind them. The sunlight glowed around Sheila's head, but her face was a shadow under the brim of her hat.

"The Dean wants to meet with us first; we have to be at Highland Hall at eight."

"Tomara's my court date, Sheila. I should plan my

defense instead of driving Zack home."

"I thought you settled it. Isn't that why you brought me flowers and champagne?"

"We didn't settle it. Stuff was stolen off of a few jobs, and the owner blames me."

Carl drove another five miles in silence.

"What I don't understand, Sheila, is why we have to come git him. If he is homesick, why can't he pack up and move himself home?"

As they reached the outskirts of the city, the sun climbed in the sky, but the scenery had changed. The bright green yards and well-tended gardens turned brown in October. The residents, most of them still getting ready for work, were absent from the sidewalks and streets. Leaves piled in yards, and household trash decayed on the curbs waiting for pickup. Even the campus appeared wilted, dreary, and asleep.

"Once you get on Live Oak Drive, turn right at the second road. It will dead-end at Highland Hall."

"Here it is!" Sheila pointed out.

"I see it," he growled.

"It's warming up outside, I don't need my coat."

"You are the one who wanted him to go to college. It's fine with me if he quits." Carl searched for a parking place. He parked within sight of the building, but they walked three city blocks to get there.

When they reached the Dean's building, the couple lumbered up thirty front steps to the impressive double steel doors guarding the offices.

"I bet there is another entrance on the first floor for the staff," Carl said, breathing heavily and wiping his brow with his handkerchief. Sheila, even in sneakers, couldn't keep up, so she followed him, stepping around the occasional wad of chewing gum and sticky pieces of food wrap.

"We made it!" she said as she struggled to breathe. "It will be all down-hill from here."

"You are right about that. Come on.".

"The Dean's Office is 121," Sheila read from her phone.

"If I was a betting man, I would say it is in a corner so the Dean would own plenty of windows," Carl stopped in the entrance hall to get his bearings. "The best view of the campus would be to our right. Let's follow the numbers this way first." The hallway was dimly lit, and as they walked, they passed portrait after portrait of prior deans all dressed in a suit and tie.

Just as Carl suspected, the Dean's office was on the right-hand corner, away from the street. He opened the door for his wife, and they ran into a secretary's desk, but no secretary. A small waiting alcove with comfortable seating occupied a sidewall.

"I guess they ain't here yet," Carl shook his head slowly back and forth. "Can you believe it?"

"Carl, I don't want you mad when we see Zack. Why don't we sit down?" Sheila took her seat while she was talking. "I brought some water; do you want some?"

"Naw, how long do you think they will make us wait?"

"Well, we are about five minutes early."

"I ain't heard no bell, but surely classes have started already."

"They don't ring a bell in college."

"Well, that explains that," Carl smiled. "Good thing I got you here with me." He reached into his pocket and extracted a breath mint from its package.

The wait was so long Carl wondered if they had come on a minor holiday only celebrated by overly educated people.

"You reckon they are shut down for Shakespeare's birthday?" he quipped.

Eventually, light from the hall shined through the transom window above the door, and they heard voices outside.

"This is crazy, Sheila. There must be a person in charge. I'd be broke if I ran my business this way."

"Should we go to his dorm?"

"I say we ransack this building first and find someone who can tell us what the hell is going on." Sheila followed Carl back into the massive hallway, relieved to see the building waking up.

"Baby, this suite looks more important than the Dean of Students Office." Carl pointed to the "Bursar's Office," sign.

"How may I help you?" A trim middle-aged woman with dark hair and eyes stood up from her desk.

"We had an appointment with Dean Ralston at eight, but no one is there," Carl said.

"Oh…" The woman looked sad. "I am so sorry. The Dean had a family emergency and won't be coming in today. Let me call his assistant, and he can meet with you." She looked up a number in a booklet by her touch-tone phone.

Soon a young man with an olive-green backpack bounded in and grinned. He dressed like faculty, worn corduroy pants, a wrinkled white shirt, and carried two pens in his breast pocket. His eyes gave him away; he appeared to be unsure of himself.

"Good morning, I am Lane Nelson." The man said as

he shook Carl's hand. "How can I help you?"—a question addressed to Carl.

Before he could answer, Sheila tried to take the lead.

"We have an appointment with the Dean of Students, but no one is in his office."

"I'm so sorry. Unfortunately, the Dean is unavailable at the moment. I don't know anything about your situation." Carl's face turned red.

"You scare the hell out of us and make us rush over for an appointment, keep us waiting, and now you are telling us to do what? Go back home?" When Carl was this mad, he could sound dangerous.

"No, sir." The junior administrator said, and he lowered his backpack to the floor. "I'm going to help you, of course. What is your child's name, and what dorm is he in?"

"Good grief," said Carl, and he sat back down in his chair.

After Sheila provided the information, Carl stood up silently to intimidate the young man again while Lane spoke rapidly.

"I am calling the person in charge of Zack's dorm now." Carl paced and Sheila stood while Nelson had a brief conversation.

"Yes, Dr. Morris," Nelson said into his cell phone. "I will send them over."

"Okay," the young man emptied his lungs of all breath and lifted his eyes to face Carl. He breathed in and steadied himself to ask, "Do you know how to get to Nicholson dorm from here?"

"Of course, we do," Carl raised his voice. "WE JUST MOVED HIM IN TWO MONTHS AGO."

"Awesome!" The young man said, rattled all over

again. "Go over there now, and Dr. Morris will meet you on the front steps. It's just a short walk from here." Carl stood up and opened the door to the hall for Sheila. They left the office with the Dean's Assistant trailing them to be sure they left the building, traveling in the right direction.

Once they arrived at Nicholson dorm, Morris guarded the front door, ready to intercept them before they entered.

"Good morning, you must be the Ewing's. I am Dr. Morris, and I am standing in for Dean Ralston." Carl stiffened and punched the palm of his left hand with his right.

"His wife died in a car wreck this morning, and we are all in a state of shock and confusion." He paused, allowing his words to sink in. "This tragedy was so sudden we are in disarray around here."

"DISARRAY? WHAT THE HELL ARE YOU TALKING ABOUT?" Carl put his right hand in his pocket to keep it under control.

"I'm sorry," Dr. Morris, said attempting to defuse him, "all I know is that Zack is in his room now, waiting for you."

CHAPTER 7

Zack unlocked his door and stole a look down the hall. Seeing no one, he locked the door again and moved to the window to look down at the quadrangle. The boy with the red shirt was standing on the grass, while the other students congregated in groups or walked to class.

He was certain this boy caused his roommate to be misplaced. Preston, or was it Paul, disappeared. One day his roommate's clothes were in the closet; the next day there was no evidence of him anywhere. So far, the boy in the red shirt had not approached him. The college boy always followed from a distance, making it difficult for Zack when he tried to describe him. Zack, who was not an artist, attempted to draw a picture.

He dragged his desk chair to the window with pencil and lined paper in hand. The college boy wore a baseball cap, but he was too far away for Zack to read the insignia. He was tall, and he was handsome, like a movie star. His hands were enormous, and he waved to entice Zack to come down.

A loud knock at the door startled him, and his paper fluttered to the floor.

"Zack, open the door."

"Son. It's Dad."

Zack gripped the pencil, holding it like a weapon.

"Unlock the door."

Zack cracked the door as if it had a chain lock.

"Dad, is that you?"

Carl used his weight and strength to push the door wide open, and Zack fell down hard.

"This room sure is a mess," he said, as Sheila followed, walking on tiptoe behind him.

"We need some leaf bags, Sheila. Here are the keys; go to the store and git some trash bags—a big box of them—while I stay with Zack."

Sheila took the keys, walked out the door, and closed it without making a sound.

Zack, wary of his mother, concentrated on his father while wrapping his arms around himself.

"While your Mama is at the store, I'm going to make some calls. Go take a shower, if you can."

Zack felt it was imperative to finish his sketch of the boy outside, but he obeyed his father. The water of the shower felt comforting as though it was holding him together, allowing his arms to be free to reach for the shampoo and soap. He was reluctant to leave the bathroom because the pelting of the hot water confirmed the boundaries of his own body versus everything else.

"Zack," he heard his father shout. "Come out. You are taking too long."

He left the water running to stand naked in the middle of the room, water pooling at his feet.

"You got a rubber band?"

Zack glanced around, feeling helpless while his father answered a phone call. He shivered as the water dripped off his matted hair.

Carl paced with the phone to his ear, ignoring Zack.

"Steve, I can't meet with you today like we planned.

Are you ready to go?" And after a few beats, Carl said, "Go ahead. It don't look like we are gonna get canceled. Get in and get out of the house as quick as you can."

When Carl finished, he threw Zack a towel and shut off the water in the shower. Pointing at the chest of drawers, he said, "You got clothes in there? Put them on." Carl resumed walking around the room. This time he was rifling through Zack's papers and checking the drawers of the desk.

Standing in front of the bureau, blocking his father's view, Zack retrieved a small plastic bag of marijuana hidden under a stack of underwear and put it in his jeans pocket. But his father had already found cigarettes.

"You smoking now?"

Zack didn't answer. He stood standing against the wall, hugging himself, and staring at the floor.

"And what is this?" his father said with controlled rage while holding a short story Zack wrote for creative writing.

"For God's sake, put on a shirt!"

Sheila's arrival with trash bags and a laundry basket, interrupted their confrontation.

"I didn't have to go far, the school has a little general store next to the bookstore, and I brought the laundry basket I keep in the car."

"Hand 'em to me." Dumping the boxes out of the basket, he handed it to Zack.

"Put your books in this." Then he pulled out three trash bags. "This bag is for trash, and the others are for stuff to take home."

"The cigarettes," Carl clenched his jaw, "are trash."

He made a great show of throwing them into the bag—emptying the package so they would fall out one by one. He still had the eight-page short story and held it over the bag for trash, but changed his mind. Zack flinched when he saw his Dad carefully fold the papers and put them in his back pocket.

By two in the afternoon, they prepared to leave.

"Zack's going to ride with me, Sheila. You take his car." Zack, fully dressed now, followed his father out of the door.

He wondered why his mother had not spoken to him once. The mother he left at home would have run up to hug him, but this woman kept her distance. He studied the floor while he followed his father out of the room and down the stairs. Sitting in his mother's car, he and his Dad watched her walk to the student's parking lot.

"I told you it was a mistake to come here. It's your mother who doesn't want the best for you."

"You were right about college. I didn't fit in." His eyes scanned the campus, looking for the boy in the red shirt.

"What the hell happened?" Carl asked.

"A few guys on campus liked to follow me around, but there was one who was creepy." Zack was highly vigilant and nervous. Every few minutes, he swiped his forehead and dragged his hand over his face to his chin.

"I'm going to teach you the ways of the world like my Daddy taught me, but remember this; if you are going to live with me, you need to be strong, 'cause I can't take weakness in people." Carl reached in his pocket for the typewritten pages. "You see this? Get a good look at it 'cause we are gonna burn it when we get home. I don't like you writing stories about me and you."

"Yes, sir." Zack made himself as small as he could for the drive.

"I want you to get a haircut and let your Mom cut them dirty fingernails."

"Yes, sir."

Zack was no more aware of what was happening to him than his mother, but he was happy to be home. By the time he and his father reached the city limits of Gower, he began to feel better. Everything was familiar, but when Zack arrived at his house, he was flooded with relief. The college boys were miles away and could not know where he lived. From the measured steps to the porch, to the staircase, and finally, the room that gave him peace, all things signaled safety now. The muscles in his face relaxed, and his brain felt extraordinarily tired, as if he had run a marathon to get there.

His tranquility was short-lived. A loud knocking on his bedroom door and the voice of his father interrupted it.

"Let's burn this before your mother gets back."

"Okay." He followed his father out the back door and to the grill on the patio. Carl turned on the gas and lit the burner with a match.

"You burn it, Son," he said, handing it to him. "I forbid you to write any more stories about us."

Zack took the typewritten pages, willing to burn everything he had to remain in the safety of his room at home.

"You can turn this around, Son, but you have to be strong. I can't tolerate weak people, and I can't stand people who tattle tale."

"I know."

After the burning, Zack went back to his room and closed the window shades before collapsing into bed. His brain spent all the energy it had. He closed his eyes and tried to sleep, but his body was restless. His limbs kept begging him to move them. After hours of walking in his room, he opened his bedroom door and went downstairs to march in the living room until his body was as tired as his head. At four AM, he walked upstairs and fell into a fitful sleep.

Sheila, relieved to drive Zack's car, needed time alone. The condition of his room—the clutter, the stench, and no sign of a roommate worried her. But the condition of Zack was worse. He had neglected himself. He neglected to get haircuts, wash his hair, shower his body, shave, or trim his fingernails. His weight loss was striking. If she passed him on the street, she would not have recognized him. It all came down to a parent's worst nightmare—he was a changeling. He was so thin, so disheveled, so wild-eyed, so foreign, that her instincts to protect him evaporated. Her husband was calm, she was the one who panicked.

CHAPTER 8

26 October 2017

Trent Wilson woke up when his alarm rang at five in the morning. He arranged his clothes on the unmade bed while still in his boxer shorts—a gray suit, white shirt, striped tie, and matching socks. Satisfied with his wardrobe, he double-checked his briefcase and drank a glass of orange juice. Without a care in the world, he put on his gym shorts and a tee-shirt. Trent lived so close to Carl he could have run by his house. Instead, he flipped a finger in Carl's direction and jogged the other way— three miles on the levee. Trent was fifty-six years old, he was in good shape, and planned to stay that way.

As he completed the loop back to his house, he slowed his pace. Breathing easier now, he climbed the four steps to his front porch. He removed each running shoe while he stood supported by the knee wall. Leaving the shoes outside, he padded into the empty house in his socks. He walked into the kitchen to flip the switch on the coffeemaker. The phone rang, but being in a hurry, he left it to voice mail and headed to the bedroom, changed into his robe, and turned on the water in the shower. He stood there a moment, testing the temperature of the water with his hand. The cold water gradually turned warm and then to hot. He stepped into the shower to wash away the sweat. There was just one minor glitch; the water was spraying a side wall instead of straight down. He automatically reached up to adjust the showerhead, and with that motion, he felt excruciating pain. His housekeeper would find him at ten when she came to clean.

Carl started his day when Sheila shook his shoulder gently.

"Aren't you going to get up this morning?" she asked. "You have court today, remember?"

"What time is it?" he was half asleep.

"It's a little after six; Do you want me to make breakfast?"

Carl sat up with a start. He rubbed his eyes and reached for his glasses.

"I've been dreaming about you," he said.

"Well, I am glad you aren't worried about today."

"No, I ain't worried," he stood up and went into the bathroom. He stuck his head out, "Don't cook anything; I don't feel like eating."

After twenty minutes Sheila, lying in bed looking at the closed bathroom door, called to him. "Are you all right in there?"

"Yeah, Baby, I'll be out in a minute."

Blue-collar men shower in the evening, so Sheila wondered why he was in the bathroom for so long.

"Carl? Are you sure you don't need—Carl! My goodness!"

"How do you like it?" he pretended to smile. Carl's clean-shaven face could not have been more dramatic than if he had shaved his head too.

"It will take me a while to get used to it."

"Do you think a man without facial hair looks more

honest?" Carl sat down on the bed beside her.

"I never thought about it."

"I think it does," he said. "Time to get dressed and get some work started first—before I go to the courthouse."

When Carl joined Sheila in the kitchen, he wore his blue suit, a white shirt, and a solid gray tie.

"Should I wake him up?" she asked.

"No, I got to keep my mind on the trial right now. What time did you go to bed?"

"I was awake until three. But I got a lot done. Zack was awake, too."

"What was he doin'?" Carl picked up his newspaper.

"Just walking around downstairs. And I have good news, too."

"What is it?"

"I found no sign of drugs in the bags we brought home yesterday."

"But we found cigarettes, Sheila. They are the gateway." Carl looked at his watch. "Time to go."

Once in the truck, he got into character by putting a breath mint in his mouth and slipping on a silver Saint Vincent's bracelet over his thick hairy wrist.

Son, give people a sign that they can trust you well before you ever speak a word to them.

While driving to the job site, he let down the driver's side window to enjoy the cool morning air while he could. Louisiana was experiencing an Indian summer, and soon, the day would be hot.

The job was about five miles from the city limits, in a rapidly growing community of folks who loved the openness of underground wires and a view of the river.

His project was the eleventh house in the subdivision and was going to be expensive. Each new house wanted to be fancier than the last.

Jimmy, the supervisor of the framing crew, waited for him. Carl jumped the curb with his truck and drove into the front yard, parked, and swung his legs out of the door first, careful to keep his suit clean.

"Boss man! Good morning," Jimmy called out and walked to the makeshift table where the house plans lay.

"I got a few questions about these plans. Couple things don't look right." He paused until Carl appeared to be ready to discuss the specifics and then spoke. "We got two windows that don't show on the detail, and the window size in the front bedroom don't meet code."

"Let me look at that," Carl shook his head. "We all know that architects ain't perfect." While he stood hunched over the table, he adjusted his bifocal glasses on his face. "You're right. We got to make it a bigger window and be sure we keep the window out to the front porch. The house would look lopsided without it. What other window is not on the detail?"

"It's the one in the bathroom upstairs."

"Yeah, I see it now. Did you notice they want all of them doors oversized?"

"I seen it. You going to church or something?"

"No, you didn't hear? They made me CEO of the paper mill one town over," Carl's blue eyes twinkled, and his naked cheeks looked rosy in the cool breeze they were enjoying.

"Funny, I didn't hear about that," Jimmy played along.

"Truth is, I got some business to take care of." Carl

lowered his voice. "Do me a favor, and watch that young man in the tight jeans and plaid shirt. I like him 'cause he ain't scared of gittin' up high, but the last time he worked for me I was short on lumber. I don't know if he took it hisself or if he called it in to someone, but I'm sure it was him."

"You want me to say something to him?"

"No, make sure he has a slight accident—maybe mess up his nail gun or something."

"I can do that." Jimmy smiled.

Carl's friends knew him to be a prankster. Among themselves, they would excuse his high jinks; "You know Carl; he is a mess." While he never targeted his friends, every new subcontractor was fair game. The scenarios he devised were juvenile, like hiding a sub-contractor's Allen wretch. While most of Carl's experienced workers loved the spectacle of a newbie frantically searching for a necessary tool; it troubled some of them.

By nine o'clock, Carl sat in Judge Hayes' courtroom waiting to begin the case of Trent Wilson vs. Carl Davis Ewing. The defendant and his lawyer were present, but everyone realized the plaintiff was missing. Carl sat motionless with his head bowed and hands off the table, while everyone else seemed restless. A supporting cast of witnesses, including two accountants, two bankers, three suppliers, and two representatives of an insurance company, were eager to testify and leave. The audience shuffled their shoes while consulting their watches and the clock on the wall.

"Mr. Lefleur, where is your client?" Judge Hayes asked Wilson's attorney. Carl couldn't help but wonder why Trent, an attorney himself, would hire a lawyer to represent him.

"I do not know, your Honor; he spoke with me last night and was ready to proceed with the trial this morning."

"Find out what happened; I'm ready to adjourn because he is late."

Carl was as still as a statue. He kept his head bowed, and his upper body crouched over the defendant's table as if his switch was turned off. His attorney whispered an explanation. Carl tilted his head and looked at the Judge. Under the desk, he was fidgeting with his wristwatch, tossing it from one hand to the other.

"I don't know what happened," his attorney said. "Sometimes the plaintiff gets cold feet and doesn't show up."

"All rise."

The watch activity ceased. Carl slid his chair back, placed his hands on the table, and rose cautiously, careful not to stand up too quickly. Once standing, he fumbled with his documents, a well-worn ledger and pictures. The photos slipped out of his hands and scattered on the floor. He remained standing, clutching his ledger, until they dismissed the court. Then, with exaggerated effort, he stooped down to gather the pictures as if they were fragile butterflies and placed them in between the ledger pages. As he turned to leave, he created the appearance of self-effacing humility and conjured his father's words.

Son, when you set up a scheme, introduce as much chaos as you can. Make the details so tangled and outrageous, that it would take two or three minds to unravel it, and al-

ways play the victim.

It was an Oscar-worthy performance.

Speaking to no one and avoiding eye contact, he left the courtroom modeling an honest man broken by the insinuations thrown at him by Wilson. The change in his demeanor began as he descended the courtroom steps; he straightened up to his full height, and a broad smile illuminated his face. He developed a swagger as he walked, and there was a spring to his step, too. Now full of energy and feeling charismatic, he was ready to mingle with the public. He passed by his truck in the parking lot and crossed the street to the coffee shop nearby.

Carl was jubilant by the time he crossed the threshold. He had never had breakfast there before, but he was a frequent lunch patron. Scanning the tables, he noticed that the breakfast crowd was smaller than the lunch crowd, much smaller. The young waitress, engaged at another table, recognized him as a customer who tipped generously. She smiled, hello.

"I will be right back to take your order!" she said as she took a rubber band out of her apron pocket and pulled her long blond hair into a ponytail. "Sit anywhere you want."

"Yes, ma'am!" he said, and he selected a booth. He took off his suit jacket, carefully folded it, and placed it on the seat beside him. He loosened his tie.

Marie returned with a glass of water and a menu.

"Oh, I know what I want," he said. "I'll have fried eggs and bacon. I was so nervous this morning I couldn't eat."

"Well, I am glad you can eat now!" she said writing

on her pad. "Do you want toast or a biscuit with that?"

"Toast." He looked her up and down. "Baby, let me borrow your cell phone for a minute. Mine is acting funny."

"Sure. Sorry, it's not smart." She handed him her flip phone. "I'll get it back after I turn in your order."

He clumsily put in the telephone number, having to correct the entry twice. The mistakes did not bother him in the least because they improved his image: an attractive, professional, clean-shaven, gray-haired man in his late fifties, trying to punch out a phone number on a tiny keypad.

He did not have to wait long for Steve to answer.

"Buddy, you know who this is," Carl said with a hearty laugh. "You did great! We need to set up a poker game. You are the best man I ever worked with. No joke, you are the best."

"Yes, sir!" Steve said, "Just call me when you're ready, and I'll be there."

"Can we do it sometime around Thanksgiving? You'd better take a brief vacation."

"I kin wait. I'm leaving out this afternoon, driving a truck to Canada, and then who knows where they'll send me."

"Good plan! Drive safe, and I'll call soon to set the date."

"Thanks, Boss."

Breakfast arrived, and Carl handed the phone over, touching Marie's fingers ever so softly.

"Thank you, ma'am!" and he looked at her as if she was the most exciting person he had ever met. Not just beautiful, but interesting. She playfully slipped her phone into her uniform pocket.

"Anytime, Carl."

The hearty breakfast was the signal for a brand-new day to start. What happened before was just a bad dream. In the time it took him to eat, the breakfast crowd increased. He searched the room again to see if there was a familiar face, and there it was at the door looking over the crowd just as he was.

"Charles!" he said loudly and motioned to his booth. "You can have my table. What are you doing here? I figured you'd be on the job by now."

"No, Carl. I was looking for you. Guess what happened?" Charles took off his cowboy hat and put it on the table as soon as he sat down. Beads of sweat poured off his face as if he ran to bring the news. He whispered, "Did you hear what happened to Trent?"

"No, all I know is that he didn't show up this morn'in."

Charles wiped his mouth with a napkin and spoke again in a conspiratorial tone.

"He had a massive heart attack. He's gone, Carl."

Carl's head jerked back; his face projected disbelief, "That's impossible! That man was fit as a fiddle, always running around the neighborhood."

"No, it's true, Carl. I heard it from Darlene in the ER. It happened this morning."

"I wouldn't wish that on anybody, but Trent was a jack," and he paused for effect and then added "rabbit."

"He was a jackass," laughed Charles.

Carl faked an angry face. "I took the entire day off for court today, but I guess there ain't going to be any more of that."

"Well, if you ain't busy, you can come help me with the shed I'm building out behind my house."

"No, as much as I would love to help you, I better go home. The wife's not feeling good."

"Look at you coming up with an excuse," Charles said jokingly as he noticed Marie walking toward them.

"Marie," Carl said, when she returned to help the new fellow, "this here is Charles, and he ain't married. He's got a good job, too." He stood up and reached deep into his pocket for cash, leaving an extra two dollars over what was customary.

"Keep the change, darlin'," he smiled. "I feeeel good."

CHAPTER 9

9 November 2017

Two weeks later, Sheila did not doubt Zack had fundamentally changed, and she was convinced drug addiction was not the cause. He never left home, no friends came to see him, and no mysterious packages arrived in the mail. And while she accepted his need for privacy and rest, his withdrawal from society was extreme. During the day, he rarely left his room for anything, not even meals. At night he roamed downstairs. He lost more weight, but his eyes troubled her more than anything else. The eyes were furtive, afraid, and unrecognizable.

Her dreams, gut-wrenching scenes of what happened at school to transform him like this, jolted her awake in the early morning hours. He was awake then, too. She could hear him muttering and opening cabinets in the kitchen. Carl disengaged; Zack became Sheila's problem now.

When she questioned Zack, he stuck to his story; the college boys did not like him. But there were no specifics. She wanted to scream and argue when he lied to her. Later, she realized Zack could not tell her the truth because he did not know it.

In a rare moment of clarity, she called the Dean of Students Office to make an appointment to discuss

Zack's problems at school, and it surprised her when the Dean wanted to come to their home rather than meet her in his office.

"You know why he wants to come to the house, don't you?" Carl growled. "He wants to leave when he is ready."

"I don't think Zack should be here when he comes."

"Suit yourself." Carl shook his head. "We send our son to college, and they send him home like this."

Zack woke up early on the day of the Dean's visit. Before his eyes could open, he felt someone patting his shoulder.

"Wake up, uncle Martin is coming." He closed his eyes and tried to go back to sleep.

"I am cooking breakfast now, so you come down in fifteen. Wear old clothes." She opened the window shades in his bedroom, and the sun came streaming in. Zack covered his eyes with his hands and sat up in bed. He rubbed his eyes in a circular motion with his fists.

While Zack's eyes adjusted to the light, he looked at her and said, "Mom?"

"Yes, Zack. It's me. It's morning, and Martin is coming to get you."

After his mother left, Zack examined the room— no concerns. He went into his bathroom, shut the door, and urinated. While checking himself in the mirror, he saw smudges on the glass resembling the letters Z, A, Y, like the "I am not a robot" test on a computer.

He had been getting strange "vibes" lately, and the message intrigued him. He reached his hand in-between the mattress and box spring of his bed, retrieved a notebook, wrote the letters in it. Then he pulled down the shades to darken the room again and finished dressing. The air outside his room reeked of bacon.

"Zack! Come here now."

He walked down the stairs, pausing on the last step while he considered going back to his room. He carefully placed his right foot on the floor. The stairwell exploded behind him. Zack jumped and took cover in the kitchen, where he saw Ruth for the first time.

She stood with her back to him while she tended the frying pan.

"Ah, there you are," she turned around. "Eat breakfast, and uncle Martin will be here to collect you." She was off-putting, but hunger got the best of him.

Before he could finish, his uncle arrived.

"Hey Buddy, guess what? We are going to a tractor auction!"

"He says great," Ruth opened the refrigerator. "Do you want anything for the road?"

"No, thanks, Sis. We are leaving straight away. As soon as Zack wipes his face with a napkin." A bit of butter was in Zack's beard. Zack wiped it and stood up.

"I'm ready," Zack said.

"All right, let's go. We'll be back between three and four this afternoon."

"Thanks, Martin."

Sheila tried to relax and prepare her questions while she waited. The Dean had lost his wife, but she had lost her son.

"Is his highness here yet?" Carl poked his head into the living room.

"No."

"You know where to find me." He spun around like a

soldier, ready for battle in his home office.

Dean Ralston arrived on time, and he brought someone with him. Sheila spotted them from an upstairs window, a tall man in a grey corduroy jacket and a young woman in a khaki trench coat. The distinguished Dr. Ralston plus his frumpy short friend made an odd couple.

"Hello, Ms. Ewing, I would like you to meet my colleague, Ms. Evans." Sheila suspected Evans was new to the job because she lacked the professional appearance of the other staff members. Clothes don't make you a lady, but they can unmake you, she thought. The blouse, the skirt, the baggy coat were all wrong as her husband would say. Sheila wondered why the Dean would bring her along.

"Ms. Evans works with the student guidance services at the University," Dr. Ralston continued. "I asked her to come to our meeting because she and Zack talked frequently."

"Carl is in his office; one moment, I'll get him."

She left them sitting beside each other on the sofa, went down the hall, and tapped lightly on Carl's office door. He opened it right away.

"I'm coming," he said.

While waiting, the two university employees exchanged glances. This was the first time for Ms. Evans to talk with parents about a sticky situation. When Carl and Sheila entered the room, they stood up, and the men shook hands. Sheila offered them coffee, which they declined, and then they sat down. Dean Ralston took the lead.

"I am well aware we fumbled the visit to pick up

Zack. I sincerely apologize. The other faculty members had no knowledge of Zack's circumstances, and I regret I could not be there for him." He turned his head to look at Evans, talking to her instead of Sheila and Carl.

"Ms. Evans and I want to make things right."

Carl interrupted, "One of you could start with why you called my wife. What happened exactly?"

Ralston spoke first. "Shortly after Zack arrived at Lee, he contacted Ms. Evans because he was being followed, or stalked, by another student. I'll let her describe what happened next."

Ms. Evans seemed nervous while she flipped through her papers. "I met Zack five days after he arrived at school." Sheila noticed that she wore a Jesuit cross around her neck. "He accused another student of stalking him." Evans swept an unruly lock of hair behind her ear. "The student was in two freshmen core classes with Zack, so they encountered each other daily. But I could find no evidence of stalking. The other student did not even know Zack." Sheila weighed every word Ms. Evans said.

"We put them in separate classes, and there were no more complaints for a few days. Then Zack complained about another boy following him. The young man he described was distinctive, red shirt and black jeans, wearing a purple baseball cap. We questioned students who were in the area when Zack saw him, and no one else saw a boy dressed like that. Even so, Zack persisted in sending me reports that he had seen him, mostly hanging around the cafeteria. Then, just before we called you, Paul's parents called requesting permission to move off campus."

"What problems did Paul have with Zack?" Sheila

interrupted.

"He raised several issues regarding Zack's behavior. Zack quit bathing, so there was an odor to the room. He bought most of his meals from vending machines and left the wrappers on the floor and on the beds. The roommate felt as though he was being crowded out by Zack's trash. One night, Paul awoke to see Zack standing by his bed and looking down at him. At that point, he moved in with some other guys who let him sleep on the floor."

"But why did you wait so long to call us?" Sheila asked, while Carl mirrored the pose of Ralston, straight back, knees at attention, hands in his lap. "You knew it, she knew it," pointing at Evans, "and his roommate's parents knew it, but you didn't tell us. We should have been the first to know."

Dr. Ralston took this question.

"College freshmen have privacy rights that may seem illogical since they depend upon their families to pay tuition and are not yet twenty-one years old. Zack signed a form that prevented us from sending you a copy of his grades or class attendance. We tried to persuade him to see a psychiatrist associated with the University for an evaluation, but Zack refused, which is his legal right to do." He shifted his weight on the cushion. Sheila thought the Dean was wary and brittle.

"When Zack demonstrated that he could not look after himself and when our investigations proved to us that his fears were irrational, we called you."

"Something else must have happened," Sheila accused him. "Was he hazed? Was he assaulted? Were students bullying him?"

"Again," the Dean breathed in, "eighteen-year-old

university students have legal rights. Zack's grade point average dropped when he stopped going to classes altogether. But Zack signed a contract that forbids us from notifying you."

"Notifying us of what? There is something you are not telling me."

The Dean wiped his brow with a handkerchief.

"He stopped eating..." Ralston leaned in. "At that point, we were well within our rights to have an ambulance pick him up and take him to the hospital. I thought the medics, the flashing lights, would frighten him. The kinder thing to do was to call you. He did go willingly, I was told."

"Nothing you have said explains why Zack is so afraid." Sheila looked at Evans for help.

"Well, since he has been here, he has been fine," said Carl. "He is out working for his uncle right now. We are all paid up, so naturally, we feel he should go back to school and finish his education unless the school is at fault."

"What does his doctor say?" Dean Ralston asked. Sheila detected a degree of disparagement in the Dean's tone.

"We didn't take him to a doctor. NOBODY told us to take him to the doctor."

"We insist that he have a doctor's evaluation before considering readmission," Ralston said with a sense of finality.

Sheila and Carl sat stupefied on the sofa.

"There are other colleges, and we need the tuition refunded," Carl said.

Ralston stood up and buttoned his suit jacket; Evans stood up, too.

"We try to do our very best for every student, and this is our best advice: convince him to see a doctor about this rough patch in his life. If you advise it, he will probably go." He offered his hand to Carl, who ignored the gesture.

"It was very nice meeting both of you, and when Zack is ready, we will welcome him back to the University."

Sheila walked them to the door, but Carl stayed seated like a stone statue in front of their fireplace. Sheila recognized this pose. He slouched in a chair, his eyes blank, and his mouth hanging open as if he did not have the energy to close it. When Carl had a brain freeze, she could do nothing but wait for him to thaw out.

Martin and Zack returned from the auction, finding Sheila home alone. She let them in, wearing a drab pair of jeans and a tee-shirt. In the foyer Sheila frowned at Martin to show she heard bad news. Zack did not linger; he immediately took the stairs to his room.

"Zack likes his privacy. He takes after Carl, who loves to be in his office." She ran her fingers through her hair. "Would you like something to drink, Martin? Come, tell me about the outing." She led him to the kitchen table to talk.

"Did you know a freshman college student could fail his classes without his parents being notified?"

"No, I didn't." Martin took off his jacket and laid it on a kitchen chair. "Sis, Zack worries me; he is not himself. I think he needs to see someone in the mental health field. He might suffer from depression." Martin lowered his voice, "You know how Carl is; he won't like this suggestion, but I think something is very wrong."

"Don't worry, Brother, we are going to do something about it," Sheila said.

"Why the beard? He looks like a mountain man."

"He won't shave, and I hate to say this, but he scares me."

CHAPTER 10

Thanksgiving Holidays, 2017

The day before Thanksgiving, Sheila vacillated between choosing a skirt or pants with a matching jacket. She usually preferred a skirt if it was going to rain.

"You babied him. He don't need a doctor. Be firm, and he'll come around." Carl said as he watched her dress.

"I didn't baby him. This is something different."

Sheila could not schedule an appointment with a psychiatrist in Gower or anywhere else until their family doctor examined Zack first.

"Hurry up, Zack. We don't want to be late."

"I don't feel like going." Zack came into their room with his pajama bottoms on.

"If you come with me now, I'll bring your meals to your room."

The windshield wipers made noise, slapping rainwater off the car as Sheila and Zack drove to Dr. Brown's office. The practice was small, but convenient. Two younger family practitioners and three nurses shared the offices. For years, Sheila's family saw Brown for minor complaints, nothing as serious as this. But even though she was familiar with him, Sheila worried he would not take her seriously. And Zack was unpredictable; would he put on a show or act normal?

"Dr. Brown is very nice," she said after she coaxed Zack into the passenger seat. "He saw you when you broke your leg. Do you remember? Uncle Martin thought your surgery looked infected, but Dr. Brown said your leg was healing."

Zack stared out the window.

"You got your meningitis shot there just before you left for college, but you only saw his nurse then. They are all nice at this office."

"Mrs. Ewing," the receptionist called. "May we see your insurance card, and I have some papers for you to fill out." Sheila was losing her patience. It took so long to get an appointment and Zack was unpredictable. The last thing she wanted to do was sit in the waiting room for an hour.

"Zack has been a patient here all of his life."

"I'm sorry, it is our policy to check on every visit."

Sheila took the questionnaire the girl slid under the glass and gave her Zack's insurance card in return. She went to her seat beside Zack to complete the questions. He fidgeted, with quick turns of his head, his knee pumped. The other patients in the waiting room kept their eyes on him. When the nurse called Zack's name, he startled.

"Mrs. Ewing, good morning," the nurse said. "This must be Zack," she smiled at him. "Zack, the doctor, will see you soon. We have set aside about twenty-five minutes today, and he would like to see you, Mrs. Ewing, first, and then Zack by himself."

Sheila was not sure this arrangement would be acceptable with Zack. She read his face for a sign.

"After Dr. Brown speaks with Zack, he will speak with you both."

Sheila turned to Zack, "I am going to see the doctor first, and then you will see him, okay?" She turned back to the nurse.

"Where does Zack go while I am talking to the doctor?"

"I'll escort him to a secondary waiting room and make sure he is comfortable."

Sheila had only seen doctors in an exam room. Today, she was directed to a leather chair in an office similar to a lawyer's office. She sat in one of the two chairs facing the desk.

"Dr. Brown will be with you right away," another nurse said and closed the door.

Sheila noticed a box of tissues placed strategically on the desk within her reach. She reapplied her lipstick just as the door opened briskly, and the doctor came looking harried in his wrinkled lab coat and holding a chart in his hand.

"Good morning, Miss Sheila," he said as he collapsed his heavy frame into his ergonomically designed swivel chair. She thought he looked as if he slept in his coat and routinely forgot to get his hair cut. Looking over the chart, he read aloud the diagnosis for each previous visit.

"Well-child, well-child, strep throat, well-child, ear infection, flu, sports physical, follow up femur fracture. He fell off a roof?" Dr. Brown's eyes peered at Sheila.

"Yes, he was helping his father at work and fell off a roof."

"Eleven years old. That's young to be doing a job like

that."

"He wasn't working. In the summer, he liked to go to work with his father; Carl is a contractor. I guess Zack was trying to help. Didn't you see him then?"

"No, my partner saw him. It must have been a bad break, a metal plate and screws."

The doctor closed the chart and laid it on the desk.

"I understand you are here to talk about problems Zack had at school. Before I visit with him, could you give me a picture of the situation as you see it?"

Sheila told her story.

"Correct me if I am wrong." he said. "His symptoms started with the onset of college studies—that's two months and add that to the time he has been home, which is about two months—that would add up to four months. Is that close to what you have calculated?"

"Yes."

"What is his mood?"

"What?"

"His mood. Is he happy, sad, angry, or afraid?" Dr. Brown gave her a verbal multiple-choice list.

"Mostly, I would say that he does not have any emotion except fear. In fact, I feel there has been a rift between him and me that I don't completely understand."

"Miss Sheila, I'd like to interview Zack by himself now, if that would be all right with you. He is eighteen years old, and we talk to young adults separately from their parents as a matter of routine."

"One more thing that might be helpful. My son uses words oddly." Sheila could pinpoint this one thing, and she hoped it would justify her concerns. She feared the doctor would dismiss Zack's problems by telling her all teenagers are moody, lazy, and stay up late.

"Can you remember something he said that struck you as odd?"

"He said the words, blood orange, bluebloods, and blood money—all in one sentence."

"We call that 'word salad' in medicine," the doctor said offhandedly. "Does he do it often?"

"It was only one time." It comforted her that the doctor was familiar with this behavior and had a name for it.

Dr. Brown pushed an extension on his phone.

"Jennifer, please bring Zack to the office."

An alarm went off in Zack's head when they ushered her out of the room as soon as he came in. Merely crossing the threshold of the door was challenging, but watching her leave so quickly—literally, as soon as he got there— was scary. She had planned something, but what?

Dr. Brown was dealing with challenges of his own. Foremost was Zack's appearance. While he stood out as a young adult with poor grooming, Zack did not look like the ordinary troubled youth. Those patients adopted a theme to their dress—goth, for instance, or tattoo enthusiast, intended to impress.

Zack had no unifying theme at all, which troubled the doctor. He was tall and was nervous—evidenced by his eyes darting in a futile effort to see everything in the room at once. He did not sit down but stood in front of the doctor's desk as if he were in front of a firing squad.

"Have a seat, Zack," the doctor said pleasantly. He wanted to say, "At ease, soldier."

"Where?" Zack looked around the room.

"Either chair would be fine."

Zack lowered himself into the chair carefully. His

eyes focused on the wall behind the doctor's head, and his right knee started jumping up and down like a jackhammer.

"I'm Dr. Brown. Do you remember me? It's been a long time since I have seen you."

Zack moved his hand to his forehead as if he were going to brush away his long hair, but instead, he dragged his hand down his face, forehead to chin.

"Can you tell me why you left school this past fall?"

Zack noticed the walls were dripping like candle wax. *When did the room start melting?*

It was hard to tear his eyes away from the dripping wall because the advancing edge was turning red, but when he looked back at the doctor, he was appalled. One of the doctor's eyes was falling out of its socket, and the noise was becoming almost unbearable.

"What happened at school, Zack?" The doctor said this a little louder to get his patient's attention.

Zack was more interested in looking at the room.

"Some college boys want to hurt me." He stole a quick glance back at the doctor.

"Why would these boys want to hurt you?"

"I don't know."

Dr. Brown saw Zack's hands clench the armrest of his chair so tightly that the knuckles turned white, and the tendons were prominent. His eyes began to roam the room again.

"Zack, what are you looking at?"

"I'm sure you are aware of it."

"Aware of what?"

Zack forced himself to look at the doctor once more. "The screaming."

"Who or what is screaming, Zack?"

"The children."

"What children?"

"The children hidden in your walls." Dr. Brown leaned into his chair. A frightened animal seemed to stare at him from inside Zack's head. There was something frightening about the eyes of his patient.

"Hearing that must be very upsetting."

"Yes, it is." *Finally, someone understands.*

"Have you ever thought of harming yourself?"

"No, someone else wants to harm me!"

Dr. Brown rearranged some things on his desk.

"Who wants to harm you?"

"Ruth." Zack looked up at Dr. Brown.

"Why would Ruth want to harm you, Zack?"

"I don't know, but she brought me here."

Sheila heard her name called. She walked in and sat next to her son. He looks agitated, she thought. Both of them look agitated.

"Mrs. Ewing, Zack, and I have talked, and I am going to refer him to another doctor who specializes in disorders of the mind. It is common for young adults to have temporary emotional setbacks, and these are best handled by a specialist. I don't want to worry you, but Zack may suffer from schizophrenia. It's too early to tell —he hasn't had symptoms long enough to make that diagnosis, and there are a handful of other illnesses that the psychiatrist will rule out."

Dr. Brown's assessment was not what Sheila wanted to hear, but it rang true.

"Zack," Dr. Brown addressed him respectfully, "I'm going to send you to a specialist. The University hospital has an excellent psychiatric department." The doctor turned his attention to his desk phone, calling the nurse.

"Jennifer, come get Zack, and let him sit in the nurses' station while I have a few words with Mrs. Ewing."

Sheila felt the deadening numbness of ice water in her veins. *His office is entirely too cold; why would they run the air conditioning in November?*

Dr. Brown walked over to sit in the chair beside her.

"I know what I have shared with you is difficult news to hear, but there is more, and this is important. Zack has delusions about you, and because of that, you could be in danger. I'll schedule an appointment with a psychiatrist as soon as I can, but I'm also sure it will take a few days before they can see him. In the meantime, be wary of Zack. If he should seem out of control, the emergency room is the place to go. Don't call the police if you can help it. There are drugs a doctor can give to calm him down."

Zack, relieved to be home again, walked up the stairs intending to go back into his room, but he became frightened before reaching the upstairs hall. He could hear the college-boys downstairs saying, *"You'd be better off dead, you crazy." They found him.* There was something else besides the boys. He couldn't figure out what, but something happened while he was away. There were more shadows than usual. There was something else, a smell. *Is it, gasoline?*

He backed away from the door and started walking in the hall, not wanting to go back downstairs, and not wanting to go into his room. Then he heard steps on the stairs getting louder and louder. At the last minute, he scrambled into his room and shut the door.

Zack got into his bed and pulled the sheets over his head. The footsteps stopped outside his door, then moved to leave him lightheaded from the weird way his heart was beating. He couldn't stay in this house much longer, now that the boys found him. He learned from experience that if he lay still and closed his eyes, the fear would subside. But terrifying thoughts were descending on him more frequently now and lasting longer.

Sheila had to share the terrible news with Carl, and she practiced how to say it. "Schizophrenia," she said out loud. *Possibly dangerous, needs psychiatric help, emergency room for emergencies.*

"Carl, we saw Dr. Brown today."

"Hey, Baby." Carl got up from his office chair and began walking away from her into the kitchen.

"He said that Zack needs to see a"—Carl kept walking like he didn't hear her.

On Thanksgiving Day, Sheila's mother, her sisters, their husbands, and six cousins gathered for a traditional meal in her home. Everyone thought Zack seemed strange, but out of respect for Sheila, they did not bring it up. Sheila noticed Zack developed a phobia about windows. He sat in a chair far away from the den window after lunch and excused himself early for reasons only Sheila understood.

The clean-up with her mother and her sisters, the best part of the holiday, distracted her. They laughed and retold family stories while they cleared the two tables, the formal one in the dining room and the one in the kitchen. When the dishes were washed, dried, and put away, her mother, Dixie, was the first to leave.

"I have leftovers for you, Mama," Sheila said, as Martin helped their mother with her coat. Sheila grabbed her jacket and walked them to his car.

"Martin has something for you, dear," Dixie said. "Help me into the car while he gets it from the trunk."

Martin motioned Sheila to join him. They stood hidden by the open trunk of the car. Martin was the youngest of the Hayward siblings, but he ran the farming business for all of them

"Here is a copy of Mama's will. Nothing surprising here. She is dividing everything equally among us. You have access to Zack's trust if you need it. I have been investing in the stock market so we can get it out quickly. I'm not trying to upset you unnecessarily, but if you need money for him now, it's available. We don't have to wait until he is twenty-one."

"Thanks, Martin."

"One other thing, Sis. Carl told me today that Zack is going to work for him. I don't think it is a good idea. You know how Carl is."

"How is he, Martin?"

"He's controlling. I don't think Zack could stand it, and I worry about you."

Her eyes were brimming with tears. The stress of her marriage, a mentally ill child, and organizing a formal dinner party had worn her down more than she realized.

"Sorry, Sis. I did not mean to make it worse. I am here for you if you need me." He handed her a legal-sized manila envelope with her name on it.

"I know it looks like I married the wrong man and I am weak." Sheila felt she had to defend herself. "But

I did the hard thing. I protected the children until they could leave. If there is any good news, Zack is eighteen. Carl no longer has power over him, but I don't think either of them realize it."

Martin circled back to the previous discussion.

"If Zack's choices are going back to school or working for Carl, there is another solution. He could work on the farm."

"Thank you. I love you so much, little brother." Sheila took a deep breath and tried to compose herself. "Give me some time to work through this. I don't think Zack can work for anyone right now—one more thing, Carl does not know about the trust."

"Yes, ma'am," Martin said, and he gave her a hug goodbye. "Thank you for a wonderful Thanksgiving party." Sheila watched him get into his car and leave before she strolled back into the house, dropping the document in a large basket she had for mail in the foyer.

Her sisters and their husbands were hugged and sent on their way home. When the last one filed out, Carl blocked the door and would not let Sheila walk them to their cars.

"We have spent the entire day with your family. You don't need to talk to them for an hour outside."

"Carl, you don't understand. They want to ask me about Zack in private, and I don't like it when you stand there, blocking the door."

"I wouldn't want to be someone like you, worried about what people think." Carl made a scowl on his face.

"Carl, nothing could be further from the truth. You worry as much as anybody, and you know it."

"I am going to the office," he said, looking at his feet.

"On Thanksgiving? It seems you are always locking

yourself up in there." Carl refused to make eye contact. "I've got some copying to do; don't wait up."

CHAPTER 11

27 November 2017

November and December are slow months for residential construction. Carl depended upon household maintenance and repairs to survive the holidays, anything from changing a lightbulb to rebuilding a deck, to pay his overhead. To that end, he cultivated a number of relationships with elderly patrons who could afford his work and who were lonely this time of year. This morning, Miss Sarah expected him. He left his house at seven, even though Sarah wanted to meet at nine. A man's gotta eat, and he has to have friends.

At seven-fifteen, Carl parked outside the Gower Airport looking over his empty appointment book when a face poked in his passenger side window.

"Hey, Randall. I'm stuck here trying to remember what the heck Sheila wanted at the hardware store."

"It happens to me, too. Sometimes my wife says something, and it goes in one ear and out the other. Are you having breakfast here?" Randall had an unpleasant halting laugh and rarely said anything interesting. Usually, Carl avoided him, but today he had time to kill.

The restaurant in the Gower airport served three meals a day, but men like Carl only ate breakfast there. The landing strip and terminal started as a hanger for crop dusters. Later, a wealthy retiree housed his private jet in the facility. When passenger service started in 1980, connecting Gower with Atlanta, Houston, and Dallas, the café flourished. Now the heart of the building is an atrium restaurant where every table enjoyed a commanding view of the tarmac.

"Where is everybody?" Carl expected busy tables at that hour.

"We're early. Look! That's the plane from Houston." Randall pointed to the sky. "Dallas will be next."

Within a few minutes, more men joined their table. Carl's "breakfast club" attended high school together; the buddies, all business owners, were fixated on gossip and politics.

The waitress brought their orders while the group conversation turned to speculation about a plan to update downtown. Bored, Carl found the 6 passengers who stepped off a plane from Dallas more engaging. One was not a local. She was stunning and confident, probably in her late twenties. A natural blonde, he thought, and possibly a model. Carl could imagine her working for Calvin Klein.

The guys at Carl's table stopped talking and watched him pop up from his chair to greet her.

"Miss, can I help you? You seem lost." She carried a briefcase which she shifted from one hand to the other.

"Thanks, I'm looking for my luggage."

"Certainly." He extended his arm to point to a corner of the waiting room.

"They place the luggage on the floor, but they take about fifteen minutes to unload the plane."

Carl kept walking toward the ticket counter where

he inquired about flight times to Atlanta and then returned to the table of friends.

"What are you doing?" his buddy to his left asked.

"Show'in off," he giggled, acting silly. Carl put five dollars on the table and finished his orange juice.

"Don't forget you are married," one of his buddies said.

"I ain't forgettin'. I'd like to stay, but if I do, I'll be late for a meeting with a client."

His buddies watched him leave and then seamlessly found another subject to discuss.

Pausing near the luggage, he pretended to search for a telephone number on his phone. His friends could not see him now. The new lady in town ignored him and read a book while she waited.

"Miss? I'm driving to town. Would you like a ride?"

Son, nothing vexes a woman more than a man faithful to his wife, but flirting doesn't count.

Her expression said yes, but she thanked him and said no.

Carl waited outside for her to leave in a cab or rental car, but no one left through the sliding glass doors for the next thirty minutes. Impatient, he placed a call.

"Miss Sarah, this is Carl. I'm running early today. Would it work for you if I came at 8:45?"

"That would be perfect. I'm expecting my granddaughter in a few minutes, and I want you two to meet."

"Yes, ma'am."

He had time to visit the car wash before Sarah's appointment in case she and her granddaughter wanted to ride in his truck to buy something. He would recommend a new refrigerator.

Once the pickup was vacuumed to his satisfaction, he paid the attendant a large tip and a compliment.

"Baby, I don't think anyone has done this job better," he said, pressing the dollar bills into her palm so she could feel his fingers against her skin.

"Thank you, Mr. Ewing. Don't be a stranger," the buxom teenager pocketed the money.

Generous tips are an investment in the future; don't be stingy.

He arrived at his appointment at eight-forty-two, drove his truck into her driveway, and parked behind a blue Honda Accord. Like an actor getting ready for a play, he channeled his feelings into the character. It took an enormous amount of energy to portray the man his client expected, but on this day, he assumed the role effortlessly. His good mood was genuine.

Armed with a breath mint in his mouth, his pink breast cancer band, and food for her dog, he stepped onto the pavement. He thought Miss Sarah may watch him from her window because she was always quick to answer the door. Just in case, he lingered a minute to admire her front yard flowers. Southern women of Miss Sarah's generation strive to have flowers all year long.

Bypassing the doorbell, Carl knocked. Only door-to-door salesmen clang a bell. For Sarah, his knock was personalized for her safety; she would always know it was him. The code was: three quick knocks, pause, and two quick knocks. The eardrum piercing bark reminded Carl to dig the treat out of his pocket just in time. When Sarah, beaming, opened the door, he rewarded her dog with a bacon-flavored strip.

"There you go, Sasha. You miss me?" Carl bent down, patting the dog's head. "I believe bacon is her favorite, Miss Sarah." He looked at her, thinking, she won't last much longer while the smell of cake engulfed him.

"Carl, good morning. I have the coffee on and banana bread in the oven."

"It smells good in here. How's the hot water heater working now?"

"It works fine," she said as they walked into the kitchen where she set up a placemat, plate, and coffee cup. "How is your family?"

"They are all good. We plan to visit the kids in Idaho soon."

"I know your wife is excited about that."

"She is," he said with a nod of his head.

Carl knew he shouldn't rush this, but it was hard to adhere to the customary ritual. On the days she baked, the work took longer.

"Did you get a new car, Miss Sarah?"

She furrowed her brow to think.

"Car? Oh no, it must be Ellen's rental." She served him a slice of banana bread with melted butter on top. "She's in the back bedroom."

Dang! "Where is she from?"

"She grew up here, but now she is a Texan," Sarah laughed. "And here she is!" Carl hoped to see the girl at the airport, and he was not disappointed. He stood up when she came into the room; head bowed, showing respect.

"I believe we just met," he said shyly and looked up to glance at her sideways. They already had two things in common, the airport and Miss Sarah.

"What a coincidence. Grandma has told me all

about you," she extended her hand. "My name is Ellen Kennedy."

"Now don't be telling any stories on me, Miss Sarah."

"Please, Sarah said, "we can sit around the table and talk. Let Carl finish his coffee."

Carl briefly stood at attention as the granddaughter took her place and then took his seat, determined not to leave a crumb on his plate.

"We are selling the house," Miss Sarah announced, "because Ellen wants me to downsize and live closer to my family who, I might add, moved away from me," she patted Ellen's forearm.

"Before we sell it, we want to update it for buyers."

The pupils in Carl's eyes dilated with excitement. Containing the emotion as best he could, he wiped his mouth with his napkin and stroked his mustache.

"I couldn't agree with you more," he said. "Family is everything." A remodel could be worth twenty thousand to five hundred thousand, depending upon what she is thinking.

"Ellen is going to help me decide how much to do," she continued as if she heard his thoughts. "I wanted to tell you sooner rather than later because you have such a good eye for design."

"It makes me sad to think about you moving, Miss Sarah." Carl invested so much time in this relationship that he was hoping she would leave him her money, but an extensive remodel is always expensive because once one opens the walls, there will always be a surprise.

"Well, seasons change, so I guess we have to change, too," she said.

"God has a plan for all of us, I know that," said Carl, nodding his head.

Sarah was an optimist, and Carl preferred working with an optimist; they spend more money.

"What do you think we should update?" Ellen asked.

"The front and back porches, he said."

"I love them," Miss Sarah said wistfully.

"Repaint them, Miss Sarah, and replace any trim that is showing signs of wear. The front door needs replacing, too. We both remember when you bought that door," he winked at her.

"Thirty years," she said. "You put that door up thirty years ago."

"As far as updates, kitchen updates are by far the most useful in making a house sell for a great price. Also, energy-efficient windows are popular. You two could think about that. I recommend you hire an interior decorator. I can give you a few names."

"Thanks, Carl, but I have a friend who lives here, and she will help us," Ellen said.

"Good deal." Carl approved of interior decorators; they raise the bar on price.

"I hadn't thought about changing the windows, but I see what you mean. They are drafty in the winter," Sarah said.

"Yes, ma'am," Carl said. "A good coat of paint, on the outside and inside, will brighten the house quite a bit, and you might consider a bathroom remodel for the master. When you and your granddaughter are ready, make me a list, and we'll get started."

Carl took his appointment book out of his breast pocket.

"How long will you be in town, Miss Ellen?" He hoped she would be in town for a long time.

"Two more days. Could we meet the day after Christmas? I'll have more time then."

"Great, that will give me time, too. I'll check out the attic and walk over the roof."

Attic equals goldmine, Son, mine it first.

Carl marked the day in his calendar

"Don't you two worry about anything; you'll be proud of the house when you finish, and the resale will give Miss Sarah a nice profit." He stood up, bent over, and hugged Sarah.

"It's a pleasure to meet you, Miss Ellen." Carl extended his hand, the one with the breast cancer bracelet on it, to shake hers; he was sure she saw it. "I can find my way out, Miss Sarah."

Ellen grabbed the dog while he left the house.

"I see what you mean, Grandma. He seems nice," Ellen said with a wide grin. "Let's get to work. I'll call Sissy Wilson today."

"Yes, call her. It's been a month since they buried her father. I don't think it's too soon."

"What happened?"

"He had a heart attack, only fifty-six years old. It was the maid that found him, poor man."

"That's terrible; I didn't know."

Zack heard the doorbell ring twice while cocooned in bed, waiting for a rim of light to appear around his blacked-out windows. Aluminum foil was not perfect, but it was all he could find in the Ewing house. Terrified, he shifted his eyes to the windows again. Now, light was streaming around the edges of the pane of glass and pooling on the floor. His eyes played tricks on him all the time, now. To identify the caller, he crept into the upstairs hall and listened while Ruth opened the door. He was ready to run if the boys came back.

"Paul, come in. He will be thrilled to see you." Zack slipped back in his room to put on a pair of jeans and walked a few steps on the stairs wearing socks.

"I'm aware you are here to see Zack, but if you don't mind, may I talk to you for a moment in the kitchen?"

"I'm sorry I can't stay, Mrs. Ewing. Could I give Zack's money to you?"

"Only a few minutes, please."

Zack tiptoed down the stairs to listen outside the door.

"Paul," he heard her say, "Zack came home from school early. Do you have any idea why?"

"No, ma'am."

"But you were his roommate; was Zack into drugs?"

"I never saw him do any, Mrs. Ewing."

"Are you telling me the truth?"

"Oh yes, ma'am!"

Zack tried to stand as still as possible.

"Paul, Zack has changed. Something must have happened to him at school, something terrible to change him like that."

"She thinks you are terrible, and you are."

"I think he was just shy," Mrs. Ewing.

"Wait right here."

Sheila bumped into Zack when she left the kitchen to find him.

"Goodness!" she said. "Come in, Paul came to see you."

Zack weighed his options. He could turn and run, or face Paul.

"Paul is bringing you a message, go ahead."

Zack walked in with Sheila. Paul stood up when they came in.

"I'll leave you boys alone," she said.

"Yes, ma'am," The boys heard her shut the front door.

"Hey, Zack, when are you coming back to school?" Paul asked, still standing.

"Never." Zack lifted his hand to his forehead and moved the palm over his face, ending at the chin.

"You probably forgot, but I borrowed twenty dollars from you for my key deposit. I wanted to pay you back and tell you, I'm sorry if I wasn't a good roommate."

"Are you here to warn me, Paul? Because if you are, they found me here."

"What?" Paul made a move to leave.

"The college boys." Zack sat down.

"No, I came to repay your money." Paul dug the dollar bills out of his pocket.

Zack licked his lips. "Are you here to warn me about her?" Zack shifted his eyes to show he was talking about the woman who just left the room.

"Who?"

"Ruth."

"No! Of course not!" Paul threw the money at the table.

Zack grabbed it but said nothing. Paul blinked and headed for the door.

"Watch out for those boys I told you about." He followed Paul out to his car. It felt comforting to watch

Paul drive away. Then he checked the house for signs of her, before returning to his room and closing the door.

A few minutes later, she was standing over him.

"You should have locked it, idiot."

"Zack, we must talk."

"What do you want me to do?" Zack lay in bed.

"Talk to me!"

Swiping his face three times, he popped out of bed, and paced back and forth a few times before confronting her.

"Ruth," Zack bared his teeth and placed his hands on her shoulders, while Sheila turned pale and tried to push him away.

"Are you finished?" His eyes riveted to hers.

"Yes, yes I am," Ruth seemed less frightening now that he had her in his grip. Her shoulders were so fragile he could crack them as easily as halving a graham cracker.

Sheila tried to back away, but she was stuck. His hands were only inches away from her neck and he was squeezing her tight. Her phone ringing in her apron pocket caused him to waver, and she ran into her bedroom and locked the door.

Sheila, out of breath from fear, not exhaustion, called Carl back.

"Yeah," he answered. Someone was sawing in the background.

"Come home right now! He is acting crazy and calling me Ruth."

"It would surprise me if Zack could hurt a fly. I bet you got it all wrong." Carl sounded annoyed.

"I don't think so."

"Well, think again. Find out what's going on."

"I am no match for him. And Dr. Brown warned me about this!"

"Well, it's not like he is a water moccasin on the porch," Carl snarled. "I'll tan his hide when I get home tonight."

"I need you now," Sheila begged.

"Baby," Carl chuckled as if he were enjoying the situation, "I can't leave work right now." As an afterthought, he said. "You know the gun I keep in the drawer by the bed? See if he has it."

CHAPTER 12

Late Afternoon, Same Day

Privacy locks, found on bedroom and bathroom doors, can be picked with a hairpin in less than two minutes. For security, a key lock is required. Exterior doors, for example, have key access on one side and a knob on the other. If you come across a lock that is accessed by a key on both sides, you are looking at the most secure lock of all, the dual cylinder deadbolt. A homeowner with a dual cylinder deadbolt lock on the bedroom door had better wear the key around her neck because the monster is in the house.

Sheila wrapped Carl's gun in a towel before sliding it between two hat boxes in her closet. Frightened her son would come in, she dragged the loveseat to block his entry, knowing furniture would only slow him down.

Poised to make the first 911 call of her life, she heard Zack running downstairs. The next sound, metal upon metal, stopped her. From her window she saw him drive away in his car, having knocked the mailbox on its side.

Carl came home later that afternoon, jubilant over his good luck; the remodel job, predominantly inside work, had the potential to carry him through the winter. The next step was to provide his client with a detailed cost estimate. Not wanting to be interrupted, he took the path from the garage to his office. By six PM, the aroma of parsley and garlic wafting from the kitchen lured him to dinner.

Sheila stood with her back to him while she boiled potatoes. She cut a chunk of butter with a dinner knife.

He made no sound in his stocking feet and waited until she felt his breath on her neck. Startled, she dropped the butter onto the gas burner.

"Carl?" She was trembling when Carl poked her in the ribs.

"What are you cooking, Mama?"

"I thought you were Zack."

"Where is he anyway?"

"He left in his car."

"Good, I'm glad he's getting out." Carl pranced around looking in the refrigerator and under the cake dome to see what she prepared for supper. "Not to change the subject, I have to meet with a client tonight." Carl stared at the floor.

"When?"

"Around eight-thirty, he's leaving for Denver to-mara morning."

"Zack and I had an argument," Sheila cleaned up the butter she spilled. "I yelled at him, and he got mad at me."

"Sheila, lose your temper. Be firm with him." Carl gave her a hug. "We should be grateful to have some time alone." He set the table for dinner and poured her a glass of wine.

Sheila reached for her carving knife to serve the roast, but it was missing. She hadn't used it since Thanksgiving.

"You will never guess what happened at work

today?" Carl had a boyish grin. "Baby, aren't you going to ask me what happened?"

"I'm waiting for you to tell me." Carl watched Shelia check every drawer in the room.

"We got this skinny plumber's helper, and he put in the garbage disposal weird, so when we turned it on, it ground itself out of the cabinet, and water went spewing everywhere. We laughed so hard, I thought I was gonna be sick. And the little guy, only five-foot-three, burst into tears and quit on the spot. I tole him, you can quit, but you got to clean this mess up first."

"Did he clean it up?"

Carl pushed the wine glass toward her. "Yep, he did."

"Aren't you worried about Zack?"

"Naw, he's eighteen years old, and it's not that late."

"Don't wait up for me." Carl walked upstairs to brush his teeth. He poked his head in again before he left. "A second-floor bedroom with a deadbolt lock is dangerous if there's a fire. I'm sure the imbecile who installed it, failed to tell you that."

Sheila checked the pantry, her box of sterling silver, and the good china cabinet trying to find the knife. Having no luck, she checked odd places, like the freezer and the wastebasket. She hated to think she accidentally threw it away and searched in inconceivable places. By the time she checked her bedside table, she thought she was losing her mind. Alone in the house, she climbed into bed to rest, afraid to fall asleep.

The RING-RING coming from somewhere in the house was unmistakable; it was Zack's phone.

Twenty minutes after Carl left home, he pulled

into the parking lot of Mickey's bar, a hangout for middle-aged men. Carl and his friends often met there to play cards. Mick tried a lady's night, but it never caught on, so he capitalized on the all-male, "no loose lips here" reputation, and it was a wise choice. The guys picked up their spirits at the counter. One employee, Chuck, served them while the owner worked the cash register.

A parking lot in the back was an unintended, but brilliant idea. While the front was lit up with neon lights, the back was dark. Carl could appreciate that "deals" were being transacted in the parking lot with no one taking notice, but Carl was paying a debt. He wanted everyone there to see his friend Steve win $2,000 in a poker game. Once inside, he spotted five potential witnesses, and then he saw Steve sitting at a booth in the far corner.

Carl passed by the other tables before shaking Steve's hand. "Hey, man, how're you?" Everyone, including Fred, the policeman, saw it.

"I'm doing fine, Boss. I love driving a truck. Takes me all over the country."

"Well, it is good to see you, brother. Can I get you something?"

"No, this one is still fresh."

Thirsty, Carl ordered a whiskey and requested a deck of cards. When he returned to Steve's table he said, "How about a game of Texas Hold 'em?"

"Chuck," he called. "Can you come over and light our candle? This old man can't see to play."

"I appreciate this," Steve whispered. "I sure need the money."

"You did great. Did the housekeeper let you in?"

"Yes, but don't worry about her. Steve finished his drink. I bet your friend was hopping mad."

Carl grinned and dealt the cards. They played for two hours, laughing and talking like best friends, and when the game was over, Steve won $2,000. Carl made sure it was all twenty-dollar bills, accumulated by many small bank withdrawals and money from cash jobs.

The only blemish of the evening was Carl's phone, which interrupted them three times, all three calls from Sheila.

"You are a good man, Steve," Carl said, refusing to appear hurried. "This'ere's my wife calling, so I'd better pick up on this one." And then he said a little louder, "Steve, you can't be beat tonight. It's time for me to quit."

Steve shook Carl's hand and left quickly to evade any "creditors" who might be lurking in the bar or parking lot.

"Hey honey," Carl said into the phone, "I just now saw you called. Our meetin' went long."

"I'm worried about Zack," she said. "He wants you to pick him up."

"What are you talking about?"

"When he ran out of the house, he left his phone. Someone, I don't know who, called to say he wants us to come get him. The address is: 121 Logtown Road in Bingham. He's not feeling well, they said."

"Damn! What business does he have going way out there?" And before Sheila could say anything else; he hissed, "Don't you worry, I'll git him."

Carl punched the address into his GPS. He was familiar with the community because he hired a man who lived there. The "sorry son of a bitch" did not have a driver's license. Every workday for three months, Carl drove him back and forth to the job site. He was talented, but Carl had to fire him when he started making mistakes, and tools disappeared.

He considered asking a friend to go with him, but decided it was better to go alone. No telling what Zack's condition would be. He opened his glove compartment and put a revolver on the seat beside him. In the dark, the lights across the cab and both side mirrors made his truck look like a mini-eighteen-wheeler. Gunning the motor, he was forced to ease out of the parking lot, because by now it was crowded.

After traveling seven miles south on the interstate, he exited to take a two-lane highway to the village of Epps, where he turned on a narrow winding road that led to Bingham. There were no street lights in Bingham, and all but one house was dark. Vehicles, mostly old trucks, decorated the front yards. When Carl was near, he saw a white frame shotgun house with Christmas lights on the porch. Cars littered the curb on both sides of the street while Rap music blared from the house. Zack was sitting alone on top of someone's car. He wore a short-sleeve shirt in 43-degree weather, hugging himself and rocking back and forth.

"Where is your coat?" Carl said when he reached him. "Son, it's warm in the truck, come on. Where is your car?" Carl kept looking for a white Toyota Camry, while Zack got into the back seat of the cab as though he were taking a taxi home. He sat looking out the rear window and his knee pumped up and down.

"Son! Answer me when I talk to you."

Zack turned around so Carl could talk to him in the

rear-view window.

"Where's your car? I understand a boy your age is gonna make mistakes, but losing your car is serious."

Zack turned again to look out his side window into the dark. The window held his attention for several minutes while Carl drove up and down the street looking for the car.

"You been drinking?"

"I want to go home." Zack rolled up one of his pants legs and started vigorously scratching.

"What were they doing at this party?"

"Nothing."

"Sure Zack, I believe that. What else were they doing?"

The ride back home was quiet; neither of them wanted to talk. Carl plotted to set things straight, and soon. He wanted to believe that Sheila was the reason his son was a disappointment, Sheila, or possibly drugs, and he planned to correct both.

"Zack, just you remember, I ain't no taxi ride for you."

Carl yelled, "SHEILA!" when they got home.

Zack walked like a zombie up the stairs.

"Sheila, we have to be tougher on him. They were doing drugs. DRUGS." He took her arm and squeezed so tightly she winced.

"We need to talk about this situation with our son." He pulled her to the sofa and pointed for her to sit down. "We can't keep treating Zack like a little boy. Look at him. He's a grown man now, and he needs to act like one."

"I know you don't see it, but Zack is sick."

"What does he do all day when I am not home?"

"He stays in his room and plays on his computer. You sleep so soundly you don't hear him, but he is roaming downstairs almost every night."

"I'll take care of the computer." Carl, irate and tired, looked at his watch; it was three o'clock in the morning.

He grabbed Zack's computer, dropped it on the driveway, and ran over it with his truck. Before going to bed, he threw it in Zack's wastebasket.

"No more fun and games."

CHAPTER 13

December 24, and 25, 2017

Zack's psychiatric appointment, scheduled on January 5, was almost two weeks away. By Christmas Eve, Sheila had not slept in five weeks. Insomnia, an alarming symptom, interfered with her ability to plan. While waking too early was manageable, sleepless nights forced her to adopt bad habits. The afternoon wine wore off by evening. Desperate, she drank bedtime wine and swallowed over-the-counter sleeping pills. By three in the morning, still wide awake, she felt adrift until, without warning, dread engulfed her in the form of noise. Every night, she threw off the covers and monitored the house.

Zack's nighttime behavior solidified her fear of him. There was nothing left of the charming boy she raised. He made unbearable noise. The muttering morphed into chanting, the kitchen antics accelerated into slamming cabinet doors, drawers and dropping dishes, *and the stairs, up and down, like a hamster on a wheel.*

At six, Carl, untroubled, woke up, and the day would start.

Sheila prepared breakfast without an appetite. Dark wrinkles gathered under her eyes, giving her the appearance of too much makeup. Carl sat reading the obituaries in the newspaper while she stood, painstakingly cutting sections of a grapefruit.

"Ole Mrs. Garrett died this week; a remodel on her house would transform it." He made a note in his appointment book so he would not miss the funeral. "Baby, I met one of her heirs at the bowling alley last year. Do you know any of them?"

"No."

Zack appeared for breakfast. Sitting opposite his dad, he poured orange juice into his glass from a carton Sheila placed on the table. Lifting the glass to eye level, he turned it around to inspect it.

"This looks like blood-orange juice, or maybe it's the blood of the Lamb. Is it Sunday yet? Blue bloods like us should be in church if it's Sunday because we have a lot of blood money to give to those who bleed." Sheila had heard this nonsense before. Carl inexplicably ignored it.

Zack ate eggs and sausage with gusto, but after a few bites, he stopped eating. Sheila could not understand why he served himself so much and left it untouched.

"Zack," Carl said. "My friend Fred found your car parked at the high school. I brought it home, but I want your set of keys."

Zack scurried to his room, reminding Sheila of a raccoon.

"I swear to God, there has to be drugs in his room." And then in a saccharine voice, he added, "Honey, I have been thinking," he parted his lips. "Maybe Zack stockpiled supplies in his room he don't want us to see… like… drugs?" he shrugged. "I don't think I am crazy to suggest a search."

"How can I do that, Carl, when he never leaves the house?" Sheila felt like throwing the extra grapefruit at him.

"I'll take him out tonight. Can you look in his room for me, Baby? 'Cause it looks like drugs to me." Carl hugged her. "And he don't have to go anywhere if it's stashed under the bed or in his closet."

Carl followed through with his promise as soon as he returned from work. Winking at her. "Come on, Son. Let's go out for a hamburger."

Soon Sheila searched Zack's bedroom as planned. Still, it was ironic. She was home doing the dirty work while Carl and Zack celebrated a new job and Christmas Eve without her.

Zack left every light turned on, the ceiling light, the desk lamp, the light on the bedside table, the bathroom, and the closet. The pictures on the walls had not changed, a famous baseball player, a poster of a rock band, the awards—Merit Scholar, First Place in the state's Literary Rally, First Prize in the Evangeline Literary Contest for Short Story, a picture of him shaking hands with an author (what was his name?) at Square Books in Oxford, Mississippi.

She patted the bed to see if Zack hid anything under the wrinkled covers. He never made his bed anymore. She felt under the mattress for items placed there and found a white and black speckled composition booklet. Zack's handwriting had changed unless someone else wrote the notes, line upon line of indecipherable letters and symbols. Her heart flipped over and shifted into high gear—Sheila dropped to sit on his bed, fearing she was about to have a heart attack. The strain of blood pumping so fast overcame her. Lightheaded, she lay on the bed, legs dangling off the side, fearing Carl and Zack would come home and find her this way. The change in position seemed to help. Another flip and the heartbeat was imperceptible again. The heaviness lifted, and she sat up slowly. She gathered her courage and tried to stand. She was fine; it was just a scare.

She replaced the notebook, examined the pillows, and patted down the blanket. Sheila was careful to leave no clues. It would inflame Zack.

She fished a flashlight out of her apron pocket to see under the bed. There she found several brown paper bags stored almost beyond her reach. She laid on the floor and slid her arm as far as she could to grasp one of them. It was an awkward position and seemed to strain her shoulder as if it might be too much contortion to bear, but she made the swipe and brought out a paper bag appropriate for a sack lunch. Inside the brown bag was a plastic sandwich bag containing a few tablespoons of a spice-like substance. She thought it was marijuana.

She left again to get a broom to push the remaining three within reach. One, a paper grocery sack, contained the carving knife. The implications were so devastating that she steeled herself for the next assault on her heart. But it did not come. Maybe she was healthier than she thought.

Two smaller brown bags contained a fraternity pin, a rabbit's foot key chain, and his senior ring. *When they amputate a rabbit's foot, is he already dead?* She would amputate a live rabbit's foot if it made all of this go away. So far, not a call from Carl, so she examined Zack's desk. The laptop Carl crushed was resting on his desk as if Zack thought it was salvageable. She pulled out the drawers looking for notes, letters, anything that would explain his behavior. His books were still in the laundry basket. His closet was next.

He moved a bean bag chair into the closet and piled it with clothes. Otherwise, everything there looked like the day he left it. She turned to search his bureau. Beginning with the top drawer, she found his wallet with 20, one-dollar bills in it, his driver's license, and his student ID. A buzzing in her apron pocket, followed by Carl's ring tone, made her jump. The anxiety of everything reared its ugly head. They were coming home.

"We'll talk when you get back," she said. She glanced around the room to see if everything appeared undisturbed and left carrying the "sample" and her carving knife. Before the boys got home, she collected all the kitchen knives and hid them in her closet. There was not enough time to secure the scissors.

Zack disappeared into his room as soon as they arrived, leaving Sheila and Carl sitting on the sofa in their living room. Her tree was sparkly, and there was a sprinkling of presents underneath. Christmas preparations this year were last minute because the family had to cancel a trip to see the grandchildren in Idaho. They could not travel with Zack as planned or leave him home.

"I guess Zack wasn't digging it," Carl said. "He seemed nervous and couldn't wait to get back." He shook his head in disbelief. "Zack acted funny, Sheila; his eyes kept darting every which way around the room like he was watching a mosquito fly." Carl imitated Zack for effect. "My friends thought he was wired." Carl nodded his head knowingly. "Did you search his room, Baby?"

"Yes, I found some stuff in a plastic bag; I'm not sure, but I think it is marijuana. There was a knife under the bed. It looks like Zack pretends to use his crushed computer—the way he has it set up on his desk."

"What about the plastic bag?"

"I hid it in the kitchen."

"Let's go look."

Sheila had hidden the bag in the drawer under the oven. She retrieved it and gave it to Carl.

He was livid when he saw it. His eyes, almost black, seemed to penetrate her. "Where did you find this?" Blood suffused his face.

"Under his bed." Sheila cowered before him.

"Damn!" Carl said as if he had become electrified. "He has disrespected me for the last time, and he is going to get it through his head right now!" Carl turned toward the stairs.

"Carl, no!" Sheila reached for him, and he grabbed her by the upper arm.

"It's your fault. You babied our son. He's taking drugs! He's smoking pot," he yelled. "And it is very dangerous for him to keep your carving knife tucked under his bed."

"Carl, you are hurting me."

"All you do is go to the Junior League and the Garden Club. I have to be the one to knock some sense into him."

She makes you do these things. Be sure she knows it.

"He sees Dr. Brown on Monday," Sheila lied. "How would it look if Zack had a black eye?"

Carl remained agitated but understood the implications. He came to an abrupt stop and turned to punch the kitchen wall while he yelled: "GOD DAMN IT!" The searing pain of a boxer's fracture evaporated the anger that consumed him only moments before. He cradled his right hand with his left and slowly sank onto the floor.

"Let me see it," Sheila said. He lowered his injured hand to let it rest in his lap. She gently examined it, bruised and starting to swell. "We have to go to the emergency room. I'll get ice for the swelling and Advil for the pain."

Carl said nothing. He had that cold, empty, defeated look on his face that she had seen far too often. She left him to get car keys and her purse, mentally making a list of the other items they would require for the trip: a pillow, insurance card, snack. What just happened was real—something she could handle.

"Here, take this," she said as she gave him three Advil tablets and a glass of water. She brought him a plastic bag with ice and a bed pillow. "Rest your hand on the pillow, put the ice on it, and then wrap the pillow around your wrist to support it. I'll bring the car around to the front door."

Carl did as he was told and supported the right forearm on the pillow, pressing it against his chest. He struggled to stand, then walked to the car where he hesitated a moment, wobbling, before accessing the front passenger seat. The ride was short and silent. Sheila dropped him off in the drive-through, and the orderly wheeled him into the hospital.

When the triage nurse, wearing an elf's cap, asked Carl what happened. He said a window fell on his hand while he was fixing it. The orderly took him for x-rays. By the time they moved him into an exam room, Sheila

118

was there, legs crossed, listening to faint Christmas carols.

"The doctor will be in shortly," the nurse sealed the door.

Dr. Patel sat at his desk and looked at Carl's information; the nurse on duty looked over his shoulder. Then, he pulled up the x-rays on his computer.

"Whoa," he said to the nurse. "I would hate to see the other guy." He shook his head, "I can guarantee this patient was not fixing a window."

Three hours later, an attendant helped Carl into the car. He was wearing a bulky split and carrying a prescription for pain medication in his pocket.

As Sheila drove them home, she unemotionally said, "Zack is not smoking it in the house; I would smell it."

Carl shifted himself in his seat to get more comfortable.

"We had a wonderful family until you let this drug stuff happen."

Carl was not a tall man, only five foot seven, but he seemed tall to people who met him for the first time. He projected confidence and strength, perhaps explaining the impression of being tall, and he was stocky in a way that looked strong. But the next morning, Carl got out of bed, lacking his characteristic good looks, strength, or power. He was weak as a kitten and appeared at least two inches shorter. Dr. Patel put a splint on him that started at his fingertips and ended just below his elbow; the awkwardness of it and the throbbing pain kept him awake all night.

"You up?" he said to his wife.

"Yes," Sheila yawned. A muffled ring-ring distracted them. "Is that your phone?"

"Yeah, I must have left it in my pocket after we came home from the ER. It's a good thing I don't have to work today." Sheila got his phone from the closet.

"It says Sarah."

"I gotta call her back." Sheila helped him return the call.

"Merry Christmas!" he said when Sarah answered.

"Merry Christmas to you and your family. Ellen and I are wondering if you can meet with us tomorrow?"

"Yes, ma'am." He made his face look cheerful to produce a generous tone of voice.

"How about eight?"

When he got off the phone, he turned to tell Sheila that the remodel contract was ready to sign.

"How are you going to sign anything?" She slipped on her robe, glad he was no longer angry.

"I can make an X with my left hand." He lay back in bed. "Sheila, get me another one of them pain pills."

Christmas day for the Ewing family was a quiet affair. Carl did not feel like coming downstairs, and Zack opened his gifts mechanically. Sheila bought him a shirt and a tie. Zack did not give any presents, and Carl gave Sheila gloves made from a buck he killed last year. Sheila brought Carl's gift upstairs.

"It's hard to choose a present for you, but I know you will use this." He looked at the present helplessly.

"I'll open it for you; see—it's four pairs of hunting socks to keep you warm."

Sheila spent the rest of Christmas day scouring the house for sharp objects and trying to think where to hide Carl's gun so no one could find it, not even him. Once again, she questioned her sanity—surely, Carl would not hurt Zack, and surely, Zack would not hurt her—but it might happen.

She gathered the scissors, remembered the ice pick, and checked Carl's tools in the garage. There were two pocket knives, several screwdrivers, and a leather punch which she confiscated. The toolbox was a mess, and she used her bare hand to shift the contents, examining it. With one sweep, she saw a glint of gold. Intrigued, she took everything out until she recovered it and held it in her hand.

It was the watch she lost when Zack left for college. Only one person would—could—have put it there.

CHAPTER 14

26 December 2017

Carl woke to go to the bathroom feeling nauseated and unsteady on his feet. The pain made him irritable; the pain pills made him sick. Overnight, the penetrating bone ache morphed into a throbbing from his hand up to his arm, leading him to believe the splint was too tight.

"Check my fingers, Sheila, and make sure I have enough circulation," Carl said when he staggered back to bed

"Let's take a look," Sheila said, taking his hand in hers. "I see more bruising and swelling, but the nail beds are pink. Can you wiggle your fingers?"

"No."

"Try again." Carl flexed his fingertips one degree.

"I don't know why they put such a big splint on you."

"What time is it?" He reached for his glasses on the bedside table.

"You should take today off." Sheila tied a knot in the belt of her robe.

"I can't. I got an appointment at eight."

"It's a quarter to seven; I'm going downstairs to make coffee." She left him to get dressed on his own.

He had no time to shave and no way to shower.

Wearing the shirt, made sleeveless on one side by the ER nurse, paired with sweat pants, the only bottoms he could put on with one hand, he swallowed more pain pills with the glass of water Sheila left on the nightstand. Descending the stairs was tricky because on the way down, the stair rail was on his right. He staggered out of the house and inched his way into his truck. The phone call came as he expected it would.

"Good morning," Sarah said. "Just reminding you that Ellen and I are ready to meet. Would you like to come now?"

Carl forced a smile.

"Miss Sarah, as a matter of fact, I am on my way." His ebullience faded once he realized he had forgotten to bring his notes from the last meeting. A sudden shift in the position of his arm created a lightning strike of pain.

Although wedged in the truck, he reluctantly swung his legs out to the running board and maneuvered the injured arm past the steering wheel while his left hand grabbed the door frame to keep from falling out. He left the motor running and entered the house by the front door.

"SHEILA, get me some pillows! I can't do anything."

"Coming," she called. While she got the pillows, Carl found the notes in the office. Sheila brought outdoor cushions and worked with Carl to stack them just the right height. By now, he had to hurry to get to Sarah's house on time.

"That's good, Sheila," he said, shooing her away. "Let me get on the road."

"You should come back as soon as you can and..." He shifted into drive and left her in mid-sentence.

Carl turned his attention to making up for the delay. *Damn old ladies, when you say you are coming, they set a timer.*

Carl arrived fifteen minutes late. *For God's sake, don't forget the list this time.*

He tore the pages out of his notebook, stuffed them into his back pocket, and began the exit procedure. It was tough, so much to remember while feeling ill. Halfway up the sidewalk, he lurched to his left and while correcting his direction, an unfamiliar black Range Rover took his attention off himself. One thought connected with another; an expensive car in this neighborhood meant a third party was in the house. Miss Sarah opened the door before he knocked.

"Carl, you are so good to come on Boxing Day. My goodness, what happened to your arm?"

"It looks worse than it is," Carl said, holding his arm up so she could see it better, "A window slammed down on my hand." He gave her the sweetest smile he could muster and inquired about her health.

"I'm not dead yet, but ready to move on," she said.

"Good! I'll do whatever you need me to do."

"Come into the kitchen; Ellen's friend Sissy is here. Come to think of it, she may want to talk to you about getting her father's house ready for sale."

"Carl, you remember, Ellen, and this is Sissy." Sarah made a formal introduction. "Sissy, this is Carl Ewing. He is helping Ellen and me update the house."

"Hello, Mr. Ewing. I'm Sissy Graham," she said primly. "I hope you don't mind if I sit in on your planning session." Sissy was short with dark eyes and straight black hair parted in the middle. She had the figure of a high school cheerleader and moved like one, too.

Ellen spoke now. "Sissy is an interior decorator, and we have been friends since high school. You may have known her dad, Trent Wilson, who passed away recently."

"Well, I am very happy to meet you; I knew your dad, and I am so sorry for your loss." Carl tried to look sad, but without the help of a mirror, the sad face was coming across as pathetic. He was caught off guard, completely off guard.

"Thank you," Sissy said. "My mother told me you and he were business partners."

Receiving no reply from Carl, Sissy continued tearfully, "I just cannot understand what happened to him. He exercised every day."

"I know it must have been a shock," Carl said, cautiously. He immediately regretted his choice of words. The good mood, the trusting mood, and the spending mood were dissipating fast. Undeterred, Sissy appeared to have an agenda.

"His neighbor said he waved to him just before he died."

Holy shit. "How long have you been in the interior decorating business?" He tried to distract her.

"Six years. My Mom said you and my dad were business partners." Carl stared at the floor, a trick his father taught him.

"We built some things together, but I wouldn't say we was partners."

Act uneducated, simple, and honest.

"What would you call your relationship then?"

125

Sissy, tilting her head sideways, tried to look him in the eyes, but he avoided her face.

"I knew him well enough to know what a fine man he was. Maybe we should talk about Miss Sarah's job another time; I could come back on Monday." Carl was feeling sick. He had a knot in his stomach.

"Please, don't go. I plan on staying quiet while you state your suggestions, and later, I will help them with the paint color and other things that don't concern you."

He planned to play the white knight, the charming grandfather, and the sexy older man, but with the three of them, it just seemed silly. Sissy was beyond his reach.

He motioned toward the kitchen, "Have a seat at the table, and I will show you my idears." They followed this suggestion without debate.

"I have two plans. One is the kitchen, and the other is the kitchen and bathrooms. No matter which one you choose, I recommend better outside lighting and upgrading the windows. This neighborhood is older, which gives it charm and the advantage of being close to the grocery store, but the trade-off is poor security. Homeowners want to feel safe."

A wave of nausea rolled over him caused by the four tablets of Advil Sheila gave him at breakfast. He pressed on.

"Consider an automatic door to the garage. A two-car garage with a door is even better. My personal opinion, Miss Sarah, safety is number one. Install outside lighting and add-on to the garage, so two cars fit in there." He had to stop talking after a disgusting taste appeared in his throat. He swallowed it back down and said, "Those are the safety issues you could address."

The three women looked at each other for comments.

"The prices are right here, Miss Sarah." He handed her the paper with his left hand.

"This looks very detailed, Carl. You always do such a wonderful job."

"Thanks." He smiled lovingly at her wrinkled face. He noticed the other two had no praise for him.

"Carl, let me walk you to the door; it was so good of you to come during the holidays." As they walked out to the porch, she said, "I'll call you Monday, don't you worry; just take care of your arm."

"I ain't worried, Miss Sarah," He stood stooped over while they talked, then turned, and lumbered into a gentle rain. Before she could close the door behind him, he called back.

"Where's your dog?"

"She's at the groomers. I know she will be sorry she missed you." Miss Sarah laughed. "Carl, you are always good medicine for me."

He tried not to throw up in her yard, but it was inevitable. The movement down the steps set it off—no more tamping it down. He limped to his truck, wrestled himself in, made the engine roar, and left.

Ellen and Sissy stayed in Miss Sarah's kitchen.

"What is going on between you and Carl Ewing?"

"Let's get out of the house; I don't want your grandmother to know." As they headed out the back door, Sissy added, "I don't think I can work with him."

The two friends sat in Sarah's garden. Southern women of Miss Sarah's generation love a well-ordered garden with a path leading to a single bench for prayer.

Sarah's backyard-retreat once had a fountain, but she let it go to ruin. Still, it had an archeological charm. Rainwater and dead leaves filled the pool until she hired Carl to clean it every spring. Once seated, Ellen was impatient.

"Now, please tell me. Something was going on in there."

"First of all, I don't trust him, and my Dad didn't trust him. They WERE partners, but they didn't get along at all."

"Tell me everything."

"Have you ever remembered an event when you were young and then revisited the memory as an adult?"

"Not really."

"I have a memory of Carl Ewing that occurred when I was young, and it bugged me for years until I finally figured him out."

"How young."

"Fourteen. Renee and I were friends."

"I never saw you two together."

"Our friendship didn't last long because of him. Anyway, one Thursday, Renee asked me to spend the night with her. School was out Friday for parent-teacher conferences, so no school, and since my mother was a teacher, she had to go to work. It seemed natural to spend the night with my friend rather than spend Friday alone at home.

"My mother dropped me off in the afternoon. We gossiped and had a great time. In the morning, Miss Sheila had to drive me home because Renee woke up with a sore throat and fever. But the plans changed when Mr. Ewing said work was slow and he offered to take me.

"We were still in their driveway when he asked if I would like to visit a house he built. I pictured it as an adventure, so I enthusiastically said yes. Remember, I was only fourteen, and he can be very charming."

"Oh my God, did he molest you?"

"No, nothing like that. Just listen to the story."

"Okay, I'm listening." Ellen crossed her arms to ward off the cold.

"We went to see the house, and he was amazing. I still use design tips he taught me when I advise my clients. But after visiting the house, he didn't take me home. He took me to the hardware store, the grocery store—if you can believe it—the gas station, and the lumberyard. At first, it was like I was along for the ride, and I admit, I enjoyed it. But later in the morning, he was having me carry packages out to his truck, handing him things off the shelf, or running back to the truck to get something he left in it. Basically, I was working for him. Just before we went to the paint store, he mentioned lunch in the next town over, as soon as we bought the paint. I balked at leaving town. When I asked about going home, he repeatedly said he would take me after we do one more thing. Mom was working, you see, and no one was at home waiting for me."

"That is strange. Couldn't you call your mother?"

"I could have, but she and I weren't getting along, and frankly, I thought it might make him mad. Anyway, I solved it myself just before he took me to lunch. While shopping with him in the paint store, I ran into a friend of my mother's. I left his side to approach her and asked if she would take me home. We didn't talk to him, and he ignored us. It was like he and I had not spent the entire morning together."

"Thank goodness, she was there."

"There is more... I left my overnight case in Mr. Ewing's truck. About thirty minutes after she took me home, I saw him walking up the sidewalk, carrying my bag. He knew I would be alone until three. The doorbell rang four times, and then the knocking started. Strong, forceful blows to the door had my teeth chattering from the stress. To get away from the noise, I hid in my mother's closet with my head between my knees.

"When my mom came home, she found the overnight bag in our garage."

"It is a queer way for a grown man to behave. Did he bother you again?"

"Never, but in a sense, he left me a message. I had my boyfriend's senior ring on a neck chain in the bag, but when I unpacked, the ring was missing. The chain was still there."

"You didn't tell your parents?"

"No. It was partly my fault. I agreed to visit the house, and he didn't do anything except boss me around. But later, much later, I realized he wanted me to feel—helpless. The same helpless feeling you would have if you got in a taxi, and the driver started driving in the wrong direction. He wanted to scare and humiliate me."

"Yes, but what about the ring?" Ellen was spellbound.

"Ah, the ring—it shows how smart he is. When I told my boyfriend, Mr. Ewing stole his ring off my chain, he didn't believe me. He was furious and crying when he said: Why don't you just tell me you lost it, instead of making up a story that no one would be stupid enough to believe."

Sissy rubbed her eyes, and her tone of voice changed to underscore that she was now an authority on the subject of Carl Ewing.

"It took me ten years to figure it out. Ewing is a sociopath; he is smart, and he has his tentacles wrapped around your grandmother."

"I'm confused. Grandma says he has been nothing but wonderful to her."

"Don't worry; that's part of his disguise. Even Mrs. Knight couldn't figure it."

"Mrs. Knight?"

"Yes, but I didn't know she was Carl's sister-in-law back then."

"Mrs. Knight, the guidance counselor?"

"Yes, don't you remember her?"

"Sure."

"She, Mrs. Knight, thought I made it up."

CHAPTER 15

30 December 2017

Funerals in Gower are followed by estate sales, even if the "estate" is small and the household refuse, ordinary. Shoppers come in droves, hoping to find a unique item worthy of salvation. On the Saturday following Christmas, Sheila's sisters, Martha and Jean, waited for her in the living room of a five-bedroom home built in the nineteen sixties. The former owners, eschewing the trend of ranch-style houses, selected a modern look. Some would say a clean look with abundant glass and a flat roof. The windows were beautiful, but the roof was a poor choice. In Louisiana, a flat roof will leak, always.

"What is wrong with Zack," Martha said to her sister Jean while browsing through the family's everyday china.

"He is having an identity crisis." Jean took some tissue from her purse and blew her nose. "This house smells moldy to me," and she blew her nose again.

"I smell it, too," said Martha. "When Sheila gets here, we can make a quick getaway for an early lunch. But back to Zack—Do you think he is depressed?"

"No, I don't think that."

"Did you ever counsel him at school?"

"A few times. Only about his college plans." Jean picked up a piece of china and turned it upside down to check the imprint. "He is experiencing an identity crisis, but he's smart and will find his way." Jean said. "Did you know he won $1,000 for a short story he wrote?" She sneezed, "I may have to cut this short; my allergies are acting up."

"I'll call Sheila and see if she is still coming." Martha took her phone from her pocket. "There is nothing of value here except the Blue Dog print in the hall."

"Hold on, Martha. I can see her at the door," Jean started waving to get Sheila's attention. "There," she said. "She saw us."

Sheila stopped several times to speak to friends while swimming through the crowd to reach her sisters.

"My God, Sheila, you look tired. Stand here and let me fix this." Martha flipped Sheila's neckline tag to the inside of the garment. Jean stared at Sheila's hair.

"I know my hair looks awful; I plan to erase the gray soon."

"Sheila, do you remember Sissy Wilson?" Martha changed the subject to lighten the somber mood.

"She was in Renee's class in high school."

"Sissy is in the hall over there," Martha said, pointing. "She's standing in front of a Blue Dog print. You might want to buy it before we leave for lunch; Jean is having a reaction to the mold."

Sheila followed Martha to the hall where empty frames and artwork hung on the wall. She took her place beside Sissy as they both gazed at the picture. Sissy was twenty-five now, but Sheila thought she had hardly changed at all. Maybe a tad taller. She had on a short skirt and tall boots that made her look artsy.

"Sissy, do you remember me? I'm Renee's mother.

It's been a long time."

"Yes, ma'am. It's good to see you again." Sissy pulled out her notebook from a fabric bag slung over her shoulder and wrote something in it. "Are you all right, Miss Sheila?"

"I'm tired." Sheila turned back to look at the print. "What do you think?" Sheila asked her.

"It is overpriced," Sissy said. "But I have a client who collects these."

"I was so sorry to hear about your father. How is your mother doing?"

"Thanks," Sissy turned away from the print to talk to Sheila. "Mom got married a few years after the divorce, and she travels a lot with her new husband. I'm the one taking it hard."

"I understand," Sheila said. "When my father died, I was devastated. Your Dad was in the prime of his life. It seems so unfair."

"I guess it's never easy. How is Renee? I regret we haven't stayed in touch."

"Great. Her daughter is almost three and they are expecting a boy."

"Has everything been going well for you?"

"Honestly, it seems I have a terrible case of insomnia." Sheila's eyes teared up. There was something about a sympathetic ear that made her want to cry.

"When you're feeling better, let's get together for coffee." Sissy gave her a business card. "I would like to talk with you, but not here, and not until you are feeling better."

A tap on Sheila's shoulder made her jump and turn around. It was Martha standing behind her.

"Jean's ready for lunch."

"I'm not feeling well. I need to go home and lie down." Martha gently took Sheila's arm to steady her.

Sheila's eyes had the dull, dead look of sleep deprivation.

"Let us drive you home. I knew something was wrong as soon as I saw you."

"No, Martha, go eat. I can drive four blocks." Sheila managed a weak smile to assure her sister she was all right. "I haven't been sleeping well; that's all it is."

"No, I insist. We'll be sure your car gets home." Martha waved at Jean to come over, and the two sisters surrounded her. "Hand over the keys."

Jean drove Sheila back to her house. "Wow, Sissy has grown up so much. She was a regular in my office when her parents were divorcing. Look how successful she is now. Did you know she and her husband have two boys?" Sheila stared out of the passenger window, not hearing anything Jean said.

When Sheila's phone rang, it lay untouched in her purse.

"There is a powder keg at my house." Sheila confided. "Zack is this close to hurting me, and Carl is this close to hurting Zack." She used her thumb and forefinger to emphasize how close. "I predict something terrible is about to happen." Sheila broke down and tears silently dripped off her face until they turned into her driveway.

Jean tried to console her, "It has to be hard to see Zack lose his confidence. Any idea what is wrong?"

"We won't get any answers until he sees a psychiatrist."

"But you must have some idea."

135

"Zack has changed so much I don't recognize him anymore. Dr. Brown mentioned schizophrenia, but it is too early to tell."

Sheila only saw the good in people. It was a trait that had gotten her into trouble more than once. This is why she was blind to Carl's manipulative behavior for years. Just when she was on the verge of taking action to free herself of him, her son became ill, destroying her confidence as a mother. The fatigue broke down her rational thought. Punching a wall—Jean had heard of it many times—is the prelude to an angry outburst that is much worse. But until this moment, Sheila had gone along with Carl's "window-sill explanation," even to the family, as if she believed it herself. *But there it was.* A hole in the kitchen wall told the story of how Carl broke his hand. Sheila sat, dumb-struck, not realizing the concrete evidence for her fears was just behind her while Jean served her lunch of sliced apple, cheese, and iced tea.

"Of all the things you have told me about Carl, this is the most telling incident. Can't you see that? The senselessness of breaking his own hand to keep himself from doing what? Who made him that mad? Zack, or you?"

"He was going to hit Zack."

"You have to take this seriously."

"It's just a wall."

"Yes, but yesterday it was just words, and today it is just a wall. Do you see a pattern?" They were interrupted by Martha ready to pick Jean up.

"Get some sleep, Sheila. When you wake up, you can order a pizza for dinner. There has to be a solution and we will find it."

When Carl came home in the afternoon, Sheila was sitting on the sofa, disheveled and sad. He thought she might have been crying.

"What's the matter, Baby?" he asked. "It seems like afternoons make you sad."

"We have to do something. I can't sleep."

"Not even with that lock you put on the door?"

"I'm not getting along with Zack. He scares me, and I can't sleep. Please try to understand that."

"Oh," said Carl, yawning. "Is he coming down for dinner?"

"No, he made himself a sandwich earlier; I just cleaned up the mess. Take me seriously for once; Zack should live somewhere else."

"Where?" Carl warmed to the idea immediately.

"I don't know. There must be someplace for young people with a problem like his."

"We don't want to send him to some cult if that is what you are thinking." He sat down and put his left arm around her, holding her close to his chest.

"You know," Carl released her and took her hand, "when we were growing up, a kid as old as Zack would be kicked out of the house. That's what my father did to my brother."

"I don't see how we can do that. It would be cruel."

"What about my camp?"

"That might work."

"Hunting season is over for me; I am about to get busy with work."

"The sooner, the better."

"You're right. Zack's too big for you to corral him if he gets riled when I'm not at home."

"I'm glad you understand. I'll never be able to sleep with Zack here. At night I hear him downstairs. He could set the house on fire."

"If we make him move out and take care of himself, do you think he really needs a doctor?"

"I do. A doctor who can help him get better."

"What boy wouldn't love living in his own house?" Carl said, putting a positive spin on the idea. "I could go out there and check on him every day if he needs it. He would have to fix his meals and clean up after himself."

"Exactly. We know Zack can make a sandwich." Sheila pursed her lips. "But will he go?"

"We'll surprise him. Don't worry." Carl sat straight up, ready for action.

"You know, when my daddy gave up on my brother, I was ten years old. All my life, I thought he liked my brother better than me, but when he kicked him out, I could see I was his favorite. My brother kept messing up, and that's what took my daddy's attention off me. When he left, I was happier than anything."

"Do you think Zack is like your brother? The doctor asked about family members."

"I don't know. I was just a kid. How would I know anything?"

CHAPTER 16

1 January 2018

On New Year's Day, the truck with lights across the top left the cul-de-sac, passed the scarred mailbox, and traveled due south. Carl fussed with the radio until country music filled the cab.

"This ere's my favorite, Son; listen to the words," Carl tapped his fingers to the rhythm of an acoustic guitar. The mournful lyrics about love and loss carried them down the highway at fifty miles an hour.

Zack sat in the back seat, balancing a mug of coffee on his lap, tensing at every bump on old highway 425 to Alexandria. Restless and fearful of spilling the bitter drink he never wanted in the first place, his knee gave way to jumping. Up and down it pumped, destabilizing the beverage.

Carl reached his right arm behind him through the gap in the bucket seats, offering a breath mint.

"Once I drop you off, you can't come back home," he said, returning the roll to his breast pocket. The road took a sharp turn, causing a wave of hot coffee to spill in Zack's lap.

"You know how your mother is. She can't stand you."

Zack rolled down his window and held the brimming cup away from himself, inching it toward the wind.

"Don't do that," Carl said, looking in his rearview mirror. The warning came too late. Zack tossed the coffee, hitting the window frame and spilling it on himself, soiling the leather seat. Carl drove faster on the rocks, kicking up dust until they parked at the camp.

Carl's hunting camp was a perfect retreat, only twenty-five miles from the Ewing residence, but isolated as if it were on the other side of the earth. Smith's Sporting Goods in Gower estimated fifty percent of their loyal customers owned hunting camps; rich or poor, it didn't matter. The store's inventory grew to include bunk beds, cabin cookware, and mosquito netting along with the traditional guns, rifles, deer stands, and duck blinds. A man's camp could be a tent, a trailer, a lean-to, or a house. Carl was fortunate to own a modest farmhouse surrounded by dense woods. He rented it from a soybean farmer, first. Two years ago, he bought the house, negotiating an agreement that included hunting rights on the farmer's property certified as wetland.

Wetlands are protected by the federal government. The water supports an ecosystem near town, but so different—worlds apart. Besides ducks, geese, and deer, the wetland forests of Louisiana are home to an exceptional variety of wildlife. Owls, snakes, salamanders, turtles, frogs, alligators, armadillos, black bears, red foxes, bobcats, cougars, feral hogs, coyotes all thrive in these designated areas.

Carl could host three of his friends in the three-bedroom, one bath house if one of them slept in the living room. The kitchen had the basics, a stove, and a refrigerator. Best of all, the wives approved of parties at Carl's house as compared to more primitive venues. Carl's camp had a washer and a dryer; the men wash the dirt and blood off their clothes before they come home.

Outside, a gas grill and a rack for hanging deer in the front yard completed the amenities. Most hunters hang the deer upside-down while the field dressing takes place. A minority of hunters, including Carl, hang the deer by the neck. A line of deer hanging by a thick rope collar is a disturbing sight for the uninitiated. Their gentle brown eyes, even in death, appear intelligent and sad. The body, eviscerated, is lifeless. Carl loved the freedom of isolation, but for Zack, the move was disorienting as soon as he got there.

The deer, five of them hanging in the yard, watched Zack. Their eyes followed him as he and his father carried four boxes of clothes, books, writing materials, and food prepared by his mother.

"Here's a rag; go clean up the mess you made in the truck." Zack fumbled with the task, distracted by the deer rack and the grill. Forrest surrounded the house. Even in winter there was enough leafy cover to filter the sun's rays and shroud the clearing in shade. He mopped the pool of coffee on the seat, wiped the window slot, and rubbed the grime on the outside door, trying to make the accident disappear. His father stopped him.

"Let me do it." Carl washed the outside with a water hose and cleaned up the leather seats with a special solution he kept in the cab. "There is food in the refrigerator and I left money on the coffee table for the grocery store. Pull yourself together, boy." Carl went inside to wash his hands before leaving.

Sarah, who had a knack for needing him on holidays, called him as soon as he finished.

"Don't worry. Ellen wants to check into costs that concern her but not me." Sarah said when she scheduled the meeting.

"Yes ma'am."

On New Year's Day, precisely on time, Carl eased out of his truck like a man in no hurry, just in case she was watching him from the window.

Son, a man in a hurry bothers folks. A builder who has time to listen always wins the contract.

When he knocked, the door opened. Ellen drew him in with a smile.

"Hi, Carl! Thanks for coming. I've laid some files on the table in the kitchen. Would you care for anything to drink? Water or coffee?"

"No, ma'am.". He kept his head low and stooped a little. "Where is Miss Sarah?"

"She had a doctor's appointment. Please have a seat," Ellen waited for him to sit down before taking her own chair across the table from him. "My grandmother asked me to look over her finances, and I discovered a few invoices..."

"Sure, show me which ones you are talking about. Miss Sarah does so many projects; I think she enjoys taking good care of her home." He leaned into the conversation. "Is she sick?"

"A fall. They wanted to check her again in the urgent care center this morning." Ellen smiled at him again. "Thank you for your concern. There are charges I don't understand."

"Let's take a look." Carl reached for his glasses and put them on. "I give all my copies to my accountant, and he sorts them out."

"This one, for example." Ellen had marked about ten with colorful post-it notes. "Here we have a bill for $15,000, and the invoice says labor."

"What is the date?" Carl said while he moved his chair to sit beside her, as if they were going to read it together. He was two inches from her face, sniffing her hair. "August of last year. Let me think," His peppermint breath stimulated the hairs on her neck.

"In August, we had some strong winds, not a tornado, but they, the winds, did some damage knocking down tree limbs and such. Well, the wind damaged the porte-cochere out there," he pointed out the window, "and some wood was rotten already, so we rebuilt and painted it, and we put a metal roof on it instead of shingles. The metal roof is tougher, and I think she got an insurance discount because she added it, and it was weather damage. I am certain her house insurance reimbursed her for part of it."

"I see." She paused and looked at him. His eyes met hers at close range.

"What about this one? Here is an invoice that says HVAC and labor, and the price is $12,000," Ellen cleared her throat. "There should be a receipt for a new unit."

"Her air conditioning quit working, and we had to replace a portion of the wall behind which had become wet and moldy from the leaking condensation. We had to tear the wall out and fix it." He started the sentence matter-of-factly, but as the end came, he sounded frustrated. "I feel you don't trust me," he said.

"I am trying to understand why my grandmother spent $50,000 on small household repairs last year."

"MA'AM, I don't come cheap, but your grandmother hires me because I AM HONEST. While I have been happy to help her, I don't think you and I should work together." Carl stood up to look down on her. "Good luck finding someone else."

Ellen's face and neck turned blotchy.

"You've been overcharging my grandmother." Ellen stood up, too.

"It just pisses me off when people like you think they know everything." Carl took off his glasses and put them into his pocket.

The rain poured down as he got in his truck and saw Ellen watching him from the window. He sat, bolt upright, staring straight ahead. For as long as she watched him, he made no effort to leave. Once she disappeared, he made a rut in Miss Sarah's yard by jumping the curb. The ground, damp from the rain, was soft, his truck heavy, so the damage was satisfying.

Carl's workers were well aware of his habit of "tit for tat." You messed with him; he messed with you. He did not shy away from a fistfight, but his talent lay in setting up "consequences." The rut in the yard was just a warning shot. He doubted Sarah was attending any appointment. *And the dog, where was she?* When he came home, he changed out of his wet clothes feeling sorry for himself. Sheila was celebrating with her family, gabbing with her sisters, and playing charades with the cousins. He opened the refrigerator, helped himself to a casserole, and grabbed a beer.

Son, if you are losing control of a woman, surprise her.

The hole in the wall stared at him while he ate lunch.

"Ricky," Carl said when his buddy answered the phone, "I am sorry to bother you on a holiday, but is there any way you could fix a hole in the wall this afternoon? I want to surprise my wife."

Ricky arrived within the hour. Carl sat on a chair watching his friend of thirty-eight years repair the wall of the breakfast nook.

"I ain't going to ask how this happened, buddy." Ricky smiled when he said it.

"And I ain't telling," Carl joked, but he was not feeling jovial.

"Thanks for coming, Sheila is so mortified; she won't invite folks inside the house until we do this."

"No problem, Carl. Who beat up the wall?"

"I ain't gonna lie, it was me," Carl held up his right wrist, which was now in a cast instead of a splint. "I got fed up with something."

"You got it better than most of us. Don't feel too sorry for yourself."

"I won't," Carl laughed.

"I always envied you in high school. You set your sights on high society." Ricky wore a short sleeve tee shirt that barely accommodated his stomach, which occupied the space between his rib cage and his hip bones. His jeans rode low on the thinnest part of his torso. Like many of Carl's friends, he sported a spindly white beard six inches long and an earring in his left earlobe.

Carl expressed his acceptance of the compliment with a good-natured chuckle. He stretched his legs out, crossed them at the shins, and rested his right arm on his stomach while he watched Ricky use a knife to make the hole more uniform.

"To tell the truth, I always envied you," Carl said with conviction.

"I don't see why," Ricky continued, "While I was looking at the legs, you were looking at the bank account. I wish I had been that smart."

"How are you and Linda? She always was a goody-two-shoes."

"Well, to be honest, I've watched her deteriorate from the most beautiful girl I ever saw, to a fat lady with back pain. What about you and Sheila?"

"We're doin' fine."

"And your boy, how's he doing?"

"He's not setting the world on fire, but he is alright, too."

"Too bad, he weren't cut out to be a contractor like you."

"He's too smart for that." Carl enjoyed the company. The shared history made it easier, and he didn't have to put on a show.

"Carl, I may cross a line here, but I think you have changed. You have a steely look, comes and goes, like you are full of rage. You got it better than most, my friend." Ricky retook the measurements.

"I know I do, and I ain't complaining. Sheila is a goose that lays golden eggs."

"What is it then?"

"What?" Carl was genuine in his curiosity.

"That look that comes over you. Your shoulders pull

in, and you frown, and you look like you want to kill somebody."

"You mean like this?" Carl made a monster face as a joke.

"No, man," Ricky said, laughing. "Not like that!" They talked about football while Ricky floated the sheetrock perfectly.

"Sheila won't see a hole anymore, but she'll have to wait a few days before she paints it," Ricky said before he left.

Sheila came home infused with energy; being with her family always boosted her spirits. Carl sat brooding in the darkened living room with a plate of cheese and crackers on his lap.

"I'm going to make hot tea. Do you want some?" She asked him before removing her coat.

"Naw, Baby, but sit with me after you make it."

"Thank you for fixing the wall," she said when she returned to sit beside him on the sofa.

"I should never have hit it. I don't know what I was thinking." He rubbed his eyes. "My mother died when I was ten. It was just my Dad and me after that. He taught me everything I know, but I didn't have a mother's touch." Sheila took his hand.

"I can't paint the wall today; the mud has to dry."

"Don't forget Zack has his appointment Friday at 2 PM. I thought it would be the best day for you."

"This Friday? Are you sure?"

"Yes, January fifth."

"I can't possibly make it Friday. Didn't I tell you? We're expecting a shipment of custom-made cabinets. Sorry, you have to take him, but I'll tell him when I call tonight."

Before she went to sleep, she checked her Facebook page for messages. Finally, a reply from Abel.

"Sheila, sorry to take so long, I rarely look at Facebook anymore. Great to connect with you after all these years. Yes! We plan to come for the thirty-fifth; I would be honored to help you plan it. Maybe we can clear any misunderstanding of the past and be friends again."

PART II

CHAPTER 17

5 January 2018

The clinic coordinator at University Hospital Psychiatric Department put down her receiver and sent a text to the doctor; the cell phone vibrated in her pocket and the screen read: *new patient-schizophrenic-confirmed for 2 PM.*

The reply—*got it. Faculty meeting today. I may be late.*

Dr. Weissman was always late. She hastily crossed the street that separated the clinic from classrooms. Her feet pounded the stairs instead of waiting for the elevator. The meeting, held on the fifth floor and on a quarterly schedule, was her first since she arrived eight weeks ago. Her stairwell in the middle of the building opened to the fifth-floor atrium where the door numbers were unconventional, causing her to go down the same hall, twice, nearly missing the double doors of the conference room. Everyone was there, waiting. Five of the doctors were complete strangers, two were recognizable, one being Dr. Lucey, the department head.

"Ladies and Gentlemen, before we begin," he caught her eye when she rushed in, "I would like to introduce our new faculty member, Dr. Elaine Weissman." It was the first time she had ever received applause.

"She is board certified in Child Psychiatry and comes to us from the Philadelphia Children's Hospital."

The psychiatrists, all in white coats (which they wore only for meetings), nodded and smiled as Dr. Weissman took her seat next to the Chief. The average age of the group was sixty years old, and they were all white. Still, like Dr. Lucey, they appeared to be a friendly and accepting group.

"Dr. Weissman, would you care to say a few words about your research?"

"Yes, thank you." She put on her glasses to look older and stood to project her voice.

"My work centers on childhood-screening for anti-social personality disorder. Five hundred students entered the study at the age of ten years, and that was four years ago. My collaborator and I hope to follow them four more years, if not longer. Of course, after they leave primary and secondary school, the follow up will be harder, but we'll try using arrest reports, divorce proceedings, obituaries, in other words, public records.

"People suffering from ASPD cause more harm to society than any other mental illness, especially if they are in jobs where there is little supervision, such as daycare operator, remodeler, night watchman, building inspector. We hope to diagnose them early and get them into treatment programs while still in their teens."

"Dr. Weissman?" one of them asked, interrupting her. "Dr. Weissman, sociopaths—forgive me for being old-fashioned—are three percent of the population. How do you propose to prevent them from choosing ordinary occupations?"

"By giving the other ninety-seven percent of the

population tools to recognize them."

Lucey jumped into the discussion to keep it short.

"Thank you, Dr. Weissman. Now we will turn to the first item on our agenda: a review and approval of the minutes of our last meeting. Mrs. Jordan?"

While the department secretary read the minutes, Weissman concocted nicknames for everyone around the table based upon hairstyle, hair color. Other interests were mannerisms, fashion sense, and meeting etiquette.

Her cell phone, like a persistent mouse in her pocket, vibrated, interrupting her thoughts. A surreptitious glance identified a text from Medical Records which could wait. The group turned its attention to a statistical analysis of patients admitted to the psych ward in the past three months. A doctor with Albert Einstein hair and a neatly trimmed beard discussed the diagnoses and average length of stay.

Her mentor and collaborator at Philadelphia Children's Hospital cautioned her. *"You are going to the deep South. Expect a certain culture shock."* Another colleague advised, *"There won't be much opportunity to network in rural Louisiana; you are likely to be the only child psychiatrist for miles."* Weissman was single, thirty-four, and ambitious. Already monitoring job listings at other teaching hospitals, she was free to move if necessary.

"Those are my concerns about faculty salaries when the new billing rules take effect," a man said after a giving a lesson in accounting. Lucey jumped into the fray.

"Have a great weekend, everyone," ending the meeting a few minutes before noon. Several of the faculty walked up to shake her hand and introduce themselves. One fellow from Great Britain lagged behind.

"Dr. Weissman, would you care to join me for lunch? There is a tavern within walking distance."

"Thank you so much, Dr. Reeves. I would love to have lunch, but I have to prepare for clinic this afternoon. Raincheck?"

"Raincheck?"

"Another day, perhaps?"

"Brilliant!" the Englishman said. "Don't worry, they will give Friday to the very next bloke who rides into town," he said, smiling.

"I don't mind, really. Statistically, the best cases come in on Friday afternoons."

"That's the spirit. We are glad to have you here."

Sheila packed her bag with two bottles of water and a canister of pepper spray. What to wear, always a challenge, evolved into a silk blouse and wool skirt. She had not seen Zack in four days. Nor had she talked to him on the phone.

"Mama hi. I'm leaving to pick up Zack. Fingers crossed."

"Good luck! When it's convenient, call me and tell me how it went."

"I will. I wish you could come, but they said only parents this time." Of all the family members, Dixie

Hayward knew the least about her grandson's decline. The rest of the family had already put two and two together.

Calling Martin, she connected her phone to the Bluetooth screen, leaving a message.

"I've finished the book-keeping, but can't meet today."

The car skimmed the road like a ski on downhill snow, gliding through turns and barreling into the country. After crossing a swollen creek, the openness of rolling pastures covered with a thin veil of frost, reminded her of jogging, a hobby she had before children.

The sun high in the sky, causing the surroundings to glow with a yellow tint. Maybe it was nerves that projected an unreality about her errand. She drove by a farm, fallow for winter, then followed a bayou, and crossed it. Sheila could count the number of times she had visited the camp on the fingers of one hand. As she rounded a sharp turn, she confronted something new, a trailer park. It was as big as a neighborhood with rows upon rows of mobile homes, all white and identical, having the same rounded shape like jelly beans—*goodness are these campers?* Each one of them had a tiny yard, the only distinguishing feature.

Some families had tricycles and baby swing sets, while others placed lawn chairs and barbeque pits in the patch of grass on the side of the trailer. Many had all these things crowded together. It did not take long for Sheila to realize that people were raising children in a space about the size of her master bedroom. *How do they do it? They have no driveways, sidewalks, garages, or fences. Do their kids grow up stronger?*

Her car sped up a small hill, and at the top, an aluminum mailbox marked the turnoff. The postman's red flag was down. She made the right turn and saw the house. She expected to see smoke rising from the chimney. He must be cold, she thought. She parked by Zack's car, which had a thin layer of dust, leaves, and bird droppings dulling the finish.

When Zack opened the door. He was thinner. His beard was longer, and his long hair was oily. She did a double-take when she realized his clothes were the same clothes he wore when he left home. She stopped three feet away from him, calculating whether she would be welcome inside the house.

"Zack, did Dad call you?"

"Dad's not here, Mom."

"Did you forget we had a doctor's appointment today?"

Zack's eyes focused upon something behind her, as if she were no longer interesting. Contradicting his demeanor, he moved aside, allowing her in. Sheila squeezed by him, carrying her open purse with her right hand, grasping the can of spray.

"You have to shower. Here, let me help you." Sheila unbuttoned his shirt with one hand. "Now, you take off your pants and socks while I get the water ready."

Zack, shivering in the cold, walked naked into the bathroom.

"Use soap and hurry. I'll lay out your clothes."

"Okay, Mom."

Sheila picked out clean clothes, socks, and shoes.

Zack emerged from the bathroom, dripping wet. Grabbing a towel, she helped him dry off. Then she assisted him in dressing and led him to sit on the bed. She combed the tangles out of his hair and tenderly washed his face.

"Mom, I feel bad."

"I'm sorry, Zack. So sorry."

The drive to the psychiatrist's office was eerily quiet, but at least he left with her willingly. He was sphinxlike while he ate a hamburger from MacDonald's in the car. Swerving in and out of lanes making up for the late start, she kept the purse still open, by her left foot. Zack fell asleep against the car door and did not wake until the traffic increased outside of Malheur.

When the structure made of electrochromic glass and steel came into view, outshining the other dull brick medical buildings and even competing with the larger University hospital, Zack pointed it out to his mother.

"Is this where we are going?" Sheila noticed his right knee, jumping. "The glass changes color with the amount of sunlight."

"How did you know that?"

"I read it somewhere." Zack performed the hand swipe.

A sign at the entrance read, "All Outpatients Are

Seen on the First Floor." Zack shuffled to the reception area. His arms did not swing when he walked, making him appear to be leading with his body, limbs to the wind.

Finding room 110, they entered a cozy waiting room—no windows here—that had five overstuffed chairs, no couch. The receptionist was behind glass.

"I am Sheila Ewing, and my son has an appointment at two." She wrote Zack's name on the sign-in sheet.

"Good afternoon, Ms. Ewing!" said a young man in scrubs behind the partition. "Brenda will be here in just a minute."

"I'm right here," Brenda said from behind a filing cabinet. She wore scrubs, too, and braided her hair in the back. Sheila took the paperwork and assessed the room. Zack preferred a far corner with a view of the receptionist and both doorways, so he led her there. It was a typical medical form except for specific questions about illnesses she had never heard of, Huntington's Chorea, anti-NMDA receptor encephalitis, porphyria. Having no family history of mental illness, Sheila could finish this quickly and turn it in. The nurse called Zack.

He stood behind Sheila, rocking on his feet and clasping his hands in front of him.

"Ms. Ewing, you may go to the coffee shop and wait there if you would be more comfortable. I can call your cell phone when the doctor is ready for you."

Sheila agreed it would be more pleasant for her to wait in a café than in the waiting room with other patients. Zack looked at his mother, folded his arms, and bounced on his feet.

Sheila assured him, "It's okay, Zack, you can go; I will be right back."

The nurse, a girl in her twenties, skinny and frail, reached out her hand, and he took it. It was a kind gesture, Sheila thought.

Zack became suspicious as soon as the door to the waiting room closed behind him. He perceived the hall as a long dim tunnel with no end. Coaxed by the nurse, he walked to a closed door where light pooled on the floor just under it. The scene reminded him of his bedroom at home, a safe place. A sign: "DR. WEISSMAN," was also reassuring because he interpreted it to say, Dr. Wise Man. Two knocks and the door opened to reveal a modern living room in someone's home. Zack approved of the design, windows on two walls, hardwood floor, and books. It was a warm, but clean look.

Dr. Weissman greeted him and showed him where to sit. He stood motionless.

"Make yourself at home. Would you like water or a coke?"

"No," he said.

"All right then," Dr. Weissman gestured again toward the couch. "Have a seat. All we do here is talk."

"I'm trying to guess where you come from," Zack said as he sat down on the couch.

"Chicago. I went to college in Boston and medical school in Michigan." Weissman took a seat in an overstuffed chair like the ones in the waiting room. She held a legal tablet on her lap and a blue fountain pen in her left hand. He thought she was exotic with black hair and brown skin. He was accustomed to the tense and frustrated faces of his parents, but this person was peaceful.

During the session, Dr. Weissman's experienced hand flew across the legal pad, producing a flurry of short-hand notes. Later, when she dictated the visit, she would rely upon the documentation to guide her. Besides looking thin and unkempt, Zack had a poker face; she wrote: *hypomimia.* He tried to look at everything in the room except her; she wrote: *lack of eye contact.* His speech sounds did not vary in pitch; she wrote: *monotone voice.* He had two quirky mannerisms, which made him appear nervous: he lifted his right hand to his forehead as if to sweep the hair out of his eyes, but instead, the motion of his hand flowed down his face to his chin as if he were wiping off a mask. The other was a constant jumping of the right knee. It reminded her of someone bouncing a baby too fast. She wrote: *complex right arm and right knee tics.*

"Zack, why are you here?" He twitched his head toward every corner of the room like a wild animal ready to flee at any moment.

His right knee kept jumping even faster.

Dr Weissman took a sip of water, "Tell me why."

He jerked as if he were avoiding something flying through the air.

"My mother. She is the reason."

"Can you tell me what is wrong?"

"Ask her." The patient said this without sarcasm. She wrote: *lack of insight.*

There was something very likable about her patient that manifested itself intermittently. She imagined the sick part, and the healthy part of his brain were in a fight for control. He had not severed his connection to reality altogether. Human eyes appeared fleetingly, but most of the time, his eyes were unfocused, as if sightless. Even when he looked into her eyes, she felt no connection was made between them. She thought: there is no medical term for this observation.

"Let's start by getting to know one another. How do you spend your day since you left school?"

"I try to stay as busy as I can," Zack said, exhibiting both tics.

"But when you are doing something, what are you doing."

"I am cracking a code. It's the first time the world has seen it." She wrote: *delusions.*

"What kind of code?" she asked, her voice soft and nonthreatening.

There was a long pause as his head tilted to the right, listening to a muse.

"Are you hearing something?" she asked.

A longer pause and a rigidly blank face. "I don't think I should tell you."

"Why don't we change the subject and talk about your family?" Weissman put down her pen and leaned forward with her hands resting on her lap. Note-taking can intimidate some patients. She considered recording the session, but thought the preparation would make Zack nervous, too. "Tell me about your mother."

"A motherboard, a metronome, a martyr. She is the glue that holds us together."

"And your father, tell me about him."

"Two-faced."

"What do you mean by two-faced? Does he have two personalities, or is he a liar?"

"Neither, he is two people; one of them is a Nazi."

"Who else lives in your home?"

"Ruth."

"Who is Ruth, Zack?"

Zack remained mute, staring at her.

"Who is she?"

Zack jumped, putting his arms across his face to protect himself, "She moved in this fall," he said

Dr. Weissman wrote: *hallucinations.*

Zack jumped, putting his arms across his face to protect himself.

"Zack, what happened?"

"They are bombing near here," he said, shaking. The lost boy in him appeared for a minute before he was swept away.

She wrote: *auditory and visual hallucinations.*

"You are safe, Zack, in this building with me." Weissman was hooked.

"I know," he said.

"Does someone want to hurt you?"

"Oh, yes." Zack smiled a goofy smile, but it was gone in an instant. "The Nazi wants to hurt me." She thought: *paranoia?* "And the college boys want to hurt me," Zack was warming up to the subject. She wrote: *paranoia.*

He left the sofa and ran to the window just behind her.

"Do you see anything outside?"

"No, there is too much smoke." He turned around. "Can I go now? I don't feel comfortable anymore." He started pacing back and forth.

"You can go, Zack. I'll ask Miss Brenda and Mr. Scott to take you to the other clinic where you will have a physical exam. The doctor will listen to your heart and check your eyes, just like Dr. Brown does when you visit with him." Weismann pressed a call button. Immediately, Scott stood by to escort him to the lab.

While Weissman was alone, she pulled Dr. Brown's notes into view and studied them again. A normal boy leaves home to attend college and has a psychotic break. Nothing in Brown's notes, and the first document was an admission to the newborn nursery, predicted this. She took a break, walking about the room, eager to leave her chair. The view from the back window turned a shade grayer, almost green, to block the afternoon sun. Three laps around the room later, Sheila arrived.

She had flyaway hair and carried a large handbag which she plopped onto the sofa when she sat down.

"How are you doing?"

"I'm up and down," she sighed.

If Sheila were to compare herself to Dr. Weissman, the young, confident physician with deep green eyes and hair styled neatly in a bun, she would slip into despair. But that's what parents do unconsciously, and the doctor knew it.

"I understand," Dr. Weissman said. "You raised a happy and healthy family and now this."

"It's taken me some time to accept it." Sheila examined the room. The huge bookcase reminded her of Martin's house, and the ubiquitous box of Kleenex reminded her of sadness.

"Sheila, may I call you Sheila?"

"Yes, please."

"Your son is highly intelligent, but he suffers from disordered thoughts. His problems are nobody's fault. Specifically, Zack's problems are not your fault."

The tension, frustration, and fear drained away, clearing her head for the first time in months. Someone had finally said the words.

"It started while he was a freshman in college, but maybe even before that." Sheila rubbed her face, smoothing out the crow's feet around her eyes. "I noticed the summer before he left, he moped around the house. You know how a boy squirms, fidgets, laughs too loud, and makes you laugh? He lacked that zest for life."

"Zack loved baseball and was on the team in high school, but this past summer he lost all interest. His friends fell away, too; I expected the opposite. It seemed so odd."

Dr. Weissman wrote: *social withdrawal* in her notes.

"In August, we packed up and moved him into his dorm room at Hillcrest College."

"Did he write to you? Or did he call?"

"No letters. But speaking of letters, my son did not write any of his thank-you notes. You know, for the graduation gifts. Normally, he would have enjoyed penning notes to people. He was competent when sending the invitations. Naturally, I was disappointed when he never took the time to thank anyone." Dr. Weissman wrote: *avolition.* "He called twice, once about money for joining a fraternity and once about someone following him, but I guess he imagined he was being followed."

Sheila described all the events leading up to his referral while Dr. Weissman listened without interrupting. Having someone listen attentively to her story was profoundly comforting to her. She gave an accurate account, no embellishments. After she finished, she confessed her latest stab of guilt.

"After we moved him to the other house, I don't believe his father ever visited him; he promised he would. I should have known better."

"His father promised he would check on him and

then didn't go?"

"From the looks of him, yes."

Dr. Weissman wrote: *father-broken promise.*

"Does your husband get along well with Zack?" Dr. Weissman honed in.

"I guess so, but you see, he was disappointed when Zack did not go into business with him after high school." She wrote: *father-poor boundaries.*

"Anything else?"

"Zack sometimes calls me Ruth instead of Mom. When he does that, it's disconcerting; the way he says it." Sheila tried to imitate him. "I can't explain why it bothers me."

"Does he frighten you?"

"Yes, he does." Dr. Weissman wrote: *Capgras syndrome.*

"Above all, Sheila, you must look after yourself. I can't emphasize that enough. You can't help him if you are overwrought."

"We found a small amount of marijuana. Carl was so mad, I thought he would hit him."

"Has he hit him before?"

"Once, but years ago."

"I don't think Zack's behavior is caused by drugs, but there seems to be a correlation between exposure to marijuana and the manifestation of schizophrenic-like symptoms." She wrote: *father has physical fights.*

"What?"

"I mean to say we don't know if marijuana plays any role in causing the disease; studies show marijuana use is common at the onset of symptoms. Whatever the cause, Zack's imagination is playing tricks on him. Zack hears sounds and sees things that are not real. He cannot tell the difference."

Sheila felt the sensation of a downward rush on a roller coaster.

"Is he dangerous to others?" she asked.

"He could be. I see here that you have no history of mental illness in the family. Are there any family members who committed suicide?"

"No."

"What about family members who are a mystery. They moved away and never kept in touch."

"Carl's brother left home when he turned eighteen. His parents are both dead."

"What does your husband say about his brother?" She wrote: *family history?*

"He says his brother was a juvenile delinquent." Sheila shifted in her seat as if tired of being interviewed. "I should tell you my husband is like a four-year old boy; he constantly tells white lies." Dr. Weissman wrote: *father-pathological lying.*

"I can see you are tired. It's been a long day, and you have the drive back. If we could visit one more thing before you go." Weissman continued. "The working diagnosis is schizophrenia. That means I am pretty sure, but not one hundred percent sure. You may think Zack would never hurt you, but the disease can cause him to think some other person is impersonating you. We call it an imposter situation. If he thinks you are an imposter, he might strike out. The good news is there is treatment. Drugs designed for schizophrenia can lessen these hallucinations. We also use psychotherapy to teach the patient insight into their disease, so they are better prepared to resist the bad thoughts that plague them."

Sheila thought about the carving knife under Zack's bed and the warning from Dr. Brown.

"So, I am right to be frightened?"

"Yes, he has delusions about you."

"I understand."

"Zack will meet with me twice a week at first."

"Do the parents of patients often seek treatment?"

"I wouldn't say often, but if you want to set up a few appointments with me for yourself, please do. As I see it, you are the parent who is shouldering the burden of a sick child. If your husband were sharing the responsibility, he would have come to this appointment. I appreciate how lonely you must feel." She wrote, *father-avoids responsibility, 5/7.*

Sheila dabbed her eyes with a tissue, "I lost myself somewhere along the way." Dr. Weissman thought, *Zack thinks so, too.*

"I'll get Brenda to make you an appointment." Dr.

Weisman wrote: *father meets criteria for ASPD.*

CHAPTER 18

8 January 2018

A common house spider surveyed the damage, climbing the scaffolding of her web in all directions, only to be swept away. Devastation marched across the facia board eliminating an entire population of spiders' homes causing them to scurry to other parts of the house on 28 Downy Drive, the one with the cat slide roof. The concrete stoop, or porch, was next. An old broom whisked the leaves, dead gnats, and accumulated dust away. The Happy New Year's wreath was replaced with another covered in purple, green, and gold plastic beads. Within an hour, trinkets hung from the Mardi Gras wreath, and ribbons, too.

Dixie Hayward sat down to wait. Jean arrived first.

"I came straight from school to help." A quick check informed her the good china tea cups and dessert plates were sitting on the dining room table. "You rest, Mama, while I put out the silver," Jean said. Martha came next.

"I dropped a cupcake on the floor at Shawn's birthday party," Martha said, while she filled the kettle and turned on the stove. "His wife Monica picked it up almost immediately—I'm sure it was less than two seconds. When she handed it back to me, she said, 'According to the two-second rule, this cupcake should be safe to eat'."

"Martha, did you eat it?" Jean winced.

"No, I just couldn't."

"Why not? I heard the two-second rule is outdated, it's five seconds now," Jean said, nodding her head to look over her reading glasses.

"You can't be serious," Martha laughed.

"I am serious. Everyone thinks it's five seconds now."

"Does the five-second rule hold when there is a dog in the house?" Martha said, willing to play along.

"How big is the dog?" Jean asked while she picked imaginary lint off her sleeve, a habit she picked up from her mother. If the sisters weren't gossiping, they were improvising.

"What difference does it make?"

"Well, the bigger the dog, the bigger the—Admit it, Jean, you know what I mean." Martha laughed so much that tears formed in her eyes.

"Mama, isn't there a five-second rule?" Jean asked her mother.

"Darling, I have only heard of the two-second rule." Dixie never could improvise meaningless conversations like her daughters, no matter how hard they tried to include her.

Jean took over, "When our kids were little, our pediatrician gave them sugar-free suckers; if they dropped the sucker on the floor, he would pick it up and stick it back in their mouth."

"Do you mean after they slobbered all over the sucker and made it sticky?" Martha said, eyes wide open.

"Yes," Jean nodded her head.

"Disgusting," Martha made a face.

"The doctor told us children should be exposed to germs to get immunity to them," Jean said.

"I don't believe that is true." said Dixie.

The doorbell silenced the discussion while Dixie got up to assist the person trying to unlock the front door.

"Sheila," she cried with delight, "Come on, we're having tea."

Martha paused as she went to the pantry to get cookies. "How did the appointment go with the psychiatrist?"

"It's complicated; basically, we are waiting for a diagnosis. But the doctor asked about Carl's brother," Sheila looked to her mother. "Do you remember anything about him or his mother, Mama?"

"Nothing about the brother. Carl's mother was eccentric. A rumor—can't remember who told me—she was afraid to leave her house."

"She drowned, right?"

"Yes, so sad. Carl's poor father had to raise a teenage boy all by himself. Here, take a cookie, I baked them this morning."

"Martha, how's the store doing?" Jean asked.

"Not great. I don't understand why people want to buy furniture at the mall. Look at Mama's house, everything is an antique. This furniture will last another hundred years." Martha pointed above her head. "Chandeliers like that one; you can't give them away now."

"How's school?" Sheila looked at Jean.

"Fifteen percent of my high schoolers are on medication for behavior problems." Jean drummed her fingers on the table. "Nobody seems worried about this trend, except for a new doctor who visited last week."

"Who?" Sheila asked.

"Dr. Weissman, she is a breath of fresh air."

"Really. You will never guess who I had coffee with this morning," Sheila said. "Sissy Graham."

The Dallas traffic on Interstate 635 was horrendous when Ellen's phone signaled a call from Sissy. Stop and go was routine at 5 PM, but stuck in a stand-still could only mean a wreck was ahead.

"When are you coming back to Gower?" Sissy asked.

"In a week, I hope. Is something going on there?"

"Not sure. Carl's wife called me, and we got together for coffee this morning."

"Really? What for?"

"She wanted to know what happened between Carl and my dad—to be sure Carl was telling her the truth." Sissy popped a potato chip into her mouth, making a crunching noise. "The last time I saw Mrs. Ewing she was falling apart; she seems put together now."

"Why now?"

"She said a few months ago, she would have defended Carl, but now she's not sure."

The traffic began to creep at a snail's pace.

"I may have to hang up soon, just so you know. Grandma is going to insist we give the remodel job to him. How can I explain he fired us?"

"No idea."

"At least I've separated her from him; she talks about Carl all the time like he was family."

"I'm convinced he did something to dad. Maybe he poisoned him."

"Like I said, Carl is charming in a snarky way. Sorry, traffic's picking up. Call you later."

Carl came home from work that evening, parked his muddy boots in his office and walked into the house carrying a package and looking for his wife. He found her in the bedroom, trying on clothes.

"Have you heard from the doctor?" He stood behind her and nibbled her neck, sending unwanted arousal throughout her body.

"No," she said.

"Let me do that," said Carl as he removed her hands from the zipper and gently closed the back of her new dress.

"They are sending the blood sample to a reference lab."

"Let me take you out tonight. You look so pretty I want to show you off." Carl tried to hug his wife, but the cast was in the way.

"How often have you been visiting Zack?"

"Why are you asking me?" Carl sulked and collapsed into a chair.

"Carl, I'm confused. Zack was not ready for the appointment when I came to pick him up."

Carl made a quick turnaround. "Look at what I bought him today." He popped up from his chair with fresh energy, spun around, and picked up a box from the bed. He opened it and struggled to lift it out of its molded packaging.

"You bought him a bow and arrows?"

"Yes, he's living in the woods already, and I've always wanted to bow hunt. We could do it together."

"Oh, my God. Do you leave your guns at the camp?" Sheila was struck by her stupidity in not thinking about this possibility.

"Sure, but I lock them in a closet." Carl fiddled with the bow to put it back in its package. "Can't a man give his son a present?"

"You can. I was just wondering why Zack would need a bow and arrows. Do you think a boy who probably has schizophrenia needs hunting equipment right now?"

"They don't know for sure, Sheila. You never go out to the camp, so you don't realize that there are black bears, bobcats, lots of dangerous animals in the woods."

"I was there Friday. Where were you? His cell phone was dead, so I had to charge it in the car on the way to the clinic. You couldn't have called him."

"You don't know when the battery failed." He stepped around the bedroom, restlessly. "We should go out to eat tonight because there is a new restaurant in town; we have never been there." He sat down on the bed. "I haven't seen you all day," he whined. "You can tell me more about the doctor's visit while we have dinner."

"I'll go with you. Should we take the bow to Zack while we are out?"

"I'll take it tomorrow."

"Did you check on him today?"

"No one wants to be around you when you are preachy. I'll go out by myself."

Son, someone is giving your wife idears, find out who it is.

CHAPTER 19

9 January 2018

An unnatural quiet enveloped the clearing, and the daylight turned dark as if an eclipse. First came a wave of needle-like rain followed by thunder and finally, stabs of lightning hitting the ground. A grand oak split nearly into, holding itself together by a thick trunk for an hour until a two -foot -wide splinter split off and, hurled by the wind, damaged an overhead electrical line. Thirty houses lost power. When the power was restored, the tenuous connection between Zack and reality was snuffed by the surge. The TV, now dead, no connection, no words or music, no heat, no buzz, no laughter, and most of all no messages, failed him. Without the distraction, time no longer had any meaning. And time had no structure. The morning news, the afternoon soap operas, and the evening police procedurals vanished in the storm.

Zack retreated to his bed once more.

"Let's see. Let's see if someone is home," the voice said. Then it said. "There has to be a person here; see the car. Hurry, I got to use it. KNOCK on the door! My hands are full!"

"I AM knocking! Why won't someone come?"

"Try the doorbell!"

The gong sounded in the hall, but the trouble was on the porch. The knocking ratcheted up and terrified him. Whoever they were, they tried to break into the house.

"Try the door, I can't wait until we get home."

"Just go in the woods," the other voice demanded.

"No! It's number 2, I would be a mess. NOBODY'S home; I'm opening the door."

Zack grabbed a kitchen knife he kept by the bed, hesitated in confusion, choosing at last to hide deep in his closet, shutting the door just as he heard the front door open.

"Anybody home?" One of them called.

"NOBODY'S HOME," said another child. "Let's just go in."

"We shouldn't."

"Then I'll go by myself. I can't wait any longer."

In the closet, Zack huddled into a corner, his heart racing. *It's demons, be careful. They will kill you if they find you and cut out your heart. Be ready.* He quivered, drooling because he couldn't swallow. *If they come in, you must slit their throat. There is no other way to kill them.* His breathing became faster, and he felt his hands cramp. Ready to strike at any moment, the voice yelled at him. *"You should have killed them, you idiot. They are inside now."*

"Do you hear something?" one of them said.

"Not really, maybe they have a cat. Where's the bathroom?"

Zack had a habit of closing, but not locking, all doors. His bedroom door, wide open in his frantic attempt to hide, invited a search.

"Okayyy," the other one said. "Just find the bathroom and let's get out."

"Here you try that door, and I'll try this one."

Zack heard footsteps walking to the closet door. The voice was being silly. "Fee, Fi, Fo, Fum, I smell the blood of an Englishman!" the knob on the door turned. Zack stood upon his knees; the knife poised like a dagger.

"I found it!" the other one said.

Zack saw the doorknob moved, but now nothing.

"Okay, you go in and potty while I stand guard."

The clack of tiny hooves retreated.

"Finally! Let's go."

Zack heard water rushing down the toilet.

"Wait. Let's leave a box of cookies. You did use their bathroom, and I am tired of carting this stuff around."

"Okay fine, but we better get out before they come home." The demon yelled.

Zack, aware the front door had closed, and the house was quiet, remained still for hours. By the time he left the closet it was twilight. When the room grew dark gradually, outside-shadows crept into the house. With his knife in hand, he walked stiffly to lock the front door and shove a chair against it before collapsing into a corner of the bedroom.

When the only light was a full moon outside, he heard a pack of coyotes' wail. The sounds they made became unbearable. Baying in a chorus with growling in between—sometimes laughing. He listened to the howling. The animals were a few feet from the house, and it lasted for at least two hours nonstop, until squealing and then quiet. No more sounds all night, and Zack was scared out of his wits.

CHAPTER 20

10 January 2018

Zack's phone call interrupted Sheila's morning bath. The ringing stopped before she put down her wash cloth, more ringing another stop. More ringing.

"Bringmeblackpaint-nails-lumber-nail-gun-staple-gun-glue-gun. I-need-an-excavator—for. The moat. With-tracks. NOW."

"Slow down. What is wrong?" A pounding—flesh and bone on something hard. A scream.

"Rope-wire-barbed wire-ties. REBAR. Sand-cinder-blocks. FLASHING." *Dead silence.*

"I am going to call your dad; stay in the house."

Sheila, with a towel wrapped around her, fumbled with her phone.

"What... is he... saying," Carl said in a sing-song voice, calmly—with a hint of irritation, no concern at all—humoring his wife.

"He is jabbering nonsense and sounds scared. I would go, but I don't know if I could handle him."

"I'll go—as soon as we finish up this house inspection."

"Carl, go now, I can see he is calling me back. Please."

"I said I was going," But he didn't rush.

A man has to eat, Carl reasoned, so he bought eight pounds of crawfish, boiled corn on the cob and potatoes, and a six-pack of Corona. The fumes of the seasoning filled the cab of his truck, and the smell made him hungry. The bow and arrows lay on the back seat. Now he was ready to check on Zack.

He selected Sheila on the blue tooth screen and called as he was leaving the restaurant.

"Hey, Baby, Zack is fine, and we are going to eat at the camp, and I will be home at six. Just letting you know." His hand danced on the steering wheel to the beat of a song playing on the radio. It was a new artist, but it reminded Carl of the music he listened to as a teenager. When the next song came on, he placed a call to Zack and left a message.

A pretty girl jogging along the road came into view. He swerved just in time to avoid hitting her. And then he saw it, a doe blending in perfectly with the surroundings. It was a mother without her fawn. She ran across the road in front of him to graze on the other side.

A few phone calls cleared Carl's schedule before he turned off the highway. Zack's car was in place. Good, he didn't go anywhere. Carl parked and grabbed the two bags of crawfish with his left hand and walked to the house. A cloud of flies swarmed over a carcass—a fresh one—three feet from the board sidewalk. For a minute, Carl wondered if Zack had killed the fawn with a knife. He set the food down, got out his key, and unlocked the door. Someone or something prevented the door from opening. He knocked and called out, "Zack," as loud as he could.

"God damn!" He ran to the truck to grab a hammer. He had a functional left hand, but he was right-handed, making a simple task much harder. The shattered pane of glass was large enough to get his arm inside and unlock the window, but he couldn't raise it. "Damn window was painted shut," he grunted under his breath. He had no choice but to break the entire window grill. There were shards of glass everywhere, sending him back to the truck for a glove before wiggling into the house.

Once inside, he took his time removing the chair wedged under the doorknob of the front door, and taking stock of the living room and kitchen. He searched every room, leaving Zack's bedroom for last, preparing himself for a suicide. The body was slouched on the floor in the far corner, chin propped on his chest.

"ZACK!" he yelled from ten feet away. Zack did not move a muscle, no startle, no recognition. Nothing indicated he was a living human being, and yet he did not seem dead. Carl walked over to this son and put his hand on his shoulder.

"Son, it's dad, wake up," but there was no response. He lifted Zack's head and could see the eyes were open but vacant. When Carl laid him on the floor, Zack's posture did not change. He was stuck in a semi-sitting position. Carl shook his son, gently.

"Wake up!" Zack was breathing. His heartbeat was steady. It was now he realized Zack had wet himself, and a butcher knife lay on the floor beside him. Suspecting his son was drugged, Carl called 911 from his cell phone. He wanted to believe it was drugs, someone to blame, and a chance for recovery. He covered him with a blanket and searched the house, no pills, no needles, no tourniquets, and no pipes.

By the time the ambulance arrived, it was close to three o'clock. Time was wasted when the EMT's passed by the driveway to overshoot it by seven miles. Carl sat on the sofa in the living room, waiting. Zack remained frozen in his bizarre position, sitting while lying on his side. He reminded Carl of a statue in a wax museum, lifelike in every respect except for the lack of motion.

The medics knocked on the door. Carl felt heavy, not yet resigned to what happened. He pointed the EMT's to the bedroom.

"He's over there. I found him sitting with his back against the wall." One medic put Zack on a cardiac monitor; the other spoke to him.

"Hey, buddy. Are you all right?" No response. He then grabbed his shoulder and said, "Buddy, are you all right?" When that failed, he put his fist in the middle of Zack's chest and ground it in forcefully. The action elicited a groan and a slight movement. The other medic who had placed him on a monitor, counted his respirations, reached for a penlight, and checked Zack's eyes. The driver of the ambulance came in next and approached Carl, who had returned to the sofa.

"Sir, I need your name and the relationship you have with the patient."

"I'm his father, and my name is Carl Ewing."

"Patient's name?"

Carl had to think a minute; he was so flustered. "Zackery Carlton Ewing."

"Does your son take any medications or street drugs, sir?"

"No, not that I know of."

"Is he allergic to any medications or foods?"

"No."

"Has he ever been hospitalized?"

"He had surgery on his leg when he broke it."

"No problems with the anesthesia?"

"No."

"How old is he?"

"Eighteen." As Carl said this, Zack's life flashed before his eyes. Preschool, ball games, birthday parties, and high school graduation.

"Tell me what happened?"

"I came out to see him. He has been living here, doing some repairs. I thought he was dead, slumped in the corner of the room, halfway sittin' up. His eyes were open, but it was like he was sleeping."

The first medic said, "No signs of injury, we can go now."

They laid him on the stretcher, still in the strange sitting position, and carried him out. Once on the ground, they released the "legs" of the cot. The wheels rolled it to the ambulance where they collapsed it again, picked it up and rolled it into the back, locking it in place.

The first medic gave a report by phone. "Yes, sir, we are leaving now for Benton."

The driver got Carl's telephone number and instructed him to follow the ambulance to the hospital emergency room. "Please look for his insurance card and bring it with you," the last man out told him.

"I'll lock up before I go," Carl said as the medics left. Lunch was lying at his feet, the plastic bags of crawfish, the six-pack of beer. He picked up a bottle of Corona to drink while he reluctantly put the rest of the beer in the refrigerator. He dug his hand into one of the crawfish bags and found three boiled potatoes. Seated now at the kitchen table, he surveyed the room again and saw something he missed before.

It was an unopened box of Thin Mints on the sofa. He walked over and picked it up to examine it thoroughly, turning the carton around as though he had never seen girl scout cookies before. Then he placed them under his right arm and walked out the door, locking it behind him.

As he drove, well below the speed limit, he moved his head around in a circle and shrugged his shoulders.

He called his wife.

"Sheila, honey," he grunted. "We are going to the ER. Zack's got a fever. What was the name of the doctor he saw?"

"Weissman. Her name is Dr. Weissman."

"No, I mean the other one."

"Brown."

The doctor in green scrubs stood in the empty waiting room at two forty-five AM, looking for Mr. Ewing.

"Mr. Ewing, may I have a word with you?"

Carl struggled to stand up. He crossed the expanse of empty chairs to talk to a doctor who stood far away from the waiting area for privacy's sake.

"Zack had an episode of not speaking and not moving that lasted about 6 hours. We stopped it by giving him a muscle relaxant. He's sleeping now, and this morning we are going to contact his psychiatrist. Were you able to get the name?"

"It's a woman doctor named Weissman at University. Zack saw her five days ago, but it don't look like she did him any good."

"I'll contact Dr. Weissman this morning before I sign off. I'm only moonlighting here, while I finish my surgery residency." The boy, standing before Carl, did not look old enough to be a doctor.

"Mr. Ewing, I don't specialize in neurology, but Zack has had a spinal tap, C T scan, MRI, and an EEG. We don't see any lesions on the brain, and his toxicology tests show no alcohol or drugs. I think he was in a catatonic state, but he is out of it now."

"What?"

"His brain shut down. We have ruled out drugs, seizures, brain tumor, brain bleed, infection. It was something else that caused it, possibly a psychiatric illness. We treated the symptoms successfully, but we don't yet have a diagnosis."

"Can I see him?"

The doctor led the way. As Carl passed through the door to the inner sanctum of the hospital, he felt a biting uneasiness. Unfamiliar sounds and smells behind that door gave way to negative messages everywhere: NO EXIT. NO ENTRANCE. HOSPITAL PERSONNEL ONLY. The doctor led him through the maze without hesitation. At last, Carl could see where he was going, the sliding glass doors with a sign above, MEDICAL ICU.

"He's in room five."

There were only five rooms with in this area partitioned by glass walls. Carl was surprised to see how little privacy the patients had; he could see everything about the patient in each room they passed, except one where the curtain was drawn. *This one is probably dead,* he thought. It was disconcerting to view the demise of old people in this fish bowl environment.

"Here he is!" the doctor informed him.

Zack was awake, lying in bed with the top half raised to a semi-sitting pose. His eyes were moving and blinking, and he was drinking through a straw from a plastic cup held by the nurse.

"Zack," the doctor said, "your dad is here to see you."

"Hi, dad," Zack said. He looked vulnerable in the pale blue hospital gown, and cold under the crisp snow-white sheets. His arm was secured to a board with intravenous fluid flowing into a mound of gauze and tape, and he had something clipped on his right index finger. The leads to his cardiac monitor had just been taken off his chest and hung loosely draped over the IV pole.

Carl's heart turned over. He still had hope.

"Are you feeling better?"

"Sort of," Zack said.

"Well, you look much better to me. What happened to you last night?"

"They were trying to kill me, dad."

"Who?" Carl felt a crushing weight on his chest.

"It was two of them."

"Did you see them, Zack?"

"No. You'd be proud, dad, I was going to kill them with my knife if they got close."

"Who were they?"

"I'm not sure." Carl could see Zack's leg seizing under the sheet.

"It's okay now, Zack. You're safe here." *Say they were burglars,* Carl prayed.

"Am I?" Zack opened his eyes wide in disbelief.

"Yes, you are. You are in a hospital."

"Look over there," and Zack pointed to an air-conditioning vent. "They are sending poisonous waves through that vent, and they travel around the room until the gas waves find me, and they come in through my mouth."

Carl covered his face with his hands. When he had composed himself, he took his hands away to look at Zack again. His phone rang, giving him little time to process the moment. "My wife's calling," he told the doctor.

A cup of coffee later, Carl sat in the empty waiting room fidgeting with his keys, waiting for the nurse and the documents to be signed. The ER doctor had "P-E-C-ed" Zack, meaning he had signed a physician emergency certificate, but because of Zack's age, Carl was asked to sign off on the referral and mode of transportation.

Carl, worn out and counting the minutes before he could cancel his appointments and go home to sleep, waited. Somebody designed a massive plate-glass window on the east wall. The sun's rays streaming in, even in January, made the dust particles in the air seem almost like a fog. Carl's eyes, always sensitive to too much light, responded with a headache.

"Excuse me, don't I know you?" a cultured man's voice said. Carl looked up and saw a vaguely familiar face. Maybe he was a preacher ready to witness. They were sitting with just one empty waiting-room seat between them, but Carl had not noticed him walk in.

"I'm Mark Lefleur," and he reached out his hand.

"Sorry," said Carl, holding up his cast.

"You look lonely, I thought you might like company." The man had a distinctive face, dimpled chin, and nose with a bump on it. Carl realized he had seen him before but couldn't place him.

"Thanks, I'm Carl Ewing."

"I know. I was Trent Wilson's attorney. It's good to see you."

"You got somebody sick?"

"No, my family is fine—knock on wood. I have a slip-and-fall complaint to file."

"How much is that worth?"

"For her, at least 100,000 dollars; she was severely injured." The lawyer switched to a sad face, "Too bad about Trent, but I guess it worked out well for you."

"You could say that." There was no inflection in Carl's voice.

"Have you ever met his daughter, Sissy?" The man shifted in his seat and crossed his legs as if they were going to have a chat.

"No, what's going on with her?"

"Sissy's a little crazy, Carl. She is requesting some of Trent's documents, which I have under lock and key. Don't worry, I'm not working for her."

"I ain't worried. I didn't do anything wrong," Carl

yawned and shifted in his chair to distance himself.

"Don't kid yourself. Trent had a strong case against you," Lefleur crossed his legs the other way. "Sissy is irrational with grief, and when it comes to you, she could be a problem."

"She's hysterical." Carl modeled disbelief.

"She is," Mark Lefleur moved in even closer.

"Why are you telling me this?"

Lefleur smiled at a few people drifting in to wait. He relaxed as if he and Carl were talking about the weather.

"I want to warn you that Trent was a well-connected guy, and he hated you." Lefleur reached into his pocket and took out a business card. "Think about it, Carl, Trent was a lawyer. Why didn't he represent himself in the lawsuit against you?" He chuckled as if Carl had said something funny. "The things he did—it's going to seem like he is reaching out from the grave to cause you trouble. But I know where the potholes are."

"Mr. Lefleur," a nurse called his name from the admitting desk. He stood up and buttoned his suit coat.

"Here's my business card. I'm the best-qualified lawyer to represent you if anything was to happen."

Carl made the card disappear into his fist. When Lefleur was out of sight, he scanned it. On the front, Lefleur's contact information and his message to potential clients: "At the Lefleur Law Firm, We Aim to Make Things Right." Below that, "We Specialize in Criminal Law, Contract law, and Litigation." On the back of the card, Lefleur had handwritten his cell phone number.

Carl's steady, well-oiled campaign to be respectable, wealthy, and powerful was falling to pieces. When the nurse brought him a clipboard, with arrows pointing out where to sign on four pieces of typed-written paper that he could hardly see to read; he blew up.

"Tell the doctor, my son is coming home with me."

"He's been PECed, sir. The doctor thinks he would be unsafe if discharged."

"Well, he is my son, and we have a doctor at home. His name is Dr. Brown and I will take Zack to see him."

"I can't sign Zack out to you. You have to speak with the doctor."

"Then get him out here so I can talk to him!"

"It's the end of his shift; he went home."

"I ain't signin' this!" Carl stood up to make his point.

"He's been PECed, and he is eighteen. They are going to transfer him whether or not you sign, Mr. Ewing."

"No, they're not; I'll go get him myself!" The nurse walked away to the receptionist area, and soon the overhead speaker announced: "CODE WHITE, MEDICAL ICU, CODE WHITE, MEDICAL ICU."

Carl stopped a housekeeper with her unwieldy cart on his way to the elevator.

"What is Code White? My son is in the ICU."

"Yes sir, nothing to worry about. It's not a patient code. Some family member must be up there having a temper fit." She handed him a bottle of water. "Why don't you find a place to sit and drink this while you wait. I wouldn't try to visit right now if I were you. It will be crawling with security."

CHAPTER 21

13 January 2018

"It's a wicked disease," said Dr. Weissman to Carl and Sheila two days after Zack's transfer to University Hospital. The two of them sat in leather chairs in an unfamiliar office on a Saturday morning. "Zack has schizophrenia that is characterized by paranoid delusions. You are probably more familiar with mental illness in the form of depression or anxiety, but those diseases are disorders of mood, while schizophrenia is a disorder of thought. We are certain of the diagnosis now.

"What you witnessed Mr. Ewing was an episode of catatonia, a known complication of the disease. While Zack is hospitalized, we will adjust the dose of his medication. The medicine is not perfect; there are side effects, which we will manage."

Carl was barely listening; instead, he was distracted about a disturbing dream he had yesterday while he was catching up on his sleep. He couldn't put it out of his mind. His concern revolved around Steve, who, in the dream, had a stab of conscience about the trick they played on Trent.

"We expect to discharge Zack in one week," she said.

"I would prefer he lives with you or a relative, some-one who could report any changes in his behavior right away."

If Steve broke down, Carl was thinking as the doctor spoke, *and told someone; who would he tell? Trent's daughter? The police? A friend?*

"Mr. Ewing, I'm glad you were able to come," Weissman continued. "Do you have any questions?" Dr. Weissman assessed Carl during her update. He seemed to be daydreaming, and his eyes were vacant. They were reptilian—cold-blooded. He showed no emotion at all upon hearing the news.

"Not that I can think of."

"I have a question for you," Dr. Weissman countered. "Do you have any close relatives, say a brother or a sister who had mental illness in any form?"

"Naw, everybody in my family was fine," Carl rubbed his eyes as he sat like a dead weight in his chair. She wrote: *father lying?*

"And your mother? Was the drowning an accident, or suicide?"

"My Daddy always thought somebody done it, but the coroner called it an accident."

"One more, if you don't mind. Do you regret not checking on Zack at the camp?" Dr. Weissman held her breath. She did not want to provoke him, but she had to know.

"Excuse me, Doc, but you have it all wrong. I was going out there every day and calling too. The only day I didn't go was the day of his appointment when my wife brought him to see you." Carl began to pout. "I don't know what my son has been telling you, but he is very ill as you have said yourself."

"I'm sorry. You are right, of course. I misunderstood him. That about wraps it up. Would you like to see Zack today? It's a short walk from here."

Sheila took her husband's hand when he offered it, and they walked out together, the picture of a mature couple still in love.

"None of this would have happened if you hadn't babied him, Sheila," Carl growled. "You should have listened to me." The words did not sting at all.

They walked out of Weissman's office and down the back hall, exiting onto the campus with its beautifully landscaped lawns, sidewalks, and winter flowers, all of nature vibrant despite cold weather. The psych unit occupied the entire fifth floor of University Hospital. On the inside the design was very much like the clinic building. The elevator traveled from the first floor to the fifth, no stops, and the doors opened to enter the nurse's station, where a ward clerk monitored who was coming and going. She also collected their guest cards, promising to give them back when they left. Sheila prayed she would not have a panic attack on this strange, gloomy, and secure hospital floor.

"I'm going to open the glass doors over there, so you

can go in," the nurse explained. "After you pass through the first set of doors, they will close behind you, and you will see a second set of doors that will not open until I open them from here. You will experience just a moment of being boxed in." Sheila felt faint, and her heart was racing.

Once inside the box, she panted until the second glass doors opened. The nurse came so quickly she must have been expecting them.

"Mr. and Mrs. Ewing, hello. I'm Karen, Zack's nurse." Karen wore colorful scrubs, and although her figure looked young, her face had the leathery skin of a chain smoker. Her bleached blond hair was already thinning, something that Sheila noticed as they walked behind her. "He is waiting for you over here." She pointed to a table on the far side of the room.

As they walked toward Zack, they passed a group of patients sitting in an assortment of sofas and armchairs. It looked as if someone had tried to construct a living room without walls in the center of a wide-open space. All the patients were wearing hospital scrubs, but they were made of paper.

"Zack has been taking a strong medicine. We are weaning it now, but he is still somewhat groggy," Karen said as they walked toward their son, sitting by himself. "You may sit here and talk, and I'll be close if you need anything."

Sheila stood, feeling helpless, with her hands clasped together, and her eyes distracted by the other patients milling around. Carl walked over to hug Zack. He tried to pull a chair away from the table to sit down and found it stuck to the floor. He accepted its location and sat, mirroring the posture and expression of Zack.

"We are glad you're feeling better," he said. Karen noted the father and son made a touching portrait, but the mother stood three feet away—speechless. They visited for fifteen minutes; Karen timed them. When they were ready to go, Carl said, "We are going to beat this thing, Son." At the next staff meeting, Karen remarked how caring Zack's father was, while his mother seemed distant. Dr. Weissman corrected her observation.

Sheila expected a sad, quiet ride home; Carl surprised her when he wanted to talk, but not about Zack.

"Insurance companies are a rip-off," he said.

"What makes you say that? We carry all kinds of insurance." She tried to seem interested.

"A buddy of mine paid insurance premiums for ten years and never filed a claim until last year when stuff was stolen off the job site. The insurance company denied it because my buddy couldn't prove the items were stolen."

"How much did he lose?" She was willing to travel down this road, realizing he was talking about the lawsuit with Wilson.

"Thirty-two thousand six hundred dollars." He tapped his hand on the steering wheel to accent the number.

"Gosh, that's a lot."

"You bet your life it is! It makes people not want to play by the rules." Sheila shifted in her seat, opened her purse, and applied lipstick. Usually, she could do this without a mirror in a moving car, but Carl hit a bump.

"Carl, do you have a tissue?" she said, looking straight ahead.

"Naw, you usually carry them." Carl was upbeat, which seemed unnatural considering their circumstances.

"Well, I didn't today." Sheila looked like she had a nosebleed. When Carl saw it, his face lit up.

"We better do something about that; I'll stop at a gas station," Carl turned his eyes back to the road. "Why were you putting on lipstick? We ain't going nowhere 'cept home." Sheila ignored the comment, but he didn't mind. "My buddy got so mad, he photographed some building supplies on a job site and stole them himself to collect the insurance money."

"I can see why someone would do that." Sheila felt sorry for Carl; he was so emotionally damaged.

"Right!" Carl said, as if he was finally being understood. "I can too." He reached in his pocket for a breath mint. "But my buddy's partner went crazy and called the cops on him."

"How much trouble did your friend get into?" Sheila felt the scabs had been removed from her eyes, and she could finally recognize her husband for what he was.

"The cops said a thief took it, so the partner sued—my friend."

"That's terrible!"

"I know!" He said, nodding his head up and down. "The judge could have made my friend pay back the money, but luckily he dismissed it before they went to trial."

"Good." She could see and having seen, she thought she was free. "Here's a grocery store. Will you buy me some tissues?"

"Sure, I would be happy to do that. It's a good look for Halloween, though." Carl suppressed a chuckle.

"If I can reproduce it exactly," Sheila agreed.

"Yeah, gettin' that lawsuit dismissed was a godsend. My friend scammed the insurance company more than once." Carl put on the right blinker. "Okay, we're here, I'll be right back."

While Carl was in the store buying tissues, she pulled down the window visor and looked at herself in the mirror. She looked and felt ridiculous. Even the tissues Carl brought her were no match for the lipstick stain, but at least now it looked like a birthmark.

"Carl," she said. "If you could pick just one day, when was the happiest day of your life?"

"That's easy. It was when my father kicked my brother out of the house. I figured you knew that. When was your happiest day, Rudolph?"

"The day before we got married."

"Oh, yeah. I remember that day," Carl said, his mind adrift.

"Sissy Wilson and I got together for coffee a while ago."

"You shouldn't be talking to her." He kept his eyes on the road, but she noticed him grasping the steering wheel tighter.

"Why?"

"She's going around town trying to ruin my reputation."

CHAPTER 22

17 January 2018

"The Motherboard Complex seeks to explain why women don't leave sociopathic husbands. They marry a man, only a mother could love, form an attachment born of misunderstanding, and never emotionally leave him."

"Your work lies within the realm of social work, not psychiatry."

"How successful are social workers, policemen, and courts?"

"How successful are you?"

"We understand why sociopathic men behave the way they do. Now is the time to study what compels the women to continue a dangerous relationship when they have the resources to leave."

"It is not our job to worry about domestic abuse, emotional or otherwise. It is a criminal matter."

"The motherboards stay, and they have children." Weissman sipped her iced tea and wiped her mouth with her napkin. "I've enjoyed our discussion so much. Sorry to rush, but I have a patient ready for discharge this afternoon. Can we continue it another time?"

"Brilliant. Thursdays are best?" A text distracted her. *Zack's mother and uncle are here.*

"Excuse me, gotta run."

Sheila had spent a week searching for a home for Zack, talking with Jean, checking out group homes, working with Martin to withdraw money from his trust. The words never left her: *"He will always require supervision by a psychiatrist, daily medication, and (this is important) a trusted guardian to monitor his day-to-day behavior."*

"Why don't you let him rent one of my houses," Martin suggested. "It makes sense financially. His trust would pay minimal rent, and I'll deduct the upkeep when I file taxes."

"You would do that for me?"

"I would do it for me," Martin laughed. "It's lonely way out there, in case you haven't noticed. I'm beginning to talk to the people in the mirror myself."

"Mmm. Carl would have to agree; it wouldn't work out otherwise."

Later, when Sheila brushed by Carl in the bedroom, hair flowing down her shoulders, and clutching a romance novel she bought at the grocery store, she guided him to the loveseat and tucked her legs in her flannel nightgown.

"You are sulking while I try to find a place for Zack."

"I ain't sulkin'," Carl whined. "Why would you say that?"

"What about moving him to the farm? Martin said he would check on him."

"He's eighteen. As far as I am concerned, he can live wherever he wants." Carl picked up a magazine and started flipping the pages."

"Are you coming to pick him up?"

"No, why should I? You two have it under control." He sat with his back slumped over, staring across the room. Sheila heaved a sigh and ran her fingers through her hair.

The full moon brightened the night sky, and for a moment, birds sang after dark. By ten PM, the houses on the cul-de-sac turned off their lights. City raccoons prowled backyards looking for signs of garbage, a lone police car drove by making its rounds, and by three AM, newspapers sailed onto driveways. Anxious and aching, Sheila lay in bed watching her husband sleep. His mouth was open ever so slightly, and his muscular arms hugged the pillow. Breathing steady, in and out, in and out. An old man's face transformed into a young man's expression of vulnerability and sorrow. His thick wiry hair, also timeless, turned sandy in the glow of the nightlight. Overwhelming everything else—his moods, his temper, his high jinks—the loss of his son to this horrible disease must torture him. It was heartbreaking to imagine his pain. It was easier for her because she was able to accept the change, he couldn't.

Midmorning, Martin waited on the highway just before the turnoff to his house in a drizzle of rain, holding a diet coke.

"I didn't want you to get the car muddy. Are you excited?"

"Honestly, I don't know what I would do if it weren't for you," Sheila said as he got into the car and he handed her the soft drink. "You are considerate and kind." Sheila drove for fifty miles, consumed with her errand. Martin, always comfortable with silence, enjoyed the tour of the countryside. At the moment, timberland, a long-term investment, interested him. When Sheila turned onto the interstate highway, her mood changed and she was ready to talk.

"It's a shame you didn't remarry. You would have made a superb husband." Once she navigated a lane change, she said, "We've talked about my marriage. Why is your marriage off-limits? Come on, tell me what happened." Martin's ex-wife floated rumors about him, but Martin never said a cross word about her.

"Twisting my arm?" Martin took a deep breath. "Okay, I'll tell you. Pam and I agreed not to get pregnant for a few years. One day by accident, I don't even know why, I checked out the trash; I found a packet of pills thrown away. Not a single pill was missing from the blister pack. It took me seconds to realize she was not taking them. So, I asked her if the pills caused her to have headaches or whatever. She told me she had no side effects, and she was happy we were waiting."

"I don't understand."

"It was a lie, Sheila. Married couples don't lie to each other."

"So, you knew right away, and you divorced her?"

"Yes. I won't say it wasn't hard, but I couldn't trust my wife."

"Why don't you look for another girl to marry?"

"Who says I haven't been looking?" Martin laughed.

"Remember when Zack broke his leg?"

"Sure, like yesterday."

"Did he seem strange when he stayed with you that summer?"

"Not in the least; I wish I could have spent more time with him. We didn't do much. Early on, I came in from the field to help him to the bathroom, but after that, we only saw each other in the evenings. We watched a little TV, and he read one of his stories to me. Then I confess I fell asleep in my chair before going to bed, but he didn't mind. All I had to do was supply him with paper and pencils to keep him busy."

"He hand-wrote them?"

"Yes. That was the year I pegged Zack to be the most likely nephew to run the farm one day. He had the proper temperament. You know, he made do with what he had, and didn't waste energy longing for something else." Sheila pondered this assessment for a moment.

"When we got back, Zack said he had more fun at the farm than he would have at the beach. Thanks for taking care of him again."

"I figure it's only fair. You saved the farm for me, and I help you with Zack." Martin pointed to his side window. "I see a parking place if you want to take it."

The meeting with Dr. Weismann was formal at first.

"We have diagnosed Zack with schizophrenia: paranoid type," she said. "I have handouts for you about the illness and about the medication he is taking. There is a third item, a pamphlet published by a colleague, informing families what to expect when they come home." The literature, neatly packaged in a folder, gave the impression Zack was one of many patients Dr. Weissman treated. Sheila thought of a stack of handouts like this one, sitting in a supply closet somewhere.

Once Weissman delivered her instructions and appointment routine, she relaxed to discuss their concerns. Sheila and Martin explained where Zack would stay after discharge.

"Oh, I see. In that case, let me give you," she looked at Martin, "some contact information, too." She handed him her business card, which, among other information, had her cell phone number on it. "He may be slow to adjust to an unfamiliar environment. A new home will disorient him at first, but living in a house beside you is the ideal choice." As she handed him a packet of patient information on schizophrenia, identical to the one Sheila received, their eyes met. She tried to make sense of him. "The most important advice I can give you is to be sure he takes his medication every day and call me immediately if he refuses to take it."

"What would a relapse look like?"

"A relapse may manifest as a complete breakdown; the patient is no longer able to sustain his life. It could also be the expression of suicidal ideas, or threats toward others. Schizophrenia waxes and wanes. In the early stages, stealth attacks from visual and auditory hallucinations occur intermittently, distracting patients from relationships, schoolwork, eating, and bathing. Voices chide them about flaws in their character, dire enemies, and impending doom. The false information leads to irrational decisions. The neighbor, the cat, the mailman is out to get them. As bizarre as this sounds to you, it is real to Zack."

"What causes it?" Martin leaned forward with his arms resting on the armrest of the chair. "I have never heard of this."

"You have asked a tough question. It is inherited, it involves neurotransmitters in the brain, but we still don't have it figured out. Our goal is to prevent these relapses with medication. The fewer psychotic episodes he has, the better his outcome." Sheila put her head in her hands and stayed quiet. Martin furrowed his brow.

"I see. In case of a relapse, do I take my nephew to the emergency room?"

"If he cannot come to see me, then yes. There may be a time when you would have to call an ambulance. There may be a time when you have to call the police, but they are the last resort. Police do not administer medication, which is what they need in a crisis; psychotic breaks almost always occur when a patient goes off his medicine.

"I will see Zack twice a week in the beginning, but I would like to talk with you every other day about his activities and attitude."

"Calling around seven in the evening would be best for me. Is that too late?"

"That works well with my schedule, too." Ordinarily, a nurse would handle these calls in their program, but Weissman took a particular interest in Zack's case; his mother was a patient, and his father, was a sociopath.

"The hospital staff provides Zack's first month of medication and will explain when and how much to dose him. You and I can talk often, so don't worry if you feel overwhelmed." She smiled.

"Zack is ready for discharge; that's the good news."

Leaving the clinic to walk in the rain, the brother and sister crossed the campus, united in their mission.

"I wonder if Zack's illness was a consequence of his fall? Maybe he had a concussion that the doctor didn't recognize, and it caused this derangement years later."

"I doubt it, Sis."

"He was clowning around on a ladder, but he shouldn't have been up there in the first place." Sheila turned her attention to access the elevator.

"You know Sheila," Martin said as they rode nonstop to the fifth floor. "Zack is terrified of heights." Sheila, too, suffered a fear of heights.

"I didn't know that. How did you find out?" Sometimes even elevators worried her.

"He told me that summer."

They found Zack sitting alone at his table finishing lunch, but there were a few stragglers at other tables. The right knee was jumping, causing his hospital slipper to flip-flop on his foot. He recognized them and stood up. Sheila hugged him, which he allowed, and Martin shook his hand. Karen brought his medication in a white paper bag. Zack changed into his jeans and a tee-shirt, followed them to the car, and promptly fell asleep in the back seat, leaning against the door.

The job site in Gower was alive with activity. A roof turns rain days into workdays. This house had a table with donuts and coffee for the men hanging sheetrock, compliments of the homeowners. Everyone joked and laughed except for the Boss, who slipped into a brooding, lifeless, off-putting stare. He assumed this pose while sitting on a pile of lumber in the unfinished dining room, a cement floor, and bare wood frame. His new foreman had a question and bounded over to ask. The dead eyes stopped him. Then Carl's phone rang, and he snapped out of it.

"Hello."

"Hey, this is Susie, I'm sorry to be so late in responding to your text."

"You remember me?"

"Sure."

"Well, I got a job for Steve but he won't answer the

phone. Does he have a different number?"

"No. he's staying in Pine Bluff. You know my brother; he likes to move around now."

"Is he still driving a truck?"

"I'm not sure what he is doing."

"Thanks, I'll keep trying."

"I'll let him know you have a job for him if he calls me."

There was one more call to make before he shook off the slump. Trying to relax the muscles in his face and force a smile, he called Ellen.

He tried to sound cheerful. "Thanks for taking my call; I've been wondering about you and Miss Sarah, and I owe you an apology. I shouldn't have acted like that. If you and Miss Sarah would like me to do the job, I promise to do a good one. It looks to me like no one has started, yet. But regardless of the decision you make, please know that I am sorry."

"Carl, it's good to hear you still want the job. I'll talk to grandma about it and get back to you." She ended the call. Minutes later, he received a call from Miss Sarah.

"Please don't mind my granddaughter. She is just trying to protect me. She doesn't know how much I relied on you over the years. You are a good man. You always answered when I called, and you always came on time." Carl sensed this was the time to stay quiet and listen for cues.

"You kept me company when I lost my daughter to that terrible disease. There was a time when we were having coffee together almost every week. I'll never forget how loyal you were. Ellen is still young, and she doesn't know what it is like to lose dear friends, a husband, and a child. The world often seems like a lonely place without them in it. I want you to do the job, and I trust you."

Ellen crushed the sheet of paper listing the names of other builders she consulted. What's definitive about Carl, she thought, is that you pay to play.

"Thank you, Miss Sarah. I am honored. You will be proud of the work, I promise." As soon as he ended the call, his foreman came over to talk.

Alone in her office, Dr. Weissman reviewed her notes in preparation for dictating Zack's discharge summary. Her desk was immaculate, no loose or stacked papers. She did not like calls from medical records. A framed copy of Dr. Peabody's essay in which he argues "the secret of the care of the patient is in caring for the patient" hung on the wall.

As she saw it, Zack, Sheila, and Martin were points on a triangle—each connected to the others. Carl stood in the center as they pinwheeled around him. He was the pin, not Sheila, not Zack; he ran the show. If Sheila could pull away from Carl, the other two would be free, too, because the pinwheel could no longer spin. But Weissman doubted Sheila had the strength of character to do it, especially at her age, and with so much shared history with her husband. By pure chance, Weissman was in a unique position to see Carl through the eyes of Sheila, Zack, and, now, Martin. *I wonder if Carl will figure this out?* She found Carl fascinating.

When Sheila returned home after leaving Zack and Martin at the farm, Carl was sitting in the living room waiting for her.

"Everyone takes me for granted." He looked as if someone had kicked him in the stomach. He rubbed his face, smoothing out his twisted look and then pressed on his eyeballs as if to stem the flow of tears. "Nobody is ever satisfied. I wish I could retire now."

"Did you forget we were going to move Zack's things out to the farm tonight? It's his first night at Martin's house, and we are supposed to be there."

"No, I didn't forget it, but I got something to do in the office first." With those words, he got up and walked to his office, closing the door behind him. He took out his bottle of bourbon and poured himself a drink. He tried Steve's number again.

"Hello," This time, Steve answered on the first ring.

"Hey, buddy, I've been trying to call you—I can't talk long. Just giving you a heads up."

"What," Steve said flatly. "You should know someone is looking into how Trent died. He died, Carl. Why didn't you tell me?"

"That's why I'm calling you now."

"Who is stirring things up?"

"His daughter, that's who. What about the maid; where is she?"

"I'm pretty sure she left town when the questions started. She ain't legal. Boss, I wish I'd never let you talk me into this." Steve sounded unhinged.

"Nothing is going to happen."

"How can you say that?" Steve's voice, shaky, "I'll never be able to come home."

"Because her lawyer is working for me. Don't worry."

"What the heck?"

"Nothing." Carl was close to shouting. "I'm taking care of it. Don't let it keep you up at night." Carl poured himself another shot.

"If you don't make this go away, your ass is on the line, too," Steve said before he hung up.

Braced by the bourbon, Carl stood up, opened his office door, and went into the house.

"I'm sorry. Let's go move Zack in."

By evening the town was quiet and everyone paused for dinner. Ellen worn out by the drive from Dallas met Sissy at the Fish House Restaurant at eight PM.

"There is my friend," Ellen told the hostess and walked over to seat herself.

"I've been looking forward to this all day," Sissy said when Ellen sat down. "Today has been crazy."

"Who has the kids?"

"Their Daddy has them. He's good with them, too." Sissy looked around the establishment, admiring the new wood paneling. "My Mom isn't a big help these days; ever since she remarried, she concentrates on him." She picked up a menu. "The food here is outstanding."

"It was a good idea to eat late. Gave me time to help my grandmother get in bed."

A male server with a white apron came and took their order, recommending the fried oysters they both selected.

"Can't you sue Carl for all the repairs he did on your grandmother's house, especially since he charged her so much for it?"

"I don't know, Sissy, but I am not up to doing it, even if it is possible. Carl called today to apologize, and Grandma wants him to do the work. She already told him he has the job."

"Well then, here's a news flash. I found the nurse who saw my dad in the ER. I bet you remember Darlene; she was two years ahead of us in high school. She said my dad had burns on a few fingers of his right hand. It might have been an electrical burn."

"Why didn't the doctor notice it?" The waiter brought Ellen a beer.

"Because my dad was dead—other patients required his attention. It was the nurse who cleaned up the body. I believe the heart attack diagnosis was just an educated guess."

"That's interesting." Ellen cocked her head at this news and then squared her face to respond. In her heart of hearts, she reasoned murder was too far-fetched, but in deference to her friend, she was willing to entertain it.

"But there is more. I talked to the maid in my broken high school Spanish, and she told me a man knocked on the door saying my dad sent him to check the fuse box. She let him in. He stayed for about an hour and left."

"Good grief, that is strange. Did your dad get a bill?" Ellen, the accountant, appreciated the value of billing records.

"No. I believe the guy works for Ewing. The maid does not know his name. She said he was short and spoke Spanish."

A piano player arrived and set up within a few feet of them. Jazz music filled the room. Ellen calculated the chance that Sissy's goal was realistic. Find the man who came, get the maid to testify, and link the man to Carl Ewing.

"Are you sure that you want to pursue this? It won't change anything."

"Wouldn't you warn the other bathers if there was a shark in the water?"

"Yes."

CHAPTER 23

8 June 2018

Six months later, the clock on the bedside table read three-forty-five. The room was pitch dark. Carl sat up in bed abruptly, wet with sweat and his heart racing. The nothingness of his surroundings terrified him until he realized the nightlight burned out. Once oriented to the room, the dream was exposed as fiction and not fact. Still, unlike many of his dreams, he remembered this one vividly. The message, a premonition, rattled his brain. He dreamt he was an outcast, no longer married to his wife, rejected by his friends, and wanted by the police. Years of building a reputation, sucking up to a proper wife, listening to endless boring conversations were wasted; how did this happen? And then a thought flew by, and he snagged it. What did, in fact, happen was a whisper campaign against him. Carl was sure of it now; he had started one or two himself. Steve warned him a story was going around, Lefleur tried to get his attention, and now he was having a hard time getting jobs. It wasn't the economy; it was his reputation. The bitch was gaining traction.

"What the school board needs is a new member,"

Frank said as soon as Carl sat down at their table. Three of his friends gathered there, but Carl was early and hoped more would come.

"Who's coming off?" Carl asked.

"Jill the pill, that's who."

"I reckon I could run," said Carl as he stared at something distant, "I've got the time."

"Hey, brother, do you need some work?" asked Ted. "I'll try to help you out."

"I'd sure appreciate that, Ted. Work is slow right now." Carl turned to the waitress, "I'll have oatmeal." He knew how to steer a conversation.

"Oatmeal!" Greg laughed. "Work must be slow." He made a show of eating his bacon. "You should try the bacon." The airport was empty except for the men at the table and the airline staff at the counters.

"Seriously, Greg," Carl whispered, "I think someone is poisoning the water. June should be my busiest month, and I got nothing."

"You might be right, buddy," Greg looked around the room and then said, "a girl is going around town asking questions about you."

"Are you kidding?"

"I am just the messenger." Greg leaned away from Carl and stretched out his arms, palms first. "You should watch your back."

"I don't mean nothing against you. It just makes my skin crawl when a female tries to ruin a man's reputation."

"Me, too." His buddy commiserated and Carl laughed.

"What kind of questions is she asking?" Carl moved in closer to his friend and spoke more softly.

"She's asking for references for no reason. You know, like if you did something wrong."

"Do you have any idea who it is?"

Frank whispered in his ear, "Graham's the last name. She's checking out your past clients and asking other contractors about you."

"I'm not worried about her." Carl made his mouth a sideways slant.

"You know her, then?" Greg put down his fork. "In that case, you may want to talk with the witch." He winked. "What didge you do—knock down a flower-pot?"

"I should discuss it with her, but I'd hate to send her back to the hospital." He could start a whisper campaign as easily as she could.

"What hospital?" Greg looked at his watch.

"Her Dad said she spent some time at Greenwell Springs," Carl whispered.

Son, when you spread malicious gossip, always give a source, so it's not coming from you.

"Really," Greg's eyes rolled.

"Yep, she's nuts," Carl nodded sagely. "Well," He stood up slowly. "I'd better go finish the job I got." He left, looking downtrodden and leaving most of his oatmeal in the bowl. If he was in a reputation war, he was going to be damn sure he won it. He texted Sheila: *I noticed the church playground fence needs some repairs. Okay, if I offer to do it for free?*

Zack's modern farmhouse insulated him from the noise outside and provided more room to pace. The windows, large enough for a fireman with an oxygen tank on his back, met the fire code, and it was reassuring to have his uncle next door. At this stage, he, unlike many patients, appreciated the medicine was helping him. Weissman attributed his gains to his intelligence and the emotional intelligence of Martin. In therapy, they worked to strengthen Zack's insight into his disorder and provide him with methods to determine what was unreal. Every morning he woke up to the unmistakable sound of his phone ringing. Martin called at six-thirty on weekdays. On weekends, it was eight o'clock.

"Good morning, Zack. Come over, and we can have breakfast. How did you sleep?"

"Good," he said.

And subsequently, the schedule continued. Up, medication, then breakfast with uncle Martin, and chores. Following chores, there was a shower, then dinner, then quiet time alone, and then lights out. They exercised together. Picking up the yard, hiking through the woods, fishing off the bank, and working on the farm machinery—all weekend activities. Zack did everything with Martin except attend church. On Sunday, Zack prepared the meal.

Even though Zack was a crack shot with a rifle, he did not enjoy hunting with his father. His walks with Martin were a pleasurable experience; they both appreciated all forms of wildlife in north Louisiana. Occasionally, Martin took him on boat rides down the bayou that formed the farm's boundary to the west. While boating, they nearly bumped the craft against an alligator, six feet long. Martin idled the outboard motor. He was not sure Zack saw it at first. Alligators, even to experienced people, look like logs floating in the water, until the head moves fast and in a straight line. Once they are moving, they attract attention. When an alligator swims, there is a big V-shaped wave behind him as the water parts. When one gets up close, the eyes draw attention. They lock eyes on you, taking your measure.

"See that gator over there? She must have a nest nearby." Martin pointed to the two large eye sockets and prehistoric snout skimming the water. "The head travels like a torpedo aimed at a target."

"I see it, uncle Martin! He's looking at us." The alligator's head disappeared under the water, and the surface became utterly calm.

"They existed when dinosaurs roamed the earth." Martin turned the boat's motor off. "He's hiding underwater to catch something. Let's hang around and see if he comes back up." After five minutes, the alligator appeared and looked around. "You would not want to be boating with an alligator under you."

"I know, uncle Martin."

"Gators usually leave people alone, but he would surely eat that dog if given a chance." Martin pointed to Zack's dog, Sybil. "Be careful of them."

"Yes, sir."

This summer was happy for both Zack and his uncle. Zack drove himself to his doctor visits, managed his medication, and the daily calls between Martin and Dr. Weissman had all but vanished. Martin felt comfortable calling her and wanted to call, but he had no legitimate reason to contact her during the summer. Zack was coping exceptionally well. He took care of himself and took care of his dog. Martin had not been disturbed during the night, and their dinner conversations, although not deep, were satisfying. It was a wholesome and healthy lifestyle for both of them.

While they ate breakfast, Martin threw out a topic for conversation. "You know what? Life gave you and me lemons, and we turned them into lemonade."

"I like lemonade."

"Me, too. What do you and Dr. Weisman talk about, if you don't mind my asking?"

"I don't mind." Zack was slow with his conversation. He seemed to be deliberately slow with every word. "Everything," he said finally.

"Do the college boys bother you anymore?"

"They don't know I am here," Zack said confidently.

Sheila called Martin several times a week to check on Zack, and she continued to see Dr. Weissman as a patient herself without her husband's knowledge. They united to provide Zack with a model environment. By now, Sheila and Martin hoped to allow Zack more freedom, and she wanted to invite them to her house for dinner to celebrate his birthday.

"You know, you have an appointment today. Why don't we talk to Dr. Weissman together about what's next in your future?" Martin showed him a list of questions concerning return to school, venturing into the community, or getting a job. "Do you mind if I go?"

Zack drove them. When they arrived, Martin followed Zack through the gardens and up the stairs to the entrance of the clinic building.

"It's on the first floor," Zack said as they passed by the elevators. Zack walked straight to the waiting room door. He had made this trip many times.

"Good afternoon, Brenda, I brought my uncle Martin." Zack put his hand on the plexiglass window while they talked to Brenda sitting behind it.

"It's good to see you again." Brenda flashed a smile.

"Is Scott here? I would like him to meet my uncle."

"He's here," Brenda said. "Right now, he is taking a patient to the lab, but I will let him know when he gets back; Zack, would you like a coke? I also have chocolate chip cookies today." Brenda glanced at Martin again.

"None for me, thanks," he said. Brenda left briefly and returned with a cheerful red can of coke and a paper plate with three cookies.

"A snack makes the waiting easier, especially in the afternoon," she said to Martin, as she handed the cookies to Zack through the window. When she passed the coke through to Zack, she looked again at Martin.

"Are you sure you don't want anything to drink, Mr. Hayward?" He was surprised that she remembered his name.

"I am sure, but I appreciate your offer. Ahh, can I talk to Dr. Weissman for a few minutes toward the end of the session?"

"Of course," Brenda beamed. "I can make that happen."

"I usually sit here," Zack said, "away from the window," He used the plate of cookies to motion to the area. They walked to the chairs and sat down. "I like coke, but I wish they had tea." Zack selected his chair and stuck his feet out, causing a trip hazard.

As promised, Scott appeared in the waiting area, looking for them.

"Hey, buddy. How are you doing?"

"Quite well, Scott. This is my uncle Martin," Zack smiled as they shook hands.

"Nice to meet you, sir." Scott held out his hand to Martin, who immediately stood up and shook it. Scott was a big young man, but his demeanor was gentle.

"It's nice to meet you. Thanks for taking such good care of my nephew."

"You're welcome. Zack and I have a lot in common." Martin admired the art on the walls. There was nothing abstract about it, and he wondered if that was intentional.

As the two men stood talking, Zack devoured the last cookie just as the nurse called him back. He bounced over to the door that frightened him so much the first time he saw it.

"See ya, Zack," Scott called after him, and left the waiting room, leaving Martin to his thoughts. In about forty minutes, the nurse guided him to Weissman's study.

"Martin, I'm so glad you came today." She stood up and motioned him to the couch beside Zack while she took the chair. Her eyes expressed concern.

"Forgive me for coming unannounced, but his mother and I have some questions. Zack is doing so well. I am proud of him."

"That is wonderful," she picked up her pen and tablet. "Zack's blood work is due today, and we are going to weigh him. We could talk while he is getting those procedures if you like." Dr. Weissman finished filling out a form and gave it to Zack. He went to the lab by himself now. When they were alone, Elaine looked concerned as she asked Martin about him.

"No, really, he is doing so well. As far as I can tell, he is taking his medication and eating healthy. He has a dog now. He takes care of the dog, and he also tends our vegetable garden. Sometimes he is in the field with a hoe." Martin remembered he had not turned off his cell phone. He reached into his pocket and turned it off. "His mother and I are interested in how we should proceed, and that is why I am here. I was wondering if he should resume his schooling, or should he try to get a job?"

Weissman started with compliments. "Zack loves and trusts you. He says you are the conductor."

"I'd say, I'm more of the chef, but I'm glad he enjoys the arrangement. The relationship is beneficial for me, too. We have a consistent routine."

"Routine is so stabilizing for any mental upset, so kudos to you for maintaining it so well, and we want him to progress in a linear fashion, but I must warn you that setbacks are so common we expect them. You should never blame yourself. It is part of the illness, just like a relapse is a recognized element in many diseases. Let me assure you of that upfront."

"You may not find this information in a textbook, but the dog is a phenomenal aid. If Zack sees something frightening, he looks at her reaction."

"She's a reality check for him." She put her pen down. "Martin, you are a Godsend for me, too; your hope and dedication is refreshing. I'd rather talk to you than a colleague because you are open-minded to new ideas. Is he doing any writing now? Sometimes they stop."

"If there is writing, I don't see it. Zack used to write all the time. I've read stories he wrote before he got sick." He shifted in his seat. "They aren't bad; in fact, they are pretty good for his age."

"Maybe you could encourage him to write stories again and read them together. It could be a nonintrusive method of monitoring Zack. Many people who have schizophrenia excel at painting, too."

"I'll suggest painting and make sure he has plenty of paper—or does he need a computer?"

"A computer for word processing is fine, but no internet under any circumstances."

"I have another question. His mother wants us to come to their house for his birthday party. We make a big deal out of birthdays in our family. Would it be all right to go?"

"It would be unwise to have a party at their house, too many memories there and too much pathology. I'm walking on a razor's edge by telling you this because of patient confidentiality. What about having it at the farm and asking only his parents and his grandmother?"

Martin was surprised to hear the words family and pathology. He suspected his sister minimized her problems.

"We will host it, then"

"As far as work and school are concerned, let's ask him if he feels ready. If he is, we can ease him into it. I think Vo-Tech is a good place to start. In another year, maybe he can go to college. But even then, I prefer him to live in an apartment, not in a dorm, and never at home."

"Never at home? What was going on there?" Martin glanced at his feet. "Sorry, I understand you can't tell me." She did not respond, and he nervously added, "Would you like to come to his party?" Martin did not know where that question came from, and he blushed.

"I wish I could, but it would be unprofessional," she said. "That is not to say that I don't very much enjoy spending time with you." Still holding his face with her eyes, she continued, "Zack should be here soon, and there is one more thing to discuss."

"Sure, but if I can interrupt, I don't want to forget to ask you this. I have a meeting in New Orleans in August. I'll be gone for four days, max. What should I do about Zack.?"

"I think he can handle four days. Someone can still check on him by phone. Zack is going to be one of the lucky ones. He may even settle down, get married, and have a proper job. It's a credit to you, Martin. Is there anything else? If there is nothing else, I have something to discuss."

"No, you have answered all my questions."

"Zack and I have talked about your relationship, and he would like us to inform you of his medical condition. In other words, he would like for me to share private information with you."

"You mean the things you tell his mom and dad; you would also tell me?"

"I mean that Zack would prefer that I share medical

information only with you."

"His parents won't like that, I am sure."

"Zack is adamant about it." Dr. Weissman conveyed the finality of Zack's decision with her facial expression. "If not you, he would insist upon someone else."

"Carl would be furious," Martin said, thinking aloud.

"We don't have to decide anything now. You have time to think about it and talk to Zack yourself. Remember, it is not unusual for a young man Zack's age to seek independence from his parents. Young adults who have schizophrenia are no exception."

The color came back into Martin's face.

"Zack and I will talk about it. But actually, I cannot imagine that his parents would agree."

"That's the point, Martin. Your nephew is old enough to make decisions like this one without their permission." Dr. Weissman looked at the clock on the wall. "Give it some thought, and we can talk about it again." There were two quick knocks on the door.

"You two can talk it over and decide what is best."

CHAPTER 24

2 July 2018

A fresh supply of first year residents gathered for morning rounds in the conference room, a few feet from the psych unit. Half the room awake and squirming while the other half was heavy-lidded and slow. Night call for a psychiatry resident is horrendous.

"Lord have mercy if it ain't the worse day of the year," croaked a nursing supervisor. "I shudda taken my vacation, no matter how hot it is. Look at 'em; they can barely walk." It's an insider joke that July is a bad time to get sick if you are going to be admitted to a teaching hospital.

"Insight," Dr. Weissman began her introduction to schizophrenia, "And by insight, I mean intuitive understanding, not incite as in inciting a riot." She assessed the young doctors as a few more straggled to their seats. None of them acknowledged her attempt at humor.

On call residents spend all night in the emergency room answering consults: psychosis, suicide attempts, manic behavior, drug abuse, conversion reactions, Munchausen's syndrome, Munchausen's syndrome by proxy, amnesia—oops this one's a brain tumor, call the neurosurgeon. They brought a vending-machine breakfast, candy bar or Honey Bun, and stale coffee. She allowed them to eat because Dr. Weissman thought the morning lecture should be informal. She kept a strict time limit, no more than 20 minutes. In truth, her morning report was merely an introduction to a ponderous reading assignment.

"When a patient has schizophrenia, they lose mental capacity in many areas, not the least of which are social context, executive planning, and sustained purposeful work. They are easy targets for hustlers. If they possess money, drugs, or anything valuable, someone will con them. Likewise, internet sites motivate them to do things they would never have thought of by themselves.

"Their own families may have difficulty in connecting with them. Schizophrenic patients have a flat affect, so the face is almost always expressionless, making ordinary social interactions awkward. They lack humor, just another trait that keeps them apart from the usual commerce of society. Figures of speech are challenging for them. As you interview your patients, keep these traits in mind.

"The problems in motivation and planning stem from a flawed ability to concentrate. The schizophrenic brain, filled with pop-up ads and sound effects, can't cope. But by far, the biggest challenge for them and their caregivers is that they lack insight into what is happening to them. They rarely seek help. Your schizophrenic patients will be referred to you by a concerned friend or relative, and most of them will wonder why they are in your office.

"Your job is to gain their trust and provide them insight into what is happening to them. It is hard work and frustrating at best. Our patients live in an alternative world often populated by free-floating paranoid delusions, and it is hard to reach them. These individuals withdraw from social interaction. They don't understand small talk, which is the ultimate ice breaker for making friends. If you think of conversation as throwing a ball back and forth, the person with schizophrenia will throw the ball back in a bizarre way. It will be too high, too low, or too far to the side for you to catch it. At other times, they don't throw the conversational ball back at all by giving no response or ending the conversation in the middle.

"As an experiment, try talking to a friend while in your mind you are concurrently subtracting sevens from one hundred, 93,86,79,72 etc. This exercise will help you experience what they feel when they have a conversation with you." Dr. Weissman could see that interest in her topic was flagging.

"All parents know their son or daughter has changed and will feel uncomfortable about it, but they are not likely to recognize that the change is due to a disease until the symptoms have advanced to psychosis, an unfortunate fact. The best time to teach the patient insight into his disease is in the early stages. The longer a patient suffers delusions before treatment, the poorer the prognosis. Consider this diagnosis, which is not rare, whenever you evaluate troubled patients, especially teenagers."

Dr. Weissman picked up her briefcase and headed toward the door as the house staff, doctors, but still learning, gathered their papers, computers, candy wrappers, and coffee cups in preparation to leave. One resident, Holly Draper, stopped her just as she was exiting the door.

"Dr. Weissman, do you have a minute?"

"Of course, Dr. Draper."

"My brother has schizophrenia. He joined the army when he turned nineteen, but he had a psychotic break in basic training, and they discharged him. As you said, I wish we had noticed the symptoms you described earlier; we could have saved him from the embarrassment."

"Early diagnosis is an exciting area of research. We suspect that if it were possible to treat the illness before the patient has suffered a psychotic break..."

"What are my chances?" Holly interrupted.

"Your chances?"

"What is my risk of developing schizophrenia?"

"Is there a family history of schizophrenia, other than your brother?"

"My aunt may have had it. She committed suicide at age thirty-six."

"In women, schizophrenia develops around the age of thirty. Your brother is a first-degree relative, and his diagnosis puts you at a 10% chance of inheriting it."

Dr. Draper lifted her backpack to her shoulder, ready to go.

"If you have any other concerns, don't hesitate to call me.".

"I won't hesitate."

Sheila sat in her mother's kitchen to wait for her sisters. A cake with white icing covered with blueberries and strawberries to look like an American Flag decorated the table.

"I've been seeing Dr. Weissman, Mama."

"Did the disease come from Carl's side, dear?" Dixie adjusted the position of the dessert plates and forks while they talked.

"I guess it must have, but he doesn't want to talk about it."

Dixie decorated her home for every holiday. July was an entire month of a patriotic theme.

"When our ancestors fought in the revolutionary war, they protected our freedom to pursue happiness. Are you happy, Sheila?"

The sheer reliability of her mother's life—every holiday observed, every funeral attended, every birthday remembered, and tea served every afternoon was soothing, if rigid.

"I loved the life you gave us."

Jean was the next to arrive. She let herself in and placed a cheesecake on the table with a flourish.

"I have news! Bill just called me. They are exhuming the body—Trent Wilson's body."

"Why?" Sheila spilled the tea she was pouring.

"Bill said, someone questioned the cause of death; he didn't say who."

"Sissy told me she was worried about her father's death, but I didn't suspect this; they buried him almost a year ago."

"Bill said that situations like this are rare, but he heard the story from a waitress at the diner, so I guess someone leaked it." Jean brought decorated paper napkins to the table.

Sheila was talked to herself because no one was listening to her. "She wanted to tell me about her father's dispute with Carl."

"Sheila, what is happening to the front of your house?" Jean asked as Martha walked in.

"Carl's bored, so he is improving our curb appeal, never a dull moment at the Ewing's." Sheila cut the cake and served everyone, while Jean made more tea, and Martha put her flowers in a vase. "It's a slow summer for him. At least he has a job that is taking longer than he expected right now." Jean motioned with her eyes to join her on the other side of the room.

"How are you and Carl doing?"

"Not too bad; it's better now it is just the two of us."

Across town, Carl arrived at Miss Sarah's house five minutes early. He parked on the curb instead of in the driveway. The fresh paint in contemporary colors contrasted with the muted neutrals of the neighborhood. Sarah insisted they allow Carl to hire the interior decorator when Sissy bowed out. Miss Sarah's gonna like this, he thought. He took a breath mint out of the package, peeled off the waxy white paper, and put it in his mouth. Something was holding him back. He stepped off the runner and then remembered his bill carefully handwritten and slipped into a standard yellow envelope. Take your time, he thought, discuss each item on the list, even if it takes three hours.

"You overcharged us, and the work is subpar," Ellen

said after reviewing his bill.

"What does your grandmother say? I'm working for her, not you. Where is she, anyway?"

"It doesn't matter what my grandmother has to say because I have her power of attorney now."

Carl exploded with the mounting fury of a man double-crossed.

"Well, don't that beat all, taking over that sweet lady's money. I should report you to the Council on Aging."

"I had a housing inspector check the house. My punch list is here, and I want the work redone before I pay the bill." Ellen stood up from the kitchen table to signal an end to the conversation.

"Oh, no, Ellen. You want to wait a month so she can live in the house a while." Carl tried a ploy: convince them; they made a promise they had not made.

"You knew we were never planning on living in it. We want to sell, and we can't until you make the repairs."

"You are going to pay me first." Carl slumped in his chair, and his eyes became vacant, cold, and unfocused.

"No, Carl, you are going to finish the work, and then I will pay you." Ellen's voice did not waver this time, but he could see that she was shaking when she recited the punch list from memory. He had never hit a woman in his life, but she tempted him to do it now. He stood up and grabbed the list out of her hand.

"You are gonna wish you hadn't tricked me." Carl tore the paper into little pieces, which fluttered to the floor. "I am entitled to the money. I did the work. Sarah would never treat me like this."

"It's time for you to go." Ellen tried to show him the door, but he blocked her.

"What if I don't go now? What if I sit down and wait for your grandmother?"

"She's not coming. She is waiting for me to pick her up and drive her to Dallas."

Carl was breathing hard but deliberately. "Don't worry, MA'AM, I'm going to fix your problem, and you're going to like it," Spinning around, he let himself out of the house. The dog followed him, and Ellen locked the door.

As soon as he could be seen from the street, he regained his composure to avoid any neighborly concern. He picked his way down the narrow sidewalk toward the gate and waved at a random person passing by in a car. The little poodle, the dog that Miss Sarah pampered like a child, followed him out and into the street. "Sarah will figure Ellen let you out, Sasha. She'll be so upset nothin' will matter except findin' her dog."

Power of attorney. He never expected it, but he should have. Carl aspired to be Sarah's sole heir. Instead, Ellen dismissed him like a hired hand. He was a chump to hold Sarah's hand while her granddaughter waited for the money. The rich git rich because they know how to do it, he thought. They know how to pull strings. Sitting in the driveway of her house, he considered Ellen's complaints. The conscientious inspector actually got up on the roof and verified that the invoice charged them for expensive shingles instead of the cheap ones, not a building code violation, but Carl would have to refund some money. How on earth did the inspector determine one coat of paint instead of two? The building code violations: safety issues, corner's cut, profound disregard for the safety of others. It was not bad, except Ellen figured out how to make it cut into his profit.

His phone, lying on the passenger seat, came to life. The screen showed a number, no identification.

"Yeah," he said.

"I thought you should know they are digging Trent's body up in the morning."

"Who is this?" Carl tried to place the voice.

"It's a friend."

"Lefleur?"

CHAPTER 25

5 July 2018

The delicious smell of marinara sauce bubbling on the gas range filled the home, even penetrating every one of five bedrooms. Green leaf lettuce, the leaves washed and patted dry by Zack, lay next to Martin, who chopped celery, olives, and onion. Dixie Hayward brought the cake, her specialty, a spice cake with caramel icing, topped with nineteen candles.

"Your folks will be here in ten minutes. Don't forget the spaghetti." Martin checked if he needed to shave. "Mama, I'm going to change my shirt. Let me know if you guys need any help."

"Between the two of us, I'm sure we can make spaghetti," Dixie turned toward the pantry. "And the bread, where is it?"

"Zack can find it. I'll be right back."

Dixie raised her four children in this house. None of them shared a room, a luxury back then. The kitchen, decorated the same as she left it, was modern again. Spacious with an enormous table and a pantry built for serious food storage. It's funny how styles change. She never had what she called a "pass-through kitchen," popular in the sixties and seventies. Dixie liked to quip the families passed through the kitchen on the way out to eat. Instead, she cooked the noon meal for ten farm-hands during the growing season. Physically fit men with healthy appetites and a love of sugared iced tea gathered at her table where today they celebrated her grandson's birthday.

"I'm president, so I have to go this year." Martin said just before dessert.

"You are Farm Bureau president?" Sheila asked.

"For the parish, not the state."

"What dates are those exactly, Martin?" Carl put down his fork and took his black leather planner out of his pocket. "I don't have any problem with Zack staying here by himself. What do you think, Sheila?" Carl looked at his wife as if he wanted guidance from her.

"If his doctor says he is ready, I think it's fine." She sat beside Zack. "We'll check on him, Martin."

After cleaning his plate, Zack glanced at the four corners of the room, like people who steal a peek around their surroundings when they perform close work.

"Weren't you plannin' on going?" Carl looked at his wife.

"Something came up with the reunion committee; I can't go." Sheila waved away an errant fly. "The cake is incredible, Mama."

"Baby, you should go; I know how much you were looking forward to it. Wait, a minute." Carl perked up, "Zack could stay with me if you're worried."

Zack's knee set off, jumping under the table. Noticing this, Martin stood up. "Mama, goodness, it is late. Would you like me to drive you home?"

"No need, we have to be going, too. Carl gets up so early in the morning." Sheila stood up and helped her mother gather her things. "We'll leave the cake plate with you and get it later. Can we help with the dishes?"

"No thanks, we have a system for dealing with supper dishes."

"Well, if it works for you..." Sheila laughed. "Happy nineteenth birthday, Zack!"

When Sheila and Carl left, Martin probed the situation cautiously.

"Is it because of the voices you heard at home?"

"It's hard to explain."

"Try."

Zack did not reply. He looked around the room again.

"But you feel safe here."

"Yes." Zack showed no emotion on his face, yet both his knees pumped up and down rapidly under the table. "I'm safer here."

"So, you would feel comfortable staying here while I go."

"I would like to stay here. I've never loved any place more."

CHAPTER 26

15 August 2018

At nine in the morning, Aunt Martha received a text from her daughter.

Mom, I'll be home at three. Danny and Joe are coming, too. Can Zack have visitors?

Sure, Martin's next door if you need him.

He's not living with his parents?

No.

Don't cook; we'll bring a pizza and eat with him.

The odometer clicked off the number of miles a man has to go when someone ruins his reputation close to home. People talk: "He could be trouble; we don't know." "It's just gossip." "Yes, but why take a chance?" "Was he or wasn't he ripping off his partner?" "Guess we'll never know for damn sure." "Yeah, since Trent is dead."

A chance to bid a job forty miles south of Gower, extended by a family from West, Texas, picked up Carl's spirits. He pitched it like a pro, causing the retired couple to cross off every other contractor on their list.

"When you are building a swimming pool, you had better use an experienced builder. Even if you don't hire me, remember a pool is complicated. It needs to be safe, and they's a lot of regulations even way out here in the parish." By the time he reached the city limits, he had calculated all the potential accouterments surrounding a backyard pool: a pool-house with bathrooms, fire pit, outdoor cooking area, and tall, very tall to be safe, fence. The homeowners conceived the pool idea; he would supply the rest in good time, not to mention the added expense he planned to add for the distance from town. Carl's brother-in-law called before he got home.

"I have something that should interest you, a family matter. Why don't you come by the office this afternoon and we can talk about it; I'll let the staff go a few minutes early."

"Sure. You got my imagination spinning, Bill." Carl produced a throaty laugh.

"Park in the back," Bill said before he ended the call.

"After a quick stop at the post office, I'll be there."

Bill's SUV was the only car outside the beige stucco building. Hidden from the street, it caught Carl's eye only when he attempted to pass through the porte-cochere. There were six empty spots in the back; Carl estimated his truck was too big and backed out to park in the space for clients. He walked behind the office to the service door. The heat caused him to sweat. Bill was quick to answer the door, as if he was standing next to it, waiting.

"Come on in, Brother. It's happy hour. Jean disapproves of alcohol, so I wind down here before going home." Carl followed him to his office. "Those Hayward girls don't realize some people have stressful jobs," Bill said, looking backward.

The paneled walls struck Carl as an interesting

choice for a stucco exterior.

"Where'd you get the pecan paneling?"

"It's native pecan from a tear-down in Lake Charles. How you like it?"

"It's light, airy, and in great condition." There were two small windows with translucent shades for privacy and expensive cushioned leather chairs. Two of them, for clients, faced the desk. Bill's credentials, modestly displayed in blonde frames on the wall behind him, were an undergraduate degree from Tulane and a diploma from LSU Paul M. Hebert Law Center in Baton Rouge. On the other wall hung a magnificent painting done with southwest colors. Bill sat in the swivel chair behind the desk and produced two bottles of Yuengling Lager from the credenza's hidden refrigerator. He leaned back into his chair and said:

"Work going well?"

"So, so," Carl said. "It's been a little slow," He accepted a beer from Bill and cradled it in his lap. "Where'd you get that painting over there?" Carl pointed to it.

"We got it in Santa Fe. Do you like it?"

"I do. Don't know nothing about art; I admit that. But I do like the picture." Carl's head turned to survey the surroundings.

"Carl," Bill said with an advocate's voice, "I have some information that might be of interest to you. The trouble is, it's sensitive. Please do not tell anyone you heard it from me."

"You know I won't tell anyone," Carl said in a solemn voice.

"The District Attorney is looking into the death of Trent Wilson. It seems he may have been electrocuted.

To me, it looks like an accident. But to his daughter Sissy, it's a homicide, and she thinks you had a motive." Bill, who had already removed his jacket, unbuttoned the top button on his shirt. "I can't fathom how she got that idea, but she is pressuring for a full investigation."

"Poor girl," Carl took a swig of beer. "Of course, she is distraught over the loss of her father. Who wouldn't be? But she is grasping at straws." Carl took another sip and observed Bill's reaction.

"I just wanted you to know what's being discussed," Bill said with an unreadable face. "Any man who works for his living is going to make someone mad; it is inevitable. This type of accusation is different. The stakes are much higher."

"They can talk about it all they want, but they can't prove anything because I had nothing to do with it." Carl shrugged it off. "I had every reason to want Trent alive because we were doing construction together in Cotton Valley. I lost money when he died."

"Yes, well, let's leave it at that. The other piece is not gossip. Your son signed a Ulysses contract with Martin." Bill shuffled through documents on his desk and handed it to Carl, who immediately saw it was "legalese" and looked up at Bill to explain it.

"A Ulysses contract is likely to be the first step to giving Martin a power of attorney for Zack. In that case, if something were to happen to Zack, Martin might inherit Zack's trust, not you."

"You mean the money we get when Miss Dixie dies?" Carl was confused because he had read and copied the will himself, and her money went straight to Sheila and him.

"No, I'm talking about the trust the Haywards created for all of their grandchildren."

Carl sat stone-faced upon hearing the news. His eyes converged on the wall behind Bill, who expected a conversational exchange and got nothing. After an uncomfortable silence, Bill felt the need to say something.

"Again, I beg you to keep the source of this information confidential."

Carl ignored the pulsation of blood in his ears and refocused on his conversation with Bill. "Thanks, but I ain't worried. Sheila would never arrange something like this behind my back."

"Sheila may or may not know about the contract with Martin because Zack is eighteen now; he is a free agent. But it gets worse. I don't know how to tell you this except just to say it. Jean told me Sheila is unhappy in the marriage."

"Who else knows about it?"

"Only Jean. It's probably not news to you, but just in case, I'm telling you now."

Carl was dumbstruck. "Is she planning on leaving me, Bill?"

"I don't know. All I can tell you is that Sheila is unhappy enough to talk to Jean about it."

"What is a Ulysses contract?" Carl recovered his composure.

"It's a special contract they often use in medicine. If a mentally ill patient is not taking his medication or if he is a danger to himself or others, the person named in the contract can force him into the hospital against his will."

"Why would anybody talk Zack into doing that?" Carl finished his drink and stood up, looking down on Bill, still seated at his desk.

"I don't know." Bill cringed when he saw Carl's face. Carl was shaking and blushing as though he was ill or might cry. He put the bottle on Bill's desk so awkwardly that it fell and exploded into a million shards of glass, which they both ignored.

"And the trust?"

"Old man Hayward left more money to his grandchildren, than he left us, my friend."

"When does Zack get his trust?"

"He gets it at eighteen, but since Martin is still managing it. I doubt Zack is knows of its existence."

"Someone's going to be sorry," Carl said as he stood up in front of Bill, who was still sitting behind the desk. Bill stood up, too.

"Carl, I was too blunt. Forgive me. Let's talk about your options in this situation. You have choices. Maybe whatever is bothering Sheila can be remedied. try counseling, and PLEASE, please don't tell her you heard it from me."

"If something was to happen to Zack, would Martin get the money, or would Sheila get it."

"Right now, Sheila would inherit it. Zack can legally leave it to whomever he chooses."

"I owe you, Bill." Carl did an about-face; and fled the office with Bill running after him.

On the farm, all lights were on, in preparation for a visit from the cousins. Danny, Becky, and Joe drove up the road to Martin's house at 5:30.

"Which house is Zack's house?" Joe asked as they waited for Martin to open the door. Becky shrugged, "I guess it's the one with Zack's car in front of it."

"Somehow, that makes sense," said Joe.

"My goodness, the whole gang is here!" Martin hugged Becky and shook hands with Danny and Joe. "It's been almost a year since I've seen you."

"We were thinking about the same thing. How do you like having Zack for a neighbor?" Becky asked.

"We're getting on great." Martin was so pleased Zack was having guests that he did not even invite them in.

"Is there anything we need to know about his decision to quit college?" Becky asked. "We don't want to say the wrong thing."

"Not really. Zack can tell you about it. We're hoping he can go back."

"Looks like rain," Joe said. A dark cloud followed them to the farm and stalled overhead, making the air cooler but menacing. "Seems like it rains every day."

"Yeah," said Danny. "We don't want it to rain on the food we brought him."

A far-away thunderclap hurried the conversation to a close.

"Y'all go on over," Martin said, pointing to Zack's house. "Tell Zack that I'm going to bed early and will say goodbye to him in the morning."

"Where are you goin'?"

"New Orleans, now git." He gave them permission to leave.

They left Martin's house, stopping at the car to grab beer and pizza before knocking on Zack's door.

Zack opened the door and grinned.

"Cuz!" Shouted Danny. "How ya doin."

"Good." He stood aside, allowing them to come in.

"We brought supper, your favorite, Sweep-the-Kitchen." He held the pizza box under Zack's nose. "Smell good?"

"Yes!"

"Where's the table?" Zack waved them toward the kitchen.

"This house is small but perfect for us. We should stay here instead of at mom's," said Danny.

Zack's dog, Sybil, who never met a stranger, and who smelled the pizza, jingled her collar charms as she ran into the kitchen.

"What a sweet puppy!" Becky squatted and offered Sybil a tiny bite of pepperoni. "Here you go. I like this dog, Zack; she looks like a Heinz fifty-seven; am I right?"

"I named her Sybil."

"Good choice."

"We brought you some beer since you are almost legal now."

"Thanks."

"In two more years, you will be able to buy your own beer." Joe surveyed the house, "Can I check out your new home?" He left them to take a quick tour.

Becky found paper plates and set them around the table. "Danny, grab those napkins from the sack and bring over the beer; the Miller light is for me."

"This is still my favorite meal after all this time," Danny was the oldest by five years.

"So, Zack, what's going on out here?" Becky asked.

"Martin is watching the corn grow, and I am trying to control the pigweed."

"Nice," Danny affirmed Zack's work. "Do you plan to join Martin in the farming operation?"

"He has asked me to."

"That works for us 'cause we don't want to lose the yearly checks we've been getting."

"I know Martin would like it; he has to be lonely,"

Becky said. She took a bite of pizza. "And," she added, "It would be awkward working for your dad."

Joe set a cold bottle of beer in front of Zack, and Zack drank it.

"Hey, I don't plan to work for my dad either," said Danny, who would later join his father in the car business.

"Nobody should ever work for their parents. It's not natural," said Joe.

"Amen to that," said Becky. "Can you imagine me sitting on a car in a bathing suit? What kind of parent asks a daughter to do that?"

The party lasted precisely two hours because Aunt Martha told them not to stay too long. She made Becky promise to get her brothers home at a decent hour and to be wary of overtiring Zack.

"Take care, Cuz," Joe said. "We love you."

"Enjoy the leftovers," Danny said.

Becky hugged him, and Danny gave him a high five.

The cousins left, and Zack consumed all the leftover beer. The effect was the opposite of his expectations. Not at all relaxed, he grew more restless and more alert. A red fox shrieked outside, sending him back to his bed. It's the beer, Zack thought, but the student yelled at him, *"It's not the beer, asshole! It's your feeble mind. You would be better off dead. Everyone would be better off if you were dead."* Zack pulled up the covers and curled into a ball. Maybe they will go away if they can't see me, he thought. Still, the college boys kept it up for hours, while the rain pounded the house until the sun began to shine, and Zack finally drifted off to sleep.

When Martin woke him at six-thirty with a phone

call, Zack had a hangover. He felt he had been awake all night. With raw determination, Zack made himself get up and walk over to Martin's house for breakfast, suffering from a headache that was splitting his head in two.

"Hey, partner," Martin was in a cheerful mood. He had cereal and milk, orange juice, and coffee set out on their dining room table. Zack slowly lowered himself into a chair.

"Zack, are you ill? You look sick to me," said Martin.

"The Chain Gang brought pizza. It made me sick."

"I'll let your mom know. Don't forget that you have your appointment with Dr. Weissman tomorrow afternoon. If you can't go, call your mom. And call to cancel your appointment."

"Okay." Zack didn't touch his food, but that was not unusual.

"I'll be in meetings and will have my phone off most of the day. And don't forget to take your pills, doctor's orders."

"I won't." Zack put his elbow on the table to prop his chin on the palm of his hand.

"I'll be back Sunday or Monday afternoon. Take your time eating breakfast and lock my door when you leave."

Martin drove three hundred miles before a pang of doubt descended upon him when he reached Metairie. He thought through his plans again. The drive home would take six hours, maximum, and Dr. Weissman stressed that Zack should be as independent as possible. Besides, both of Zack's parents were close by. But doubt transformed into indecision, and indecision transformed into action. The only action available— phone calls. Like a nervous parent, he cast about for reassurances by calling people, Sheila, his farmhand, and Zack.

Thirty minutes from New Orleans, his call to Sheila went to voice mail.

"Hey, I am almost to the hotel in New Orleans. Just calling to tell you that Zack has an appointment with Dr. Weissman tomorrow, and he has a stomach virus, not bad. Would you or Carl check on him? I am about to be in meetings and will have my phone turned off."

"Tom's call: "I ain't seen him today, but I kin check when I turn off the irrigation."

He then placed a call to Zack's cell phone. No answer.

A few minutes later, Zack called. "Uncle Martin?"

"Hey, buddy, I'm just calling to remind you about your appointment and see how your stomach is doing."

There was no answer from Zack. Martin sensed he was on the phone but not talking.

"Zack, are you there?"

"Uncle Martin?"

"How are you doing?" The minute the words fell out of his mouth, he regretted it. Zack must hate everyone inquiring about his health, his mental health, so often.

"Fine."

"Don't forget your appointment with Dr. Weissman tomorrow."

"Yes."

"You sound tired. How is your day going?"

Zack looked around his room while lying in bed. His uncle's call awakened him. The cousins had left a mess of dirty plastic plates, beer bottles, ashes, and vomit. *Or had he made the mess?* Afraid that his uncle would somehow be aware of it, he got to his feet and tried to clean up while he continued to hold the phone to his ear.

"Good, uncle Martin."

At first, Zack had no idea he had slept the entire morning, and he could not remember if he had taken his pill or not.

"What did you and the cousins do?"

"Cleaning now. The Chain Gang left a mess." Zack had always been a creator of nicknames. Some might say Martha's children were rabble-rousers, but Zack lovingly referred to them as the Chain Gang since he was twelve.

"I'm sure they did," Martin chuckled. "I'll let you get back to it and will call you tomorrow."

"*Zack, I hate to tell you this, but you are the worse nephew I have. I am going to call your Dad and ask him to teach you a lesson.*"

"Uncle Martin, please don't call my dad."

"*And he will come over and set you straight. You'd better get your shit together and get a job.*"

"It wasn't a setback; it was a misunderstanding," Zack said. "I am better now."

"*That's wonderful, but I have been talking to Dr. Weissman, and we think you are pathetic and lazy*"

"I am trying very, very hard to get better."

"*I didn't know that.*"

"I am, I swear!"

"*Tell him you'd rather be dead than living with the Nazi.*" That voice came out of nowhere.

"*You got to toughen up and learn how to take it, Zack. You can't cry like a baby,*" another voice said.

"I begged the college counselor. I begged, one more chance, please one more chance."

"*It's for your own good, and your parents love you,*" Ms. Evans said.

"Why does everyone hate me?"

"Because you are a dick, that's why," the college boy yelled.

Then Dr. Weissman said, *"you are different, Zack. You don't need medication anymore."*

Damn phone! Martin thought, when he lost his connection amidst the morass of New Orleans traffic. He had to wait until he got to the hotel to try calling him back.

"Hi! Zack. Sorry, I lost our call. Don't forget to go to your appointment tomorrow."

Zack replied: "Okay."

Martin then sent a text to Sheila that he had checked in with Zack, and everything was fine.

Zack suffered from the physical effects of too much drinking. The alcohol lowered his blood sugar and dehydrated him. But more than that, the experience disoriented a finely tuned connection to reality. Zack's thinking felt fuzzy, and he could not remember if he had taken his medicine or not. He tried to resume his usual routine, according to Martin's handwritten schedule posted on the door of his bathroom. He always showered before eating supper with his uncle. Then he had three hours of free time followed by brushing his teeth, changing into his pajamas, and in bed by nine. He was tired, but he wasn't sleepy, and he could not remember if he went to his weekly appointment or not.

"Missing your medication is a big mistake," Dr. Weissman said. *"Double dosing your medication is a bigger mistake,"* the college boy said.

Before going to bed, he let Sybil out to urinate, then he brushed his teeth and put on his pajamas. Martin refused to allow him to cover his windows to keep out the light as he had done at home and school, saying that night and day outside would help him get his sleep rhythms back. His curtains were thin and transparent, but he closed them every night.

After hours of lying in bed, his thoughts began to recede, and the lids of his eyes became heavy. Sleep fell upon him, and Sybil's steady breathing at the foot of his bed was soothing whenever he twitched awake. His visions were exceptionally vivid. In his dream, he was flying like a bird in empty outer space until he reached bodies of light. He picked up speed as he flew by the planets. There was a sense of peace with his trajectory created by a million distant stars. Suddenly, though still in sleep, the peacefulness was shattered. There was more and more light becoming more and more intense. Soon he would crash into the sun or ignite from the white-hot heat emanating from the direction he was flying. His legs stiffened in an attempt to slow himself down. He arched his back and held his arms out to change his course from the light that was blinding him.

"GRANDDAD, I'M OVER HERE!"

Awake, surrounded by a terribly bright light, so bright he was blind, he sobbed, frozen with fear. All that remained was a sense of touch. He could not see, he could not move, and he could not hear because there was no sound. Sybil nudged his face with her nose. The light, brighter than day, persisted for at least an hour before abruptly extinguishing, leaving him in a dark room with flames of light lingering in his eyeballs until they grew dim; and he saw his dog, his bed, and his window in the moonlight.

Rattled, he suffered from insomnia and was unable

to go back to sleep until daybreak. But sleeping during the morning was interrupted by phone calls. Too terrified to take them, he listened to the messages instead.

"Zack, this is Ruth. We wish you were never born."

"Zack, this is uncle Martin. I'm thinking about never coming home.

Hi, Zack! This is Brenda at Dr. Weissman's office. We are cutting you off."

He attempted to follow his schedule but found it too hard. Did he, or didn't he, take his medicine this morning? He could not remember. Later he tried to get dressed and leave the house, but fear and fatigue kept him from going anywhere. Thoughts of something grisly outside the house haunted him.

"GRANDDAD, I'M OVER BY THE PICKER." But his grandfather did not hear him because of the noise; the roar of the cotton picker drowned out everything now.

Sheila called Zack to remind him about his appointment, but failed to reach him. After trying several times, she got in her car, determined to check on him. Carl's phone call stopped her before she got out of the cul-de-sac.

"Hey Baby, I'm going to the Martin Plantation this afternoon to check up with Zack. Since Martin ain't there, I'd better go today."

"Can you go now? I'm worried because he doesn't answer his phone, and he has a doctor's appointment this afternoon."

"Sure. I've been trying to call him, too. I bet his phone is out of battery or broken," Carl said.

"Martin talked to him last night."

"Then I'll be the one to see him today." Carl used his

syrupy voice, implying infinite patience.

Sybil heard someone at the door and started barking.

"Violet, this is your Dad," said Carl, banging. "I am right outside your house. Are you home? I see your car out here."

The door opened tentatively, and Zack stood in his boxer shorts.

"Dad?"

"Gosh, Son. What are you doing in your pajamas?" Carl sounded patient and kind, almost warm.

"Nothing." Zack felt naked and afraid. The college boys left, but they might be back any minute, and he heard the picker right outside his window.

"You missed your appointment. The doctor's office has been calling us." It was the Nazi, and he carried a handgun.

"They have?" Zack stood in the doorway. Carl had to brush by him to get into the house. Zack jerked back.

"Oh, you're surprised at what I brought you? Is that it?"

Zack stared at the gun.

"I brought you this gun for protection." He carried an old leather bag on his shoulder. "This here is a handgun. You remember how to shoot it, right?" Carl walked into the kitchen and placed the gun gently on the table. Reaching into the large leather bag, Carl said, "There's ammo, too." He put the extra bullets neatly beside the weapon. "In case you need more." Carl looked in the refrigerator.

"Martin left you out here all by yourself, and I figured you needed protection. You never know what's in the woods behind the cornfield."

Zack stood there, confused. He looked at the clock, wondering if the appointment was yesterday.

"I'm leaving now; take care of yourself, Violet. Martin ain't here to protect you."

Carl excelled as a puppet master on the job site. Each sub and both homeowners, unwilling participants in a pitiful farce of misunderstandings, while Carl alone controlled the production. He was the writer, director, and producer of twenty months of live-action, if the project was a new house. Years of experience prepared him to direct off-site and in other venues.

"Zack's doing good, Baby. He is dressed and planning to drive to his appointment soon. The phone? Oh yeah, he dropped his cell phone in the commode, and it don't work now. That's why you can't call him."

By nightfall the second night, Zack was barely rational.

Exhausted, he lay in bed with his eyes closed. Was he asleep or not? Around midnight, he woke up abruptly to see light streaming into his room again from the window. The light was so intense he saw it with his eyes closed. Grasping for reality checks, he looked for his phone, but it was lost. The wall clock in the kitchen read twelve o'clock, but he had no idea if it was midnight or noon. Sybil seemed spooked, but she was not barking.

From the kitchen, he saw the light coming from one direction—the north window of his bedroom, something he had not noticed the night before. On the other side of the house, the windows were dark. He got in bed with the covers over his head to hide. For an hour, he lay in bed, clutching the bedclothes and shaking with dread. The light was so powerful it shone through the sheets, and it was through the bedsheets that he observed it extinguish itself suddenly. It took five more hours for him to recognize that daylight was dawning. He looked at the kitchen clock and saw it was six o'clock. *Six o'clock in the morning or in the afternoon? Is it time for my medicine, or did I take it already?*

Spotlighting was a sport Carl discovered while still a teenager. In high school, he and his buddies would liven up the weekend by harassing people at night in their own homes. If caught, they planned to plead it was a harmless trick, but they were never even suspected. They targeted females with a three-night exposure employing police-grade floodlights mounted to a truck's side mirror or door rim. Intense high beam lights are expensive, and illegal to use for deer hunting. Still, hunters buy them and store them in the garage, unsecured. It was easy for teenaged boys to pick one up for the night.

Once, in high school, Carl and his friends targeted a teacher whose husband left her for another woman. They could tell she was vulnerable by the look in her eyes as she tried to teach them algebra two. She could hardly make it through class without giving them an assignment to do, while she hid her face behind a book until she composed herself.

The first day after they spotlighted her, she looked tired and shaky. The second day after spotlighting, she overlooked buttoning a button on her blouse, and she wore a pair of shoes that were similar but did not match, which they found hilarious. On the third day, she called in sick, and they elbowed each other playfully when it was apparent they would have no math home-work for the weekend. Three days of spotlighting will make anyone crazy.

When the teacher did not show up on the Monday morning after the no-homework weekend, a friend told him a rumor was going around: her ex-husband was trying to spook her, and she left town. Three nights of spotlighting would create chaos. Carl was sure of that.

CHAPTER 27

18 August 2018

By the third day, Zack suspected the brilliant burst of light coming from an open field signified an enemy invasion. Once the aliens landed, they stealthily moved to headquarters at the trailer park nearby, which he now nicknamed the trainer park. There they learned to pass as humans, infiltrating every aspect of society. Everything makes sense now—except for time. Time peeled away. What month? What day? What time?

He fasted, neglected his dog, and failed to power his dead phone. Moreover, Zack was afraid to sleep. The aliens would eventually notice he was watching them.

"Don't take too many pills; it will kill you," Brenda said.

He occupied himself frenetically typing on the laptop (not connected to the internet), pacing the floor, and chewing his fingernails so that his fingertips had scabs. He had not bathed or brushed his teeth, and his medication was forgotten altogether. By nightfall, he was hysterical.

Martin called Sheila. "Dr. Weissman's office called this morning to say Zack missed his appointment."

"Why didn't they call me?" She said.

"I'll explain later, but check on him," Martin said.

"But they should have called me."

"Go now."

"Carl is there now."

"Okay, good. Let me know if I need to come home."

"Don't worry, Baby, I was just there and got his phone. If the store can't fix it, I'll buy him a new one, promise."

"Good. but I'm going to the farm now," Sheila informed him. "Martin says Zack never went to his appointment yesterday."

"Sure, he'll be glad to see you."

Thirty minutes later, Sheila called him back.

"My car won't start."

"Baby, I can't do everything. I'm here getting the phone fixed, and in two hours, I have to stake the corners of the swimming pool."

An hour later, *"Hi Mom, Dad brought my phone back. Can I call you later?"*

Around eight, she got another text: *"Sorry Mom, I forgot to call. Now I'm tired. I'll call you in the morning. You are the best mother in the world. I'm sorry if I scared you."*

On the third day, Zack lay in bed shaking, covers over his head, gun in his mouth, waiting for darkness and light.

"Stupid boy," the college boy spit at him. *"Stupid, stupid, stupid, stupid. You'll see what happens to boys like you. You would be better off if you killed yourself now."* They kept it up for hours.

The black truck drove, headlights leading the way through the night, windshield wipers intermittingly erasing a drizzle of rain. No sign of life in any of the three houses at the end of the gravel road. At the half-way mark, the truck left the rocks for a muddy ditch, climbing up the other side and bumping along the rows of beans before plowing its way to a turn row next to corn six feet high. Behind him, a wake of rutted earth marked his route. In front of him, the little house to the left of the big one sat still and dark.

Son, your brother ain't right; he has to go.

"It's alright, Baby," he said when Sheila's call lit up his phone. "I'm just remeasuring the dimensions on the Rafferty's job. I'm concerned they ain't right, and the trucks will be coming as early as 3 AM on Monday to dig the hole." He took a bite of a roast beef sandwich he purchased from Mickey's bar before leaving for Zack's house. "Sheila, what do you hear from your brother?"

"Nothing except he's leaving New Orleans tomor-row afternoon. So, you are not with Zack now."

"Naw, Baby. I dropped the phone off to him ages ago. Didn't he call you?"

"He didn't call, but he sent a text."

"You're too nervous. I wish you wouldn't worry so much."

Zack was awake, expecting a sudden flash of light on the third night. Unable to move a muscle, his wide-eyed stare paralyzed his face. The ideas were gone; his brain was numb, but he wasn't caught by surprise this time. He sat there, motionless, waiting it out.

A knock at the door. *Barking.*

The rigidity of his tense muscles interfered with getting out of bed to stand up. In a crouched stance, he pointed the gun at the knocking door.

"Son, it's me, your dad."

It was his father's voice. Something was fake about it.

"*Look out, he's going to kill you,*" the college boy said. "*You are so stupid; he will kill you, and you'd be better off dead.*"

"Zack, come out here; we need to talk."

"*Don't do it,*" yelled the college boy.

"I am not calling the ambulance again," Carl yelled.

No response from Zack.

"I'm leaving now. You are not getting any second chances. Zack, if you sign any contracts with Martin, I'll kill you." Carl reached for the doorknob intending to enter the house, then drew his hand back. "I'm not afraid of you, Zack. Just remember that." He placed Zack's phone on the porch swing and slogged through the mud to the cab of his truck.

"*Get out! Get out! Now! You heard what he said,*" the college boy screamed. "*Don't be stupid, stupid.*"

Zack couldn't see anything; the light blinded him. He reached deep in his jeans pocket, got the keys for his car, and started wandering in the rest of the house where it was dark.

"*Get in the car and drive like hell,*" Ms. Evans said.

Then he heard his uncle's voice.

"*Zack, the bombings, the lightning strikes, and the screaming you hear, it is your imagination.*"

"I know, uncle Martin. You told me before." At that moment, he felt something try to grab his leg, a hand coming out of the floor.

"GRANDDAD, I'M RIGHT HERE." The blast was brief. He heard shrieking and whimpering. "*It's in your imagination,"* Martin said again.

No! the light is real, he thought, and powerful. If he looked directly at the window with the light, he was afraid he would go blind because it was so intense. A laser from outer space? Part of the alien invasion? He twitched uncontrollably now and muttered nonsense words, blinding, blinders, eye-stopping, blindfold, scorched, incinerated, burned to the bone. The gun, clutched in his hands, his finger on the trigger, even though the trigger finger was numb.

"You are no good," the college boys hissed. *"You would be better off dead! You should turn that gun on yourself."*

CHAPTER 28

19 August 2018

It was 1 AM on Sunday when Martin reached the last stretch of Highway 80 to his home. He was thirty hours early, but he had an intuitive sense something was wrong. A missed appointment, broken phone, the battery in Sheila's car died—did not add up.

His sister's comment came back to haunt him. "You don't have children, Martin, so you don't know what it is like." Well, he knew what it was like now, having taken on the responsibility for his nephew. It was unlike anything he had ever experienced; Sheila was right about this one thing. Children become the priority when you have them. And for the first time, he understood Pam's motivation to deceive him. She was using pregnancy to handcuff him in the relationship.

Rain clouds eliminated the moon and the stars, making the cloak of darkness thick and heavy. He had trouble staying awake and was afraid he would miss the turn, but there it was, thank goodness! At first, he thought it was a fire, and the adrenaline poured through his veins. He was wide awake now. Would Zack know what to do? But in mid-turn, he did not see flames; It was electric light as if a crew from Hollywood was on the farm filming a movie. Maybe it was deer hunters, but if it was hunters, why was the light focused only upon Zack's house?

Martin cut the turn short to remain on the main road and reached for his phone to call the police. And then he understood: these were not hunters. The powerful spotlight shone on Zack's house, only as a deliberate attempt to scare him. Headlights off now, he slowed down so as not to create much noise. The light was so powerful it wiped out everything behind it, but Martin assumed a vehicle was in the field. He parked on the side of the road and doubled back on foot, walking in the rows of corn. Estimating where to exit the field to arrive at the phantom vehicle from behind, Martin held his breath. Success, he was standing behind a truck.

It was black, shaped like a Ford, with a black or dark grey toolbox in the back. The truck had a double cab with lights across the top. No teenager would own a truck like that, too expensive. The floodlight was top of the line. He knew who it was.

The motor was running to feed the air conditioner. Martin stood peering at the license plate. He wanted to be sure he got this number accurately, and the bright light in front of him was making it hard to focus on the license in the shadow. He took a flashlight out of his pocket, and he could read it now. It was a Louisiana plate 33890557 exp. 11/19. Martin then turned off his flashlight and made his way back to his pickup undetected. By the time Martin reached his own truck, Carl turned the spotlight off and accelerated the motor.

Up to now, Martin thought he knew Carl. But this, this trick was evil. There was nothing funny about it. To what purpose? What could this prank accomplish? His sister's words flooded him with sympathy. "You don't know what it is like to have children. I did the hard thing and did not leave him while they were minors."

Turning his attention toward Zack, he imagined the worst. Would Zack be dead with fright or suicide? Would he suffer a second psychotic break? Would he have run away in the dark?

There was no light coming from Zack's house. Martin knocked on the door—no barking. In case Zack was too frightened to open it, he called Zack's phone to warn him. The RING-RING coming from the swing on the porch startled him. The door was unlocked. He entered the house and flipped on the light switch. The smell in the house, rancid, sour, concerning. Martin noticed there was clutter. Bottles, pizza boxes, vomitus on the floor, but no smell of death. A search for Zack ended in the bedroom where he found him safe in the bed, clutching a gun and pointing it at him.

When Zack saw him, he said in a sing-song voice.

"Annie, get your gun. Get your gun, get your gun, get your gun, Annie."

"Zack, it's Martin."

"Get your gun; there were a million lumens in here, a million volts, a million watts, a million rays of light, bright white, LED, and fluorescent. Blinded by the light!"

"It was someone playing a trick on you. Everything is safe; you are safe."

"It wasn't a blue light. It was a bright light. We flew too close to the sun. It was too close; the light was magnified."

"Where did you get this handgun?"

Zack looked blankly at Martin.

"The gun, Zack, where did you get it?"

"The Nazi. Or maybe Annie brought it. Annie, get

your gun."

Dr. Weissman prepared Martin for a scenario like this when she learned he could give injections.

"Zack, I am going to give you your medicine. Help me," Martin said gently. Zack stretched his arm out willingly, and Martin gave a dose of Haldol.

"Do you remember when you stayed here for two weeks in the summer..."

When Zack fell asleep, Martin removed the gun from Zack's hand and went into the kitchen to get juice if he woke up. His lips looked dry, almost parched. When Martin returned, he noticed the dog had not moved from her spot on the floor.

Martin got a bowl of water and wet his index finger, and rubbed the dog's lips. She stretched out her tongue, to touch the moisture. Sticky blood covered her left leg. He tended to the wound, racking his mind over who brought Zack the gun and why Carl would want to scare him. A rifle was one thing, all boys in Gower had rifles, but a handgun was another. Its sole purpose is to shoot someone at close range.

Exhausted, Martin made another trip to his house, punched in the key code to open his gun safe, and locked both pistols, his and Zack's, there.

The empty beer bottles on the floor, of course, the chain gang did this; but Carl, why would he make it worse? And who left the pistol at Zack's house? Bewildered, Martin dozed off while sitting on the couch in Zack's living room.

CHAPTER 29

"Good morning, class." Dr. Weissman stood at the wooden podium facing 200 medical students in stadium seating. Four video monitors dropped from the ceiling. "Today the topic is antisocial personality disorder, formally known as sociopathic Personality. She glanced at the eager faces and estimated six sociopaths could be in an audience this large. It would be impossible to evaluate the body language of everyone. Still, already she noticed a young man in the front row who appeared to be far more interested in the topic than the others.

"Throughout history, there have been thousands and thousands of references to unprincipled and manipulative people. There are many cautionary tales in literature across the ages. I like the poem, 'The Spider and the Fly'." The essence of the disorder is the spider in this tale for children, who uses charming words to attain his goal. I guarantee you will encounter the wolf in sheep's clothing, but you are not likely to see sociopaths as patients. They do not seek therapy. Instead, you are certain to treat patients who fall into a sociopath's snare. As long as they hypnotize your patient by the spell of charm, you cannot help them. Do yourselves a favor and learn as much as you can about antisocial personality, even though this topic will never be a large portion of your board exam.

"The prevailing notion is sociopaths are not born the way they are. Rather, adverse life experiences create them. This theory supports their universal excuse: they are the victim and need our sympathy. Another notion, they are con men, but they are not. Here is the difference.

"Think of the ordinary con artist in New York City. He is not a sociopath. He will show a tourist a fake Rolex watch with a discount price. If the tourist tells him a firm "No!" He immediately starts looking for another mark. He's not mad; he just moves on to someone more gullible. People with ASDP are different. They persist and persist. If you turn them down, they'll send you flowers every day or offer you basketball tickets, a stay in their summer house, or a seat at an important table. The charm, the well-developed appearance of empathy, and the absence of remorse confound psychiatrists, social workers, and even Judges. Sociopaths hold grudges, they don't give up, and there is no line they will not cross.

"These emotionally stunted people cause harm out of proportion to their perceived abilities. Often, they carry out complicated scams that make no sense.

"In the video, you will see a financier who bilked billions of dollars from investors by creating the biggest Ponzi scheme in the history of the United States. He is being interviewed in prison by a professional journalist. Pay close attention to the words while he tells one lie after another. Note the charm he exudes when he gives the female reporter his undivided attention. Watch him cast about for something they have in common. And find the three follow-up questions he asks, in an attempt to surprise her with his insight. Notice the innocence of having no remorse whatsoever."

Dr. Weissman took the microphone from her lapel and turned it off. After the thirty-minute clip, she dismissed the class. The boy in the front row was slow to leave. He shyly made eye contact with her and looked at her for too long, before walking out the door.

Martin awoke bathed in the sunlight streaming through the window of the living room. Except for Zack's snoring, the house was quiet. The pill count confirmed his nephew had forgotten to take his medication. He picked up the trash and mopped the floor, leaving Zack to rest. Fortified with a cup of coffee, Martin went outside and stood on the porch as he placed the call.

"Carl," Martin said when he answered, "We need to talk."

"Hey buddy, what's going on?"

"Can you meet me at the farm this afternoon? I don't want to interfere with your working hours."

"Sure, what time will you get back from New Orleans?"

"How about 4:30?"

"I'll drop by then. Do I need to bring anything to Zack?"

"No, we'll just talk."

Martin was a natural-born peacemaker, and he was eager to refrain from causing any conflict between himself and Carl. He knew Carl was cunning. But the trick he played on Zack was dangerous. And the gun, there was an ominous message in the discovery of a handgun. The question he put to himself was: Is Carl that stupid, or is he that smart? And either way, why?"

The knock, precisely at 4:30, disturbed Martin. Carl was pretending nothing happened. At least Zack was still asleep in the cottage.

"Carl, thanks for coming."

"No problem, I ain't that busy today; How was your meetin'?"

"Good. Have a seat."

"Did you go to any good restaurants?"

"Acme Oyster, I always go there. Would you like something to drink?"

"Naw, I'm fine. You have a good stand of corn this year. Zack and I wandered all over this weekend." Carl did not sit down.

"I wanted to talk to you about spotlighting Zack's house last night." Martin got directly to the point in a non-threatening way, but Carl took it hard.

"Someone spotlighted Zack's house? Way out here? We got to do something about that jerk."

"Carl, I know it was you who did it," Martin said, trying to keep on point.

"That's just not true, Martin. I did not do that." Carl stepped around like a boxer in the ring.

"It was your truck."

"It wasn't my truck. Somebody is steering you wrong. Who told you this?"

"I wrote down the license plate number. See, I have it right here." Martin tried to give Carl the piece of paper, but he wouldn't accept it.

"I don't like that you are accusing me of something I didn't do. It wasn't me!"

"Let's compare this number with your license."

"This number you wrote don't prove nothing," Carl claimed. "If it's my license plate number you wrote on this paper, it's because someone is trying to frame me." Carl stuck his hands in his pockets.

"It's detrimental for Zack to become scared and disoriented."

"What does this conversation have to do with me? You should be talking to the son of a bitch that done it."

Martin blurted out, "You tried to scare Zack last night by spotlighting his house, and he has suffered."

Carl assumed a friendly and cheerful look. "Professor, I just don't know what you are talking about, but you have it all wrong. I can see how a father might play a joke on his son. The son would get his rifle, come out to investigate, and find the joker was his dad. The two of them would laugh it off and go into the house to share a beer. But I didn't do it, I swear!"

Martin retreated. It was impossible to connect with this man. "Why did you give him a gun? The doctor said he could be a suicide risk."

"It was your idea to leave him alone out here. He could have stayed with us."

Martin ignored the accusation. "Someone gave Zack a handgun."

"Zack has always had guns, and I taught him how to use them safely. Of course, I brought his gun to him. What father wouldn't do that? You are the one who left him out here by himself."

"Well then, I guess we have nothing more to talk about." Martin walked to the front door and opened it wide.

"I think you don't trust me, Martin. I like you, but I live a completely different life from you. You don't have a wife and children. You don't have grandchildren. As a MAN, I have taken on responsibilities you will never understand." Without another word, Carl left the house, got in his truck, and drove away.

Carl dialed Sheila's number once the farm was out of sight. "Hey, I'm over here at Zack's house. Somebody spotlighted him last night. Zack's okay, just a little scared. We've been trying to figure out who could have done it, but don't talk about it. We're gonna catch the jerk, so Martin and me don't mind if he does it again, now that Martin's back home."

"Who would do something so cruel?"

"A teenager. Anyway, don't worry. If it happens again, we'll call the police."

"When will you be home?" Sheila held a letter from Abel in her hand, still unopened.

His letter began with Dear Sheila, and he told her how happy he was to hear from her. It was formal until the end. My life has been full, and I married a wonderful woman—my best friend. We look forward to the reunion. Keep in touch. P.S. here is the letter I mentioned. Not sure why I kept it.

The second page was old paper and creased in such a way as it might tear when opened. The contents, written in Times Roman, comprised of three typewritten sentences.

Dear Lowell,

I have great and surprising news. Carl and I are pregnant, and no one knows but us, and now, you. He has asked me to marry him, and I will.

Your friend,
S.H.

In Dallas, Ellen spent her day cleaning up her townhouse. Exhausted, she showered and got into her bed with a book. After reading one chapter, her phone rang.

"Ellen, Sissy said, I am reading the doctor's report as we speak. The pathologist documented the burns on Dad's right hand. The heart was not enlarged and showed no sign of arterial blockage. The lungs are congested with blood and edema. The patient most likely died from heart arrhythmia, and with the burns on his hand, it could have been an electrocution. The cause of death is not conclusive." Sissy let the words speak for themselves. "It is signed by the Chief of Forensic Pathology."

"Gosh, sounds like you were right."

"It's conclusive now, at least in my mind. I'm going to get the new owners to send someone over to check the shower. The house passed its inspection when they bought it, but an inspector would not think to check for this."

If Ellen thought Sissy was on a fool's errand, she did not believe it now.

"I'm so sorry you are going through all of this and for so long." Ellen's cat jumped in her lap for attention. "I'm flying in tomorrow at 7:30 to see if he is finishing up on Grandma's house. Do you think Carl knows what you are doing?"

"I don't know, and I don't care. I'll pick you up at the airport."

CHAPTER 30

25 August 2018

At the crack of dawn, Sheila and Jean drove to Martha's antique store in the heart of downtown Gower.

"Sheila, did you remember the peach preserves?"

"Yes, and I made black and white cookies."

"Like they have in New York?"

"Why not? Martha says the food brings in more customers during the Peach Week than anything else."

Gower's peach parade and corresponding community events bring three thousand visitors and six-hundred thousand dollars into the city every summer. Everyone in town wears a Peach Festival tee shirt, eats peach ice cream, and buys homemade crafts to give away at Christmas.

"Do you remember Marianne Temple?" Sheila asked.

"Sure, is she here?"

"Not that I know of, but Lowell—you remember him—sent me a letter he received from someone pretending to be me over thirty years ago."

"You think Marianne sent it?"

"I wouldn't put it past her. She was conniving in high school. The letter said that Carl and I were getting married—shotgun. But the date on the envelope was a week before we started dating."

"She predicted it, the marriage, I mean. I know it wasn't shotgun."

"She must have wanted Lowell for herself." Sheila checked her hair with her hand.

"Your hair looks great; I love the color. Feeling better?" Jean parked. "What about Carl?"

"There is nothing simmering right now. And frankly, I can only deal with one family crisis at a time." She applied her lipstick. "Yes, I'm feeling much better."

"You definitely look better, well rested and happy." Jean turned off the motor and grabbed a box.

Sissy stood in the airport atrium and stared out the window with a view of the tarmac. She was searching the sky for Ellen's plane, expected to land any minute. Six other greeters surrounded her in an otherwise deserted area, twenty feet from the restaurant. A group of men sat in the café, engrossed in conversation. She could almost make out what they were saying from her outpost near the entrance until she unmistakably heard her name. She eased into the center of her small crowd and stood behind a man holding a sign for Hines Grain. Partly hidden by the sign now, raucous laughter behind her, she stole a glance at the table. They reminded her of a pack of dogs, and the leader was obvious. All heads turned toward him and mimicked his posture. Relieved that he did not see her, she insinuated herself deeper behind the other people to hide while keenly listening to the table's conversation. She noticed the chatter stopped as a plane came in from the west, circled the airport, and gently landed in front of her.

On the landing strip, workers wedged blocks under the plane's wheels and rolled the passenger stairs to place them in front of the plane's exit door. As Sissy watched their progress, she felt something on her neck like a breeze; no, it was a warm peppermint breath. Carl's disembodied voice said:

"You'd better watch your back." She turned to face him, but Carl turned his back toward her. He was already on his way to the men's room.

When Ellen walked into the terminal, she saw Sissy's ashen face.

"What's wrong? You look like a ghost."

"Carl Ewing, he threatened me just now."

Carl, seated at his table, tried not to stare at Ellen and Sissy. He wanted to, but he had to pay attention to what his friend was saying.

"I don't want to mess with you, but I got some news about that jack ass partner you had," Frank said.

Carl smiled his most engaging smile. "What's it got to do with me?"

"Nothing, just that his daughter is stirring up trouble by complaining the death was not a heart attack, and I heard through the grapevine that she has proof now."

"I guess they will determine the cause of death, eventually," Carl came across as very tired. "I've resigned myself to her antics." To the waitress, he said, "I'd love a refill of coffee. I was up late fixing leaky plumbing at Martin's house."

"Your brother-in-law can't do much on his own, I hear." one of them said, laughing. "That wife of his, she's married to a rich guy in Florida now. Bet you didn't know that."

"To tell you the truth. If he weren't Sheila's brother, I wouldn't trade nickels with him, but she loves him, so I gotta love him, too," Carl chuckled. His voice was confident, sensual, masculine—like music.

"Is your son living in a house on Martin's place?" Frank asked.

"Where did you hear that?" said Carl.

"I heard it standing in line at the grocery store. It was a couple of women talking about it."

"Zack's helping him out with repairs; hopefully, we'll get finished soon." Carl let his eyes wander to watch Ellen and Sissy leave the airport. "Sheila and I think he is going to change his mind and go into business with me."

Martin and Zack reestablished their routine after Zack's psychotic break. No one understood more than Martin how close they had come to disaster, not even Sheila, who was slow to understand what really sent her son over a cliff. They had been lucky, no ambulance, no ER, no inpatient stay. Martin, who had been at Zack's side every minute of the day since he came home from his meeting, made resolutions and he shared them with his sister, but not with the rest of us. Today would be the first day he left Zack alone since the meltdown.

Beginning with breakfast, which Martin brought to Zack's house, he made a mental list. He checked the front door of Zack's cottage. Zack had not locked it the night before. He needs a cue to lock his door at night, Martin thought. He set the breakfast box on the table and looked around the house—dirty dishes in the sink and towels on the floor. He would address housekeeping and security later.

"Zack, wake up. Yes, it's uncle Martin. Time to get up."

"What?"

"Time to get up, Zack. I have your favorite breakfast right here."

"Cheerios?"

"Yes, get up and eat. You have to be starving."

Zack sat up in bed. "Is that coffee I smell?"

"Yes, and Zack, Sybil, is already up and needs to go pee."

"Okay, Okay, I am coming."

Zack got up and opened the door; Sybil limped out to the yard. When Zack came back in, he went to the bathroom before he returned to the table.

So far, so good, thought Martin. Now the hard part.

"Who brought you the gun?"

"I'm not sure who brought it. I found it on the table."

"Where did you get the beer?"

"Birthday presents from the Chain Gang."

"Okay, good. Here is your medication—let's take it now." Zack did not object.

"Zack, today is going to be a beautiful day. I want you to work outside. We will change the locks on your door so no one can bother you. If you need anything, my friend, Tom, is plowing the field behind your house. You'll meet him this afternoon, but if you need anything this morning, I wrote his cell phone number on this paper." Zack said nothing and ate his breakfast. Soon, Sybil scratched at the door.

"What is that?" Martin asked as he turned to look at the door.

"Sybil wants back in," answered Zack, nonchalantly.

"Good deal." He cleared the table and walked home to call Sheila.

"Martin," she answered on the first ring.

"Sis, I hate to tell you this, but Carl was messing with Zack while I was gone."

"What?" she gasped, "Are you sure?"

"Let's get together for lunch at Mama's house. We need to talk about the power of attorney for Zack—I'm ready to do it."

"Martin, did you forget? The Peach Festival is today."

"I did forget. Not today then, but soon. I'd better get downtown before it is teeming with people."

Martin left Zack and drove to the hardware store, where he bought new key-locks for Zack's front and back doors. He scheduled the installation of security cameras so he could monitor the property twenty-four hours a day on his phone. He found a dementia-clock that indicated morning or night, calendar date, and day of the week. Preventing forgotten pills was more challenging. Martin could dispense them daily when he was home, but Zack should be as independent as he could. He opted for day-of-the-week pill boxes.

Next on Martin's list was to call Dr. Weissman. "I'm ready to take full responsibility for my nephew. Is there a chance we could meet for dinner?"

"When?"

"Tonight."

They met at the Fish House restaurant; he arrived early, securing a large table. A briefcase and writing material lay at one end. He stood up when she came in, a southern custom that she liked.

"Dr. Weissman, Thanks for taking the time to meet with me. And on a Saturday."

"Please, call me Elaine."

"Yes, ma'am." Martin sat back down as she assumed

a chair opposite his. "It's a preliminary plan I want to run by you before I proceed. But first, let's order dinner. While we eat, I'll fill you in, and when we finish, I can make notes of your suggestions. How does that sound?"

"Perfect."

The waiter took the orders, leaving them alone to talk.

"Zack's mother loves him, but she needs help with his care. She asked me to manage his affairs indefinitely. After the events of this past weekend, I'm ready to assume the contract responsibilities you suggested. Carl is immature, reckless even, with regard to his son. It sounds cruel, but I want to limit his control over Zack."

"I see," she said. They paused the conversation while the waiter served their drinks. When the waiter left, Martin continued.

"I'm hiring a man to live on the farm. He will be responsible for many things, but also responsible for, and capable of, handling Zack if he becomes upset when I am away."

"You have been busy."

"I have. But as I said, we have a big problem, and that is his father. Help me understand what he did and why." Martin told her the story about the spotlighting and the weapon Carl brought to Zack's house while he was away.

"I trust you, Martin; we can talk about my patient's well-being. Carl operates behind the scenes blurring fact, tweaking opinion, distorting the truth. Sheila has talked about it with me on several occasions."

"She never told me that."

"I cannot discuss the specifics with you, but Carl can be malignant, and Sheila is aware of this. You should be aware of it too." Elaine unfolded her napkin, put it in her lap, and took a sip of her iced tea. "As to why? He may see you as a competitor for the attentions of his son and his wife. I can't be certain. It's an educated guess."

"Believe me, I've witnessed how stupid he can be. That's why I want to do this."

In one of Sheila's scrapbooks, there was a picture that haunted her. It was so compelling, "Bayou Expressions" wrote an article about it. Carl, determined to marry her during their senior summer, sent her a message by climbing up the town's water tower and painting it for all to see: CARL EWING LOVES SHEILA HAYWARD. It was outrageous, daring, and endearing all at the same time. Back then, she wondered, why me? But the doubt soon dissolved when he asked her father for her hand.

Her father was dead set against it. "College first, then we will think about it." But Carl would not give up; he agreed to wait, and the longer he waited, the more her doubts began to fade. He went to work for his father's construction business, and every weekend he visited her at Hillcrest College. During her summer vacation, Carl was a dinner guest at her house at least once a week. He courted her father as much, or more than he courted her. If nothing else, she basked in his tenacity in the beginning, but in the end, she fell in love and sealed her fate.

The marriage was a success—thirty years is a long time. Carl had never had an affair, but he got into scrapes. A fist-fight once, several lawsuits, a bad investment that lost them fifty thousand dollars, and of course, the lying. Dr. Weissman called it pathological lying.

When Sheila learned of Carl's latest caper, she was

appalled.

"What on earth were you thinking when you scared Zack half to death by lighting up his house!"

"You have no idear what you are talking about."

"You tried to scare him."

"No. You and Martin have it all wrong. Zack did not want you and Martin to know that he was afraid to stay at the farm alone. He wanted me to keep him safe, so I told him I would watch the house at night, and he would know it because he would see the light from my truck."

"You gave him a gun."

"Yes, I gave him a gun BECAUSE he was afraid. I told you all along he was weak, but you insisted we send him to that college, and the stress drove him crazy."

As Sheila stopped the argument by checking the time; he noticed she was wearing the gold watch her mother gave her for the wedding. Up to now, he would have expected to hear all about her finding it. Sheila was without guile—another thing he loved about her. She was incapable of holding back, concealing her opinion, or hiding her plans. But he had underestimated her, and now he suspected she was sending him a message.

"Sheila. For some reason, I have been so tired."

"I've noticed," she said without emotion.

He registered a sea change in his wife's behavior. He would have to get to know her all over again.

Dr. Weissman advised Sheila that Carl was likely to react to a divorce with a public display of affection similar to the water tower announcement. He would reach out to her friends, neighbors, pastor, and family to convince her that she was making a mistake.

He would shower her with "attention," and he would always know where she was in a small town. She also advised Sheila to steel herself to withstand gut-wrenching scenes with him—angry, crying, swearing, and the underlying revenge—roofing nails in her driveway and snakes in the mailbox. To Sheila's surprise, Dr. Weissman also advised that the wisest option was to relocate out of state, but Sheila was too tied to place and family. She had no desire to leave Gower, and the suggestion that she might be forced to leave, paradoxically made her brave.

"You can do it and stay in Gower," Dr. Weissman said, "but you have to brace yourself and warn your family."

Before retiring to bed, she circled October 6th on the calendar, her birthday.

PART III

CHAPTER 31

24 September 2018

A year and one month after Zack became ill, Dr. Weissman wrote the reading assignment on a whiteboard and continued her lecture series to a new group of interns.

"We are wrapping up our talks on schizophrenia today. A brief review before we begin the study of bipolar disorder. Although the word schizophrenia means split-brain. Patients with schizophrenia do not have split or multiple personalities. They suffer from unpleasant, sometimes incapacitating, hallucinations and delusions.

"Hallucinations can take the form of voices, noises, body sensations, and smells. The patient perceives voices as emanating from other people, real and imagined. Sometimes the voice comes from an inanimate object such as a house, or from a device implanted in their body, like a radio transmitter.

"Delusions are false convictions: conspiracy theories, persecution, special missions, drafted to a cause. Delusions are also egocentric. Whatever is going on in their world, they are at the epicenter of it.

"As bizarre as this may sound to you, the disease is common. Patients with schizophrenia make up one percent of the population, so you will encounter this disorder, no matter what specialty you choose.

"Several reasons the public does not appreciate the prevalence of schizophrenia: The first is stigma. Relatives often keep a diagnosis of schizophrenia a secret. In other situations, a coexisting drug or alcohol dependency distracts professionals, leading to misdiagnosis. Last, many schizophrenic patients get lost and therefore uncounted; they die by suicide or homicide, or they live among the homeless population."

Carl confidently battled his insecurities about his marriage until he received a letter from the IRS. The letter stuck to his sweaty hands as he read it with disbelief. The news could not have come at a worse time. His wife of thirty-two years was a stranger to him. It appeared he could do nothing to charm her, and God knows he tried. Bill suggested marriage counseling, and Carl agreed, willing to do anything. But now this, and he had to tell her before agents filled the house.

He searched his desk drawer for Lefleur's card without success. He took everything out one piece at a time, searching again. No luck. Carl was familiar with the consequences of an IRS investigation. Two local business owners went to prison for tax evasion, and he knew both of them. He was so consumed by worry he got a speeding ticket on the way home from the post office, which he threw on the kitchen counter for Sheila to see, except she wasn't there. A note in her handwriting explained where to find his dinner. Too nervous to eat, he took action.

His office was untidy. It would make sense to create a look of order—law and order. Organize everything to make a good impression, he thought. The magazines had to go. He shoved "Qualified Remodeler" and "Construction" into the wastebasket and dumped it in the trashcan outside. Returning to his office, he saw the key rack on the wall—a key from every house he built. Trent's house key was hanging on a hook, too. He hid them in the attic. Carl always regretted his attic. In the garage, a pull-down ladder gracefully descended to the concrete floor to land in the middle of Sheila's place to park. Thank goodness, she was not home.

He climbed up the ladder, switched on the dim light, and crawled in a sea of air conditioning and heating ducts. It was 90 degrees in the unconditioned space. He forgot gloves, so his hands and knees crunched dead spiders along the way. He stopped every few feet to wipe a spiderweb off his face. At the end of the line, he deposited his keys, certain no city slicker would get this far. By now, he was hungry and yearned for a shower.

Sheila slipped in while he was upstairs in the bathroom. She removed her sweater and checked the kitchen before going to the bedroom to check her email. With Jean's help, Sheila rented a house and prepared to walk out one day with only her purse and the clothes on her back. Make the split clean, Dr. Weissman warned her, don't do a half-hearted break-up—the goal is to leave and never talk to him again.

Carl came out of the bathroom wearing a robe belted at the waist. He walked over to sit on the loveseat and put his head on her lap.

"Honey, you smell so good. I got a letter from the IRS."

"Are they auditing us—or your business."

He pretended to be consumed with sleep.

CHAPTER 32

4 October 2018

Carl continued his campaign to win Sheila's heart again, and he believed he had finally succeeded when she agreed to have sexual relations; the first time in a long time. She was different now, but still malleable. Obviously, the audit upset her, but she maintained calm.

"Anyone can get audited, especially business owners, because there is a fluidity between personal and business accounts," he told her. "A contractor must hold money that belongs to someone else—the suppliers, the subcontractors, the permit office, the client." Naturally, Sheila did not understand why he diverted money, temporarily, intending to pay it back. "Everyone does it." Lefleur coached him well.

For Sheila, October sixth was coming up fast. She felt at peace and even generous, but she was no less resolute in her plans until her attorney stopped her.

"It might be wise to wait and see what you are facing with the audit," her lawyer advised, "Serving Carl with divorce papers might send a message to the IRS that you are in a hurry to avoid something you and Carl committed together." Sheila had to agree; it was only common sense. And the waiting was not that hard because he changed so much. He bought Zack a hunting dog with blue eyes and helped train the dog to fetch a frisbee, an activity Zack looked forward to every day.

"What did he say exactly when he apologized?" Jean asked Martin while she and Sheila showed him the house they rented.

"Well, something like this: 'Martin, I owe you and Zack an apology.' I accepted it on the spot. Besides, it doesn't matter anymore because I have a power of attorney now, and he knows it."

Sheila nodded her head.

"I think we can all get along." Martin hugged her. "The crisis is over, and we are all still here."

By four o'clock in the afternoon, Martin was in his yard treating ant beds with pesticide when Carl's truck pulled up in front of Zack's house. Carl made a habit of visiting his son three times a week as soon as his work day was over.

"Carl," Martin called out to him. "Do you have time to talk?"

"Sure, Zack and I are training Justice."

"The shop roof is leaking. Do you know where I can get a ladder that tall? I need to get up there and put a tarp over it."

"How tall is it?" Carl said, studying the roofline.

"It's eighteen feet to the eave. Normally, I would stand on the top of the picker, but we got it torn up—servicing it now."

"I don't have a ladder that high, I'm sorry." Carl said. "I know a guy who builds them though. He comes to the job site and builds them for us all the time. We burn 'em when we are finished, but you could store it in your shop. I think it would fit."

"How long would it take? I could order a ladder but I might have to wait a week."

"Not long, a few hours if they ain't busy. I got the number right here." Carl reached for his appointment book and found the number. "I'll put it in a message and send it to you."

"That would be a lifesaver; we are predicting rain next week."

Carl beamed. "The guy's name is Chico Garcia. He's got a good crew."

"Okay, thanks, I'll call him. Oh, and Zack made zucchini bread today, be sure to try it."

"No, kidding. I guess he takes after his mother."

Martin waited until evening to call Chico.

"Probly be two months," Chico said with a thick Spanish accent.

"Can you do it sooner? I need it now; Carl Ewing referred me to you."

"Si. Okay, next week, we measure and construct it. It's gonna cost fifty dollars for labor. Cost for supplies depends how high—we make you a ticket—you pay the lumber supply store. Two men, $25 each. I call before we come."

"How about tomorrow?"

"Forty dollars each."

"Okay!"

The next day two workmen came out at two in the afternoon and finished at four. Carl had told Martin to pay them in cash, so he had the money ready in small denominations. Carl also warned that most of Garcia's crew came from Guatemala and spoke broken English, but Martin negotiated the transaction smoothly. No one seemed to be the boss, so Martin handed out the pay in equal shares to each man, shook his hand, and thanked them. They circled him, all smiles and laughter after they received the money. Then they loaded the sawing equipment, the hammers, and leftover nails. When the clean-up was complete, they said, "Where?"

"Right there is fine," Martin said, pointing to the ladder lying on the ground.

Chatting in Spanish, they got in the truck and it sputtered to life. Martin saw the man in the passenger seat making a call on his cell phone. He smiled and waved goodbye before they sped along to the highway. Zack came out of his house when he heard the men leave; Sybil, and the new dog, followed him.

"Zack, can you help me carry the ladder and put it up on the shop?"

"Sure," said Zack, and they bent down to pick it up, stopping when they saw Carl driving in.

"Hey, sorry, I'm late," he said. "I meant to git here earlier, but I got a call about a security alarm going off on one of my jobs, and I had to attend to it first. How did it go?"

"Everything went great," Martin said. "They are a nice bunch of guys."

"They are, and they work very hard for what they git," Carl said decidedly. "Most people don't appreciate how hard they work. How're you doin', Zack?" Carl hugged Zack and roughed up his hair. "I believe the farm life is good for you, buddy."

"Okay," Zack said using his hand to keep the sun out of his eyes.

"We're going to prop the ladder on the shop so I can get up there now and see what the dickens is wrong. I just can't figure it out. We had rain on Wednesday, and the roof started leaking. Something doesn't seem right; I just replaced it two years ago."

"Yeah," said Carl. "A leak can cause a lot of damage before it gets fixed. Maybe you got some hail out here."

"Like I said, the picker's in there so we can work on it, and it sure doesn't need any water falling into the motor."

"Reckon it will rain tomara?" Carl asked.

Zack said nothing as he stood between them. He alternated looking at Martin, then looking at his father and then looking back at Martin again with an expressionless face. Carl left Zack's side, walked closer to the ladder, and said, "Let me help you stand it up; we put a wider board up top to make it easier to get down."

Carl reached for the ladder first and held the rails, checking its stability. He and Martin picked up the ladder together, raising it straight in the air and then positioning it against the shop. Carl rechecked it. "Yep, looks real stable. You want me to go up, Martin? I know some people are afraid of heights."

Zack looked at the ladder, then at Carl, and then at Martin. He walked in circles, an eccentricity of Zack's that Martin had learned to ignore. Taking Martin's lead, Carl ignored it, too.

"No thanks. I can manage." Carl walked over to stand by Zack, while Martin ascended the ladder slowly. Halfway up, Zack screamed like a maniac.

"No, no, no, not this, not this, not this, not this, not this," and he buried his head in his hands. Zack had Martin's attention now, and Martin managed a half turn, enough to glance down and back at Zack while he held on to the rail with one hand.

"Don't worry, Martin, I've got him," Carl said as he walked over to Zack, "Son, what's gotten into you? Everything is alright. Martin is checking the roof."

"God, no!" Zack said as he pushed his father away. "God no, God no, God no!"

"It's okay, Martin," Carl yelled, "Zack is fearfully afraid of heights."

Martin continued his climb.

"Zack, come on, Son. You need to go inside. It's too stressful for you out here."

Martin stopped within five steps of the top rung, and again holding one hand on the rail, he turned to look down at his nephew. Zack was hysterical. Martin carefully placed his free hand back on the handrail, and instead of going up as Carl was encouraging him to do, he gingerly stepped in the middle of the rung below him, one after another until he was on the ground.

"Everything is fine, Zack. You can look now."

Zack stopped shouting. He had tears in his eyes, and he was breathing heavily.

"I guess we will do this another day." Martin said as if nothing was wrong, although he was feeling palpitations in his chest.

"I'll watch Zack," Carl said with an exaggerated smile. "You do what you got to do."

"Thanks, but I can wait. Zack is terrified, and I don't want to upset him."

"It seems a shame you can't get this done because of the boy," Carl said. Zack sat on the ground, calming himself by performing the head swipe repeatedly.

"It's not a problem. I'll get up on the roof tomorrow morning before he gets up."

"Do you want me to come over and help you?"

"If you want to, but I'll be fine on my own. I just remembered something I need to do first. I'll get up there tomorrow."

"It seems a shame you can't get this done because of the boy," Carl said again.

"No, I am done for today," Martin said with a sense of finality. "Would you like to come in and have a drink before you leave?"

Carl was reluctant to go, but he could not think of a legitimate reason to stay.

"Naw, Martin. As much as I would like to, buddy, Sheila, expects me home soon. She has something special planned for supper tonight. We've been married for thirty-two years, and I have been building houses for longer than that. I know you and I have had our differences, but we sure appreciate all you do for Zack."

"Thank you for helping me get my ladder. I'll climb it tomorrow before Zack gets up."

"Sure, that's a good idea. Let me know what you find. I know of a real good roofer."

"Absolutely, I will call you."

It was time for Carl to go, but he stayed awkwardly, trying to fathom a reason why he should remain with his brother-in-law and his son.

It was Carl's hesitation that alerted Martin that something was happening besides what was obvious. Does Carl want to be the only witness who is not insane?

"Carl, are you sure you don't want to come in for a drink?" Martin extended an invitation, knowing it would not be accepted.

"No." Carl waved his right hand at them and walked to his truck, dragging his feet and feeling heavier by the minute. His left arm swung uselessly by his side, and he had to make two tries to step on the running board and hoist himself into his seat. Carl knew the smart thing to do was stay and be a victim of his prank, but his head hurt.

While Martin stood watching Carl leave, Zack sat on the ground, worn out by all the exertion. When Carl's dust cleared, Martin extended his hand to Zack and helped him stand up.

"Zack, could you help me with something? Let's check out this ladder." Zack helped Martin pull the ladder away from the shop to stand straight-up and then lower it backward and gently place it on the ground. Zack watched as Martin went over the ladder, checking rung by rung, starting from the bottom until he found it. The fifth one from the top, seventeen feet high, was designed to break. Zack stood there with his chest heaving. The fear in Zack's eyes was tangible.

Martin stared at the ladder, imagining what would have happened if he had climbed to the top.

"Zack, when you broke your leg, were you on a ladder?"

"Oh yes," he said.

"You need to tell Dr. Weissman and me what happened."

"My Dad told me to climb a ladder to the top."

The light went out of Carl's eyes as he drove home. He felt numb, weak, and deflated. He was in no condition to see Sheila just yet, so he attempted to avoid her. Entering the house through his office door, he lurched into his desk chair and shivered as he poured himself a shot of bourbon, sloshing much of the liquor on his desk papers. Enervated, he closed his eyes and tried to relax, but the hint of a headache he had earlier was getting stronger, much stronger now. By the time Sheila found him, he couldn't speak.

CHAPTER 33

18 December 2018

Family-owned farms in Louisiana are disappearing fast, but not because they are unprofitable. Instead, the repeated subdivision cuts a farm to pieces of undivided interest. Then personalities clash until everyone throws in the towel and cashes out for the money.

Mr. Hayward foresaw the implications for his kin, living in a community property state. Carl never imagined a significant portion of the Hayward family wealth would skip a generation and flow to the grandchildren, before they were old enough to marry. So much time and work to lose the prize. Unable to speak and paralyzed on the left side, Carl lay in a hospital for six weeks seething every minute of every day.

"Carl," Dr. Brown said, "It is a good sign you have improved so soon. Many patients regain the ability to speak, even walk with physical therapy. Your wife is preparing a room downstairs for your convalescence at home. Congratulations, you are ready to leave the hospital."

Carl wrote on a tablet, "Thank you, doctor." He tried to smile, but his face drooped. A thumbs up with his right hand signified his good will, instead.

The staff loaded him into an ambulance and delivered him to the sunroom of his home. Sheila organized the placement of things and thanked the crew. Zack stood by to help. The two of them duplicated his hospital room: a potty chair next to the bed, a wheelchair in the corner, a bedtable for his meals. The windows in the sunroom never captured a sunrise or sunset allowing it to stay cool. Sheila brought the omnipresent tumbler of ice water with a straw. A sick room isn't complete without it, she thought.

"Are you thirsty?"

He nodded and looked around the bed for a tablet.

"The doctor said you should try to speak as much as possible." He shook his head. "I have a tablet and pen." She reached into a basket on a shelf and placed the pen and paper on the bedtable.

"If you need something else, you can write it here."

Sheila was grateful to have her phone ring in the kitchen.

"Zack, sit with your dad, while I answer the phone."

"Hey," Jean said. "I know you are busy, but I am going to the grocery store, and thought you might need something."

"Nothing I can think of."

"What's it like having him home?"

"Exhausting, and it's only the first few hours. Dr. Brown says he sees improvement in most patients. It just takes a little time." Sheila ran her fingers through her hair. "He's regressing."

"What?"

"I have to change his diaper like he is a baby."

"In rehab, he used a bedside toilet. What changed?"

"Dr. Brown says he is getting depressed in the hospital, so they hurried him home."

"It's too much," Jean said, "first Zack, and now Carl."

"I'm in the middle of Carl's audit, and now I have a patient in my sunroom."

"Martin would like to see you. How about I babysit Carl so you can leave for a few hours?"

"Thank you. I need to get out of the house for a while. Give me a few minutes to make myself presentable."

Martin waited for his sister on the porch, relaxing.

"Sheila, I've missed you." She sat down and took the glass he offered.

"I know I look awful. My sleep problems are coming back, and my head feels like cotton. But something new is bothering me. I've been rolling it over in my mind and can't get a handle on it."

"New? What do you mean?"

"What if he never gets better?" Sheila's eyes were two pools of tears.

"You should get rid of him."

"So many things I suspect, but can't prove. Carl tells one lie after another until I don't know where the truth is."

"You are delusional. He's bad news." Martin put his tea on the coffee table and leaned toward her to get a good look at her face.

"What woman deserts her husband of thirty-two years, ONLY when he becomes disabled?"

"I figure a woman is exempt from the rules if they married a terrorist." Martin's face reddened. She had never seen him look so angry. "Promise me this."

"What?" She tucked her chin in, defiantly.

"For God's sake, stop being the victim! Promise me you will question and test everything he says. Verify the truth, no matter how trivial his proposition. Promise me!" Martin turned his face away from her. "It's like he has brainwashed you." He rubbed his eyes. "What is it called? The Stockholm Syndrome?"

Sheila stood up. "Jean's probably ready to go home, so I should get back."

"Where is Zack?"

"He's visiting with his dad."

When Sheila came home, Carl was sleeping; Zack was leaving.

"How'd it go?" Jean asked.

"I am having a nervous breakdown. Why do I subject myself to so much criticism?"

"Tell me how I can help." Jean said, "Shall I do some cleaning? A load of wash?"

"Come help me sort the documents for Carl's audit. Take my mind off all the hurtful words Martin said."

She led Jean to the dining room table where there were six boxes of files. "How are you able to stand this mess?"

"THIS is nothing; look in the living room! Invoices and bank statements cover the furniture." Sheila placed her arms akimbo. "I take one day at a time, I guess."

"So, what do I do?"

"We pull papers from his files and place them in the appropriate pile in the dining room—the most recent date on the top and so on."

"I would let the accountant do it," Jean advised.

"Do you have any idea how much that would cost? At least I can sort while I cannot leave the house."

After an hour of filing, the sisters relaxed and made it a game.

"What about correspondence?" Jean asked.

"That's a good question. Let's index it by job if you can, and if you can't, by the name on the letter. What if it is neither?"

"Then take a match to it."

"All right, here's another one to categorize."

"What is it?"

"It's a magazine article stapled to a hand-drawn design. The title of the article is 'Contractors Need to be Aware of the Dangers of Connecting the Neutral to the Ground in the Subpanel'."

"Let me see that," Sheila held out her hand. While Jean continued working, Sheila read the entire article and studied the pencil-drawing attached to it. When she finished, she stood up and said, "You know what? I'm getting tired. We can quit for the day."

When Jean left, Sheila filed the article under a new category called Designs, which she created in Carl's filing cabinet.

Bell ringing insistently.

Sheila stood up and braced herself.

Carl wrote: *bourbon and coke.* When Sheila read it, something tripped in her mind to visualize, like a movie, the rest of her life.

"I will not make you a drink. I'm not going to get you anything right now." She marched out of the room.

The bell rang again.

When she came back in, he was writing on his tablet. *Bath?*

Sheila reluctantly bathed him. While she wet the washcloth in the basin of water, the words spilled out of her mouth. "You tortured me about Zack's illness when you knew almost immediately what was wrong with him. You tried to convince me he was taking drugs, and it was my fault. You stole the watch my mother gave me and put it in the toolbox. Just now, I found a written plan for trying to electrocute a person in the shower. I think that is pretty incriminating, don't you? Wait until I have the police over to talk to you about it."

Sheila came closer to his face. "You told Zack to climb a flimsy homemade ladder when he was only eleven years old. You engineered the construction of a ladder that could have killed Martin. WHAT IS THE MATTER WITH YOU?"

Lying helpless on the bed, he wrote: *gun.*

"No!" she said. "I don't have time for you."

Carl scribbled: *Please, I can't live like this.* He tried to talk, but it was pathetic, slurred, unintelligible speech. "Peas, peas, un."

"NO."

If you loved me, you would give me a choice, he wrote.

"I'm leaving the room now." Sheila walked out and then turned. "You will be lucky if I ever come back."

Sheila retreated to her bedroom and threw herself on the bed. It was pitch dark outside, except for lightning behind a distant cloud. It was beautiful, almost like a silver lining. Carl started rapidly texting. *Come back, Baby, I need you—It would kill your mother—Zack needs me—You got it all wrong—All wrong—all wrong— that diagram helped us make the subpanel connections safe —We weren't working on Trent's house.*

Rational thought eluded her because of the noise of her phone notifying her repeatedly with a whine and flash of light. The terrifying thought crossed her mind that she should kill Carl herself, shut him up forever. Spare him the pain of doing it, and get this man out of her life, no matter the consequences. Otherwise, he would stick to her like glue.

The last text was the confirmation she needed.

"I didn't hide the carving knife under Zack's bed". It triggered a memory. When she told Carl about finding a knife under Zack's bed, she did not identify it as the carving knife, yet he assumed it was. Now Sheila was sure Carl put it under Zack's bed.

Sheila turned her phone off so she could think. No proof, but clues everywhere she looked. The children saw it; she was sure of that now. It explains why her daughters don't want to come home for holidays. What blinded her? Sobbing until she had no tears left, Sheila fell asleep far from the nerve-racking bell and with her phone off. She would not spare him anything.

Just before sunrise, she appeared like a ghost in his room. There was just enough light from the moon shining through the windows to walk confidently to his bed, and the low light produced by night-lights made her appear deranged. Her face red and swollen, her eyes mere slits, her skin blackened by mascara, caused Carl's eyes to open wide in fear. Sheila's hair clung to a twisted face. He had never seen her so full of hate. Standing over him, she lifted her arm to show him the handgun he kept in the bedroom.

He shut his eyes tight. She waited for him to open them. She placed the gun in his hand and turned to leave. He took the gun and put it in his mouth watching her.

"I don't want to see you do it," she said. He nodded

agreement

She was halfway to the door when Carl raised the gun to point it at her back. He held it steady as a rock, furrowed his brow and opened his mouth while he pulled the trigger.

For a moment, the room turned black. Sheila felt she was going to swoon at the sound of a click. More clicks allowed her to turn and face the gun pointed at her. The weight of her evidence dealt a crushing blow.

Carl put the gun down and started writing. He looked at her with adoring eyes before finishing his note.

Unable to stand the sight of him, she felt as though she were sinking in quicksand. He held it up so she could see: *It's not what you think.*

"WHAT PART OF HELL DID YOU COME FROM?"

Carl tried to get out of bed, he stumbled, but he got back up. He walked leaning to one side. Even with her extra ten pounds, she was much faster, and Carl was no match for her now. Instinct took over as she headed for the stairs heaving, not out of breath, but because of fear. Reaching the top, she slammed the master bedroom door and realized she did not have the key to the dead bolt. She pushed in the privacy button and dialed 911.

When the 911 operator answered, "What is your emergency?" Sheila's voice wavered as she said: "My husband tried to kill me with his gun, please send the police."

The soothing sound of sirens coming in the cul-de-sac slowed her racing heart. He will deny it, she thought, because he never admits to anything.

The officers forced the front door and found Carl on the floor at the foot of the stairs. His face frozen, his limbs not moving. The emergency room doctor diagnosed his death as a second and more massive stroke.

A week to the day after Carl died, Sheila's mother died.

CHAPTER 34

Thanksgiving Day, 2019

Sheila, surrounded by her loved ones, including her daughters and their families, hosted yet another Thanksgiving. Zack was at her side all day, cooking and serving. Martin brought his new girlfriend, Jennie. Sissy and her family came, too. Sheila had become a surrogate grandmother to Sissy's kids, Michael, age seven, and Ryan, age five. The District Attorney never brought charges against anyone for Trent Wilson's death, claiming the evidence was inconclusive and both suspects were dead. Steve, who performed the work, died in a car accident. Some said it was suicide, because he drove off a bridge. Ellen and her grandmother are living in Dallas and attending all the museums that the Metroplex has to offer. Sheila stayed in the house Carl built.

"Sheila," Sissy said after dinner. "The boys are dying to play in your backyard. Do you mind? Jeff will watch them while we clean up."

"I don't mind at all. I love having the boys come over." Sheila watched them outside from the window above her sink. It brought back wonderful memories of her children playing there.

"Thanks for having us. My Mom is so infatuated with her new husband we barely see her. He's retired, so they take one trip after another—they have a bucket list, I think."

Martin brought the last serving dish from the dining room. "The cousins are going to a movie. Can we toast you now?"

"Sure, you get the glasses, and I'll get the Champagne."

"Zack, are you coming with us to the movie?" Becky asked with her new husband in tow.

"What are you going to see?"

"You pick."

"Okay, I'll check the listings." Zack took out his phone. "Uncle Martin wants to get back to the farm by ten."

"We should have plenty of time," Becky said.

When the guests said goodbyes, Michael and Ryan ran back into the house, their faces flushed from playing outside. Michael pretended he didn't see Ryan stop near the stove and ran into him. Ryan jumped up and attempted to tackle Michael.

"Boys!" said their dad. "We are in Miss Sheila's house now. Where are your manners?"

Sheila took charge, "You two look like you need water before you head home," She handed them each a cup; both cups were identical in every respect.

Before Sissy left, Sheila stopped her. "I have something for you." She reached into the basket for mail in the foyer and pulled out a small box wrapped in pink paper.

"Oh, my," Sissy said when she opened it and saw her boyfriend's ring.

"There is something else, too."

Sissy took out a folded note and read it out loud.

I found this class ring among my husband's things after he died. Respectfully, Sheila Ewing.

CHAPTER 35

2 December 2019

The Monday after Thanksgiving, at eight AM, Sheila's phone rang, an unrecognizable caller ID.

"Hello," she said.

"Is this Sheila Ewing?"

"Yes, can I help you?"

"I hope so. You don't know me, but your niece Becky told me to call."

"What is this about?"

"My name is Tonia Peters. My grandfather was Butch Peters, and he owned around 700 acres of farmland in Bosco."

"I know where that is."

"He died three weeks ago."

"I'm so sorry."

"We are devastated. But we have to make a decision now."

"What is the situation?"

"Granddad had five daughters, all of whom are married with children. Of course, he left the farm to them, but nobody knows anything about farming, and we are dealing with ten people, the daughters plus their husbands. We are debating whether to sell the land as soon as we can, or come up with the property taxes, and try to keep it going."

"It's a common problem these days," Sheila said to herself as much as to Tonia. "I can make sense of his records and advise you. If you keep it, I can help you manage it, including finishing up this crop year."

"What do you charge?"

"Five percent of what you make either way."

"You are a godsend. With multiple heirs, we need someone to guide our decisions. Getting the husbands on board is tough."

"Great, when can we get together and talk about it?"

Medical Grand Rounds is the highlight of the month for students, interns, and residents at the University Hospital. A member of the house staff presents the case, and a professor gives a lecture highlighting a new or rare manifestation of the disease expressed in the teaching case. The patient does not attend the meeting except on rare occasions when the teaching case focuses on the patient's experience of the disease.

Zack had represented himself so well with a student video project that Elaine asked him to attend Grand Rounds and speak for himself. She discussed this with Zack and Martin, and they both agreed. Still, she was nervous about Zack. He would address an audience of one hundred fifty people composed of residents, faculty, and students looking down at him. If necessary, she was ready to abort the interview if he seemed uncomfortable.

"Good morning. We are fortunate to have a patient who has been diagnosed with schizophrenia here with us. He brought his dog, Sybil, who is his constant companion. Zack, please join me on stage."

There was a tense pause as she waited for him to appear, but he walked to center stage on cue, shuffling his feet. She led him to an armchair.

"Zack," she began, "this is your chair."

He sat down, and his dog looked over the audience before laying down at his feet.

Weissman helped him with his microphone and sat down to interview him.

"Zack, would you tell us why you agreed to come here today."

"Yes."

"Why?"

"I want to tell people what it is like to get sick with schizophrenia."

"What symptoms were you having?"

"I was in college, and I couldn't study anymore. I couldn't write either."

"What made it hard for you to study?"

"Reading sentences was hard. By the time I got to the end of the sentence, I had forgotten how it started. It made studying very hard."

"And your writing? How did the disease affect your writing?"

"When I got sick, I could still write, but most of what I wrote was nonsense. I did not know at the time I was writing nonsense. I only noticed it when I tried to read what I had written."

"We should tell our audience that before you got sick, you were a talented writer."

"Yes," he said.

"Have you read the stories you wrote before you became ill?"

"Yes."

"What do you think when you read them now?"

"I think I used to be a good writer."

"I believe you told me you won some prizes for your short stories when you were in high school."

"The Nazi burned them—the ones that won prizes."

"I see."

Zack remained expressionless. She could tell he was checking with Sybil every few seconds, and he drummed his fingers as if he were nervous, but the knee stayed in place.

"Tell us about your dog."

"My uncle Martin gave me this dog to comfort me when I see scary things."

Zack's eyes scanned the room every 2 to 3 minutes. He shifted in his chair; otherwise, no muscle moved except the muscles of the drumming fingers. "I am like a skittish horse without her."

"Do you have an agreement with your uncle?"

"Yes."

"What is your agreement?"

"He has agreed to protect me."

"May I ask how?"

"When my brain is playing tricks on me, he will keep me safe. uncle Martin keeps me safe."

"Zack, thank you so much for coming to the hospital to talk to us today. I am sure you were nervous, but you knocked it out of the park."

"I don't play baseball anymore."

Elaine stood up and took his hand to lead him to the side curtain where she handed him off to Martin, who had been standing in the wings in case they needed him.

Returning to the podium and speaking to the audience, she said, "Zack and his uncle have instituted measures to keep Zack oriented to reality when his brain is bombarding him with hallucinations and delusions. They also agreed to enter into a special type of legal contract A local attorney, Mr. Lawson, will discuss the proper wording of a Ulysses contract and when and how to use them in medicine."

Meanwhile, backstage, Martin was complimenting Zack upon his interview.

"You did a great job. Were you nervous?"

"Not really."

"Good. We can go home now."

"We should tell her goodbye."

"That's okay, we'll see her soon."

Before Martin realized it, Zack walked back on stage to tell Dr. Weissman goodbye while the lawyer was speaking. Sybil stayed with Martin.

"So, you are the one suffering stage fright," he said to the dog as he watched Zack, as proud as a father would have been.

Zack stood at the door with the porch light on and watched his mother disappear into the darkness. On the farm with no trees, power lines, or skyscrapers the night sky enveloped him, revealing Venus, the constellations, and a crescent-moon so close he thought he could touch it. Sheila waved; he didn't see it. And with that, his mom was nothing but tail lights that drove away.

Martin saw the taillights too, from his window, and walked over to join Zack standing on the porch. He pointed to the swing as an invitation to sit down.

"Hey, Zack," he said. "Let's have a nightcap before bed."

Martin handed him a bottle of coke, and they shared a bag of potato chips while they sat on a swing together, looking at the moon. The winter night was still.

"How do you like it here, Zack?"

"I feel safe here, uncle Martin," Zack's knee was still. "Granddad is near."

"Good. You know the family almost lost the farm when your grandfather died."

"Lost it, how?" Zack accepted a potato chip from the bag.

"Granddaddy got sick, but he didn't tell anyone because he thought he could keep going, at least long enough to harvest the crops. It was your mom and grandma, who made sure we fulfilled our obligations."

"I didn't know about it."

"Well, you were a kid. I am telling you this story because I want you to know that your mom is the most loyal and loving person I have ever met. You have an illness that causes you to view her as bad sometimes, but it is a false belief."

www.ingramcontent.com/pod-product-compliance
Lightning Source LLC
Chambersburg PA
CBHW071444170626
46811CB00007B/2476